Chaotic

Orne Yvonne E.S.

Chaotic

Vanguard Press

*Vanguard Press is an imprint of
Pegasus Elliot Mackenzie Publishers Ltd.*
www.pegasuspublishers.com

**Vanguard Press
Sheraton House Castle Park
Cambridge England**

Printed & Bound in Great Britain

Acknowledgements

Much appreciation to Mr Cornelius Glasgow of St Vincent and the Grenadines, from whom I first heard the Dum Dum stories.

Chapter 1

Ruth walked quickly, but she felt like flying. Her 'A' levels were over at last. She had not lingered to discuss the maths paper with her friends. She was on her way to see her boyfriend Jamie. She had not seen him all week due to her exams and she felt starved. She loved him so much.

She lifted her eyes to the sky as her spirit soared. She smiled and noted that the cumulus white clouds seemed low. How was that? She wondered absently. White clouds hanging low? Or was it her imagination? Anyway, the breeze was cool and gentle in the mild afternoon sun, and the fragrance of the poui blossoms wafted pleasantly about her nostrils. She inhaled deeply. Life was beautiful.

Ruth was smartly dressed in a sleeveless, drop waist, polka dot, blue and white dress; the bodice was white with blue dots, and the gathered skirt blue with white dots. She was wearing a matching pair of sky blue thimble heeled shoes and a shoulder length white purse with a blue clasp. Her chestnut coloured hair was drawn back and held together with a round white comb. She did not wear make-up, just light powder and lip gloss on her rose pink lips. Her moss green eyes always had a suggestion of a twinkle. Standing five foot nine inches, she was more than beautiful.

She stepped onto the road and avoided the damaged wire fence that was projecting onto the sidewalk. Now she had to pick her way through the potholes and pebbles to prevent her heels getting bruised. Five meters on, she stepped back onto the sidewalk. She wondered what Jamie was doing and then laughed foolishly to herself. Of course, he was working. There was still fifteen more minutes before he was off work. He was twenty-one and a junior accountant at Laynes Brothers. Ruth herself, planned to look for a job. She was not ready for university. Once again she stepped onto the road, and after about ten meters, descended a few steps which led to the post office compound. She was taking a short cut through Halifax Street.

When she exited the post office, she turned left. She was now walking alongside the Barclays compound. She could not resist the temptation to peer over the wall to admire the sleek expensive cars that were parked there. She loved sleek cars. It was one of the first things she planned to buy within a year of work. She waited at the crossing, since it was not a controlled one, it seemed like forever. As usual, a number of admiring glances lingered in her direction. She paid no mind. She had eyes only for Jamie. Finally a black sports car gave way and she crossed. The cheeky blond driver blew her a kiss, and sticking his head dangerously out of the window asked, "Want my number?" She smiled and stepped onto the sidewalk.

Jamie was blond, also, but very tall and bronze with sharp blue eyes. After about a year of dating, just the sight of him still did things to her. She had just turned eighteen, but already she was thinking about marriage. She did not believe in this prolonged seemingly fashionable engagement. For her, three years was the limit.

She reached the end of the block and turned right onto North River Road. She was expecting to be greeted by a harbor view that always lifted her. That was: a few ships in the harbor, old Woman's point jutting out to sea with a few small houses clinging to its sides, and the cloud-strewn horizon. But instead she gasped and momentarily halted. There, in the harbor was the largest cruise liner that she had ever seen. In fact, it was massively gigantic.

She stopped and stared. It seemed twenty storey's high with thousands of portholes. *M.V. Tulip*, perhaps it was from Holland. She started walking again, slowly. Perhaps she and Jamie could honeymoon on a ship like that. With a lingering look, she turned into Middle Street and her excitement increased as she could see the broad, open doorway of Laynes Bros.

Ruth walked carefully. Middle Street was built with cobbled stones and they were very smooth. She looked like a model as she stepped gracefully to the end of a building that was directly opposite the open doorway of

Laynes Bros. She struck a pose and stood there, poised. From where she stood, Jamie would be able to see her, long before he reached the exit and she would be able to see him too. She loved to watch him. He was always immaculately dressed. It was not the uniform, but he wore only white shirts and black pants to work, with either a black or grey tie.

The street was busy with passers-by, shoppers and street vendors hawking their trade, but Ruth was oblivious to it all. Her gaze and attention was concentrated on the store so that she would not miss the moment when Jamie emerged from the office and came towards her.

"Sweetheart, are you waiting for me?" Startled, she turned towards the voice. A handsome black man with a bald head and well pronounced Roman nose, of a golden brown complexion, stood obliquely in front of her. He was about her height. He had a camera in his hand. She looked at the camera and thought, 'He's not getting my photograph,' then looked him in the eye and said, "No." Their eyes met and held and Ruth couldn't stop looking. It seemed that something akin passed between them. Then Ruth caught herself, smiled nervously, and looked down, then away. She shifted her pose and continued, "I am waiting for my boyfriend."

"I," said the man with a pause, "have been waiting all of my life for you."

Ruth looked at her watch and then into the store. Then the man gave her a tender caressing look and walked on. But he had a treasure, unethical though it was, it was his. For when she was standing there, resplendent in all her beauty, oblivious to everyone he had taken her photo: several snaps.

Ruth was clearly shaken. She looked at his retreating figure and noted that he had an athletic physique. Then she turned her attention to Jamie and tried to steady herself. She felt like a traitor. There were more blacks on the island than whites and a well-balanced population at her college, but nothing like this had ever happened before. Although asked several times, she had never dated a black guy. She had thought that that was going too far.

It was now five o'clock. The workers most of them black, came pouring out. Then she saw him. He had to bend slightly to avoid hitting his head on the lintel of the door, Ruth's heart leapt and she smiled, radiantly. As he descended the slope towards the upper ground floor, he saw her and smiled too. He seemed pleased to see her. He was clearly the tallest of the lot that were coming towards the door, so she had no trouble keeping her eyes on him.

Just then, a blonde young lady sidled up to him and engaged him in a conversation. They seems to know each other well, because they were almost touching, laughing and looking at each other. He was no longer looking at Ruth. Ruth did not find this funny. The smile was wiped from her face. When Jamie and the young lady stepped onto the road, he stood and said something to her, upon which she looked towards Ruth with a frown and a sweeping un-appraising glance. She then turned her gaze back to Jamie and, resting her hand on his arm, she smiled into his face, and said something and moved off without another glance in Ruth's direction.

Ruth felt offended without knowing why, but she did not have enough time to think about it. In a few long strides, Jamie hand crossed the road. He smiled down at her. "Hi, sweetness," he greeted her. Ruth frowned.

"You know that I don't like that term!"

"But you have never said why you don't like it." He moved off and she fell in beside him.

"Isn't my not liking it enough reason for you to stop using it?" she asked slightly annoyed.

"Your wishes are not my command, honey."

Ruth was stumped for a second. Then she said, thinking aloud:

"But if two persons are trying to build a relationship, they should make a effort to be cognizant of each other's wishes and as much as possible, try to compromise for the good of the relationship."

"But one could compromise until one has nothing left of himself," Jamie rejoined sharply.

"But if you lose yourselves to each other, then you become one."

"Well," countered Jamie, "I don't want to become one, I wish to remain me."

Ruth did not like the trend of the conversation. She felt piqued. She had so much looked forward to seeing Jamie. Now they were bordering on a quarrel. She touched his arm. "I have to go to the library. I'll see you another time." Without waiting for a response, she turned on her heels and retraced her steps.

Jamie shrugged his shoulders and let her go. Damn, he thought. Becoming one, becoming one, that's all she could talk about. She should be a pastor like his father. That is why he had left home and gotten his own apartment. "Son, you look for a good girl and get married. It's better to marry than to burn," his father often said. Now her with this becoming one hinting at marriage! He would marry when he was forty. Moreso, she did not want to give him sex, why should he marry her, for her beauty? He had to refrain from giving her the impression that she was his only woman.

Chapter 2

Ruth and Jamie were born in St. Vincent, a former colony of the United Kingdom. During slavery, Ruth's fore-parents used to be overseers on the cotton and tobacco plantations. Jamie's fore-parents came to St. Vincent as missionaries and the spreading of the gospel had continued in the family. After the abolition of slavery, a number of the colonist repatriated but many stayed. Because the white men outnumbered the white women, some of the men married black women while others went back to the UK to secure a wife and then returned to St. Vincent. Ruth's and Jamie's parents were among the latter.

Ruth's parent went into merchandising. They started off with groceries and gradually anything that a housewife could use in and around her home was sold at Sandison's. Ruth's older siblings had married and migrated, to the USA and the UK. The unwritten law was that the youngest child should hang around to be there for the parents, Ruth's lot.

Jamie oldest brother was married and now serving as a missionary in Lebanon. Mark, the older, was practicing law in St. Vincent but was already married at the age of twenty-five. Now the pressure was on Jamie, but he would have none of it. This marrying for sex Christian thing was not for him. Women were falling at his feet. Why should he marry?

Jamie and Ruth were from the same community. They had known each other from childhood but had never spoken to each other. She had attended private school and had never come to Sunday school. He had always liked her though, and as she grew older and matured, she became even more beautiful. Jamie did not think that is was right for some man outside the community to claim her and outdo him, but he really did not know how to break down the wall between them. The thing was, Jamie had only approached girls who had shown an interest in him. Ruth was the only girl in the community who did not show any interest in him. It was not that she was deliberately trying to avoid him, as some girls do. She just did not seem to be aware of him, and it hurt and undermined his self-confidence.

Thus it was, about a year earlier, when she was seventeen and he was twenty, they were approaching each other on a village road, on opposite sides of the road when she said, "Hi Jamie." He had stood shocked, taken aback with his jaw dropped and had said nothing. And she had passed on wondering if he was stupid. Ruth did not normally believed in saying hello to boys. She did not wish for them to misinterpret her actions. She had overheard boys bragging about girls who they claimed seemed to like them simply because 'she's always calling out to me'. So she had always ignored them.

But Jamie, he was different. He was very handsome. All of the girls seemed to like him, but somehow, Ruth had a suspicion that he liked her. At seventeen, she was beginning to feel like a woman and she liked him too. She did not feel snubbed when he did not return her greeting, just disappointed, wondering if he was not as smart as he looked.

Jamie was devastated. A girl, that girl, had greeted him and he could not answer. He was glad that his friends had not witnessed the incident. They would have blasted him with jibes. What would Ruth think of him? Worse, suppose she did not wish to speak to him again. Jamie stood there for about ten minutes, too emotionally drained to continue up the road. But he knew what he had to do and he turned on his heels and went in the same direction that Ruth had gone. She was nowhere in sight so he went to her home.

Jamie's courage had begun to waver as soon as Ruth's home came into view and by the time he had gotten to the front gate, his legs were actually wobbling. But he was determined and more-so; it was too late to turn back. Ruth had emerged from their shop with a glass of something in her hand. He was captivated by her stunning looks and just stared. Her long brown hair was flowing over almost bare shoulders, since she was wearing a spaghetti strap top and short pants, all white with red slippers.

She saw him and went through the gate between the shop and the house and then she approached the front gate at which Jamie was standing. She sipped the drink that she was carrying and the action made her lips even more desirable to Jamie. She had said hi to this young man once, and here he was. She was right all along. Good thing she had not greeted all the others.

"Want something Jamie?" she asked stopping at the gate, looking up at him. He looked down at her and swallowed. He swallowed again. "I...er...I was so shocked when you hailed me back then, that I was lost for words. It was a welcome surprise. I love you." He blushed and his jaw dropped again. That had slipped out. You didn't tell a girl that you love her the very first time that you speak to her. Oh no. Oh God. What had she done?

Ruth saw his consternation and felt sorry for him. She was excited and her throat felt parched. She sipped her drink. "I love you too," she replied. "come in." Jamie opened the gate and went in. after he had bolted it shut, he turned and watched her. He felt as if he was walking on water. He was wondering if he had heard right and was afraid to ask. He thought that perhaps he was watching a movie. Ruth wondered if she was reading a fairy tale.

After they had looked at each other for what seemed like eternity, Ruth came back to earth and asked, "Would you like some lemonade?"

"Yes, thanks," said Jamie, still in a trance. She asked him to hold her glass and went back to the shop. As soon as she had turned her back, Jamie pinched himself several times. It was really happening, and if he was not dreaming, she had said that she loved him too.

Ruth went across to the snackette section of the shop. "Mom, could I have another glass of lemonade, please? Pastor McKenzie's last son is visiting with me. We'll be on the porch."

"He seems to be a nice lad," said Mrs. Sandison. "But don't let him tell you anything about that Jesus stuff."

"Oh, mom lay off. I can think for myself," responded Ruth blowing her mother a kiss as she left.

Jamie was still standing there as if rooted to the spot. She smiled. As she came through the side gate, she said, "Come, let's sit on the porch." Jamie did as he was told. Ruth drew up a patio table and put down the drink, push it towards Jamie and reaching for hers.

"That's alright," said Jamie, I'll keep this one."

They were sitting obliquely opposite each other and therefore did not have to look at each other. Each was relieved for that respite. Each was savouring the other's company and thinking. More-so, right then, they did not know what to say but both like being there at that moment. Twilight was approaching on a longer summer's day. Was this her knight in shining armour? Was she going to get married and live happily ever

after? Was he really sitting on Ruth Sandison's porch?
His friends would not believe him.

Chapter 3

As Ruth retraced her steps, she was fuming. What was wrong with Jamie? She did not know, but she had her suspicions. She had not gone with him to his apartment and he claimed that she was giving him the distant treatment. She felt that he was trying to make her feel guilty. Why would she give the man she loved and hope to marry, the distance? She was just looking out for herself.

The thing was, she did not trust herself to be exclusively alone with Jamie. She wasn't sure that she could say no to him if they were all alone. And she did not wish to judge Jamie, but she couldn't help the feeling that he was pressuring her to go against her wishes and have sex before marriage.

"Ruth!" she turned. It was Sally, "Girl", continued Sally, "where did you disappear to after the exam? That paper was tricky, eh?"

"Yes, it was but I think that I did well. I studied hard," replied Ruth.

"You alright?" Sally asked, peering into Ruth's face with concern, her girlie pigtails swinging at her breast.

"Why?" asked Ruth, feeling affronted.

You don't sound like you, I mean, bubbly, happy, sure, you know." Ruth laughed and turned her head away. "Jamie giving you problems?" asked sally.

"Why did you pick on Jamie?" responded Ruth defensively.

"If it were me, you would have told me off. If it were your parents, you would have told me. But you are always defending Jamie. Why?"

"I love him," replied Ruth simply.

"Yeah, I know. But can't you see that he is different now that he is living in the capital, away from you? How often do you see him now?" asked Sally.

"Oh Sally, I was busy with exams. Lay off him, will you?"

"I'm your friend, sweetie. I just don't want you to get hurt."

"Jamie loves me, Sally. But lovers do have their ups and downs."

They were now on North River Road, about to turn down Halifax Street.

"Did you see the large ship in the harbour?" asked Ruth, changing the conversation.

"How could anyone miss it!"

"Wouldn't it be great to honeymoon on a ship like that?" fancied Ruth.

"You're a hopeless romantic, Ruth. I think you used to read too many fairy tales. You don't believe that a young good-looking man, with women falling at his feet is going to marry at age twenty-one, do you?"

"I can wait for another two years, Sally. More-so, I need a job and some savings before I marry. I wasn't exactly talking about tomorrow," responded Ruth, seemingly offended.

"But you talk too much about marriage, Ruth, that you might scare Jamie away."

"Why should two persons in love be scared of marriage?"

"Not marriage, really some men don't like commitment."

"Sally, where have you gotten all of this wisdom? What do you know about men, anyway?"

"I've dated quite a few guys. I've listened to them talk, but most of all, I've observed what is happening with my friends and villagers. I don't have to be wise to see what you can't see. Jamie is your first boyfriend, and you talk and talk about marriage."

"A lot of people marry their...."

"Who is that man?" asked Sally, her long lashes dropping.

It was the same handsome black man who had approached Ruth earlier. Anyone who cared to, would have noted that his eyes were glued on Ruth as he came towards her. Ruth had not noticed him until he was just about five meters away, fully engaged with Sally in conversation. He stopped in front of Ruth blocking her path, but she sidestepped him and continued walking.

He quickly turned on his heels and fell alongside them, next to sally.

"What's your friend's name?" he asked Sally.

"I can tell you mine," replied Sally, with a smile, "but you will have to ask her hers, yourself."

The man looked at Sally. She had nice contemplative, dark eyes with long drooping lashes and full mouth but it did not amount to beauty. She was OK, but it was Ruth that had captivated him. Sally, on the other hand, was wondering how she had never seen that man before in a small town like this.

Ruth was uncomfortable. "Sally, I was on my way to the library when you met me. Call me later." And she turned and went back up Halifax Street.

Tony wanted to follow her but he decided against it, choosing to stick with Sally. At least, he knew her name and might be able to elicit information from Sally about Ruth.

***

Jamie walked home slowly in deep meditation. He was somewhat irked. Of course he knew that he loved Ruth, had loved her for all of his young life, it seemed to him. But as far as he was concerned, she was damn selfish. She wanted to maintain her virginity. "For what?" he wondered. What about his needs? He was a healthy young man. Sex is a physiological need. He was therefore forced to have extra relationships to meet his sexual needs and it bothered his conscience. He was using those girls and women.

Jamie had challenged Ruth. "You are not a Christian, "he had stormed. "Why are you practicing chastity?"

She had retorted, "Christians preach chastity, but many do not practise it. More-so, there are many religious and tribal groups who are not Christians who actually do practise chastity."

"Why?" Jamie had asked.

"Because they are saving themselves for the one they love," she had replied.

"So, don't you love me?" he had asked, expectantly.

"Yes, I do," she had said softly. "But we are not married."

"Why do two persons in love have to get married to make love?" asked Jamie angrily, exasperated.

"Because the Bible says so," said Ruth demurely. Jamie had exploded.

"Oh yeah! You disregard everything else that the Bible says, but conveniently, you know what it says about marriage. That makes you a hypocrite, Ruth."

Ruth's eyes had flashed and brows converged. "Really, you are the biggest hypocrite, because you are the one who claims to be a Christian, and yet you are forcing me to have sex outside of marriage."

Jamie was stumped and he was hurt. Those words had put a root of bitterness in his heart and had instigated his extra relationship, unknown to Ruth.

It was 5:45 when he opened the door to his almost two month-old apartment. As he stopped inside, he felt a burden with the stress of work, problems with Ruth and so much more. He wished then that he had a pair of loving arms to greet him, perhaps run his bath and bring him a glass of cold lemonade. He knew them, that if he ever married, he wanted a housewife. He did not want a working wife. Why was he so stupid? It was his dad. He was tired of him encouraging him to follow in his brother's footsteps and get married. Now he had to do everything for himself and he did not like it. Now he had to buy a car because his father's was no longer available. Jamie picked up the phone and called his latest annexation. Sheridan.

Chapter 4

Ruth did not need to use the library. She had just used it as an excuse to get away from that man. She did not hate him. His aura just troubled her, made her feel afraid and unsure of herself. And she held to the belief that he who can't fight must run, as Joseph in the Bible ran from Potiphar's wife. She crossed North River Road and walked about twenty metres along Grandby Street and then turned into the library.

As she stood within the door, she could hear the voices of some of her classmates behind the partition, but she did not wish to tarry so she did not attract their attention. She knew for sure that they were not doing research. They were just hanging out.

She waited for about ten minutes, to be sure that Sally and that man were too distant to espy her movements and then she exited the library, turned left, then left again and followed a long route to Bay Street. She steered clear of both Middle and Halifax Streets, so as not to risk running into Jamie or Sally and that man.

Bay Street was teeming with tourists, most likely from the large cruise liner. They were all white, speaking a foreign language, and they were all wearing shorts. She smiled. Was this what was called stereotyped? She stood aside and watched them. For once the blacks were outnumbered. Then she observed something: they were all matured or middle aged. There were no young people or children.

Ruth looked again at the giant ship. Perhaps cruising wasn't the trendy thing for her to do on her honeymoon, after all. Why wasn't there any youth among those thousands? She moved on. She did not look at the ship again for it no longer supported her fantasy.

***

Tony glanced at Sally. Now that Ruth was not around, she did not look to bad, in fact, she was really cute. It was just her nose, stuck on like half damson plum that subtracted greatly from her looks. She was looking at him too but it was his nose that gave significance to his face and she could not tell why. His eyes seemed to say, "I know all about you."

"Why did your friend run away?" asked Tony.

"She did not run away," replied Sally.

"You know that she did," countered Tony. "Is she a racist?"

Sally stopped arms akimbo. "Ruth is not a racist. She gets along with everyone in class."

"So why did she run away from me?" he persisted. Sally was annoyed.

"Perhaps you're too damn obtrusive and annoying," snapped Sally.

"Would you like a drink?" he asked, changing the subject.

"I think I deserve one," in a tone of recrimination.

They walked a few paces and stepped into the first bar and restaurant that they came to. Sally ordered a malt and Tony a beer. Tony was quietly triumphant. He had achieved his goal. He was sure that Sally was not even aware that she had let Ruth's name slip.

"So," tony began, looking innocently at Sally. "What is your friend's name?"

"I told you, you'll have to ask her," Sallly replied. Tony shrugged.

"Well then, what is your name?"

"I am Sally."

"Where do you live?"

"Here in town."

"Then you can help me find an apartment," Tony persisted.

Sally lowered her lashes and swept a glance over his face.

"I know nothing about you, not even your name and you want me to help you to find an apartment. Do I look foolish to you?"

"No, no, no," hastened Tony, trying to clasp his palm around her hand as she held the bottle, but she withdrew. "Please, please forgive my presumption. My name is Tony Blake. I am from Biabou. I have just returned from University in the U.K. I will be working at Gren-TV soon, so I need a place that is close to work. I would be grateful for your help."

Sally was attracted to him and he knew it but she sensed his arrogance and would have none of it. Imagine asking her for help before even telling her his name. Who did the think he was?

Sally pulled back her chair, her drink unfinished and stood up. "Thank you for the drink, but I have to go."

"I'll go with you," said Tony, pulling back his chair.

"No!" said Sally sharply, as if rebuking a child. "Finish your drink."

Tony reached for Sally.

"I've offended you," he stated questioningly.

"No. It's alright, "responded Sally, stepping haughtily out without looking back.

But it was not alright. Sally was offended, very offended. Perhaps she was a little oversensitive, but it was clear that, that man suspected that she was interested in him and on that notion alone, he was ready to take her for granted. She couldn't understand the human race. Love them, they take you for granted. Don't love them, they cry foul. She sucked her teeth in exasperation and decided to go to the library to meet Ruth.

The sidewalks were now crowded with most people off work. They engaged in unabashed stares at each other or little covert glances, sizing each other up. In most cases, Sally would get a second look as if they wanted to ascertain what she really was, a schoolgirl or an unsophisticated young woman?

At eighteen, Sally was still wearing her long black hair in two pigtails. She had a full shapely body, 38-26-38. Today she was wearing a black mini skirt, a white short sleeved shirt with a black border down the front and pocket, with gold buttons. These were accessorized with black and gold leaf earrings, white medium high shoes with black tip and a black purse hanging from her left shoulder. Except for a daub of lipstick, she wore no make-up.

Sally stepped into the library and went straight to the gang's corner. Judy and Alma were there, but not Ruth.

"Where is Ruth?" asked Sally. Everyone looked blankly at her.

"Did not Ruth come here about half an hour ago?" she asked again.

"No," chorused Judy and Alma.

Alma and Judy had been best friends since their primary school days, and on Judy's invitation, the two pairs became a clique. But with the two pairs favouring each other when push because a shove.

Sally sat down. "Ruth and I were going down the road about half an hour ago. This black gentleman joined us and upset Ruth. So she left us, stating that she was going to the library. Now where could she be?" wondered Sally.

"Sally you've forgotten that Ruth indicated earlier that as soon as the exam was over she was going to wait for Jamie," ventured Judy.

"She did meet Jamie," returned Sally, "but apparently they had a quarrel. It was after the quarrel that I met her."

"Since she was upset, she has probably gone home. And since it is getting on for 6:00 p.m. we should do the same and call each other later," advised Alma.

They all agreed with an air of resignation and got up to go. Sally lived close to the centre of the capital, and Alma and Judy lived within walking distance of it. Ruth lived two miles from the capital.

Chapter 5

Sheridan was not yet at home. Jamie left a message for her to call him. Sheridan lived in the capital but she had not hurried home. Why should she? Her legs and heart were weighed down by the sight of Ruth that afternoon. She had to admit that the girl was beautiful. Sheridan had a face that was neither ugly nor pretty. The only significant feature about her face was that it was almost triangular. She felt ugly next to Ruth and decided that she would start to wear make-up.

Sheridan had fallen in love with Jamie from the first day that he had begun to work for Laynes Bros, but he had not begun to notice her until about two months earlier. She had suspected that he had a girlfriend but had never met Ruth before. How could she compete with that girl? More-so, Sheridan suspected that Ruth was younger than she was. She was the same age as Jamie.

Sheridan completed the block, turned down Egmont Street and headed up Bay Street to her favourite restaurant and bar. On the other side of the street were thousands of tourists going in the opposite direction. In the bay was a gigantic cruise liner. On another day, she would have stopped and gawked, as a number of people were doing, but not today. All that she could think about was that girl and Jamie. Why were other women always taking her men away? What was wrong with her? She was walking fast but her legs felt like lead, just like her heart.

Sheridan entered the Eat Out restaurant and sat down. She ordered a beef roti and a glass of red wine. She was not hungry but slow chewing helped her to think. She was not going to give up Jamie. Why should she? True, Jamie had not made her feel a sense of belonging. They had gone to the cinema twice, had sex once and he had never kissed her. But she was willing to give him time.

Sheridan chewed and chewed. The roti seemed hard to swallow but the wine was finished and she ordered another glass. Then again, thought Sheridan, perhaps that girl was before her. Perhaps that was the reason that Jamie had not noticed her before. Perhaps she should back off. Leave him with this girl. Then she got angry. Why should she? He was not married, so he was game for anyone. She would not give him up. She ordered another glass of wine, then another, then another and another. It was 7:45 p.m. before she paid her bill and got up to leave.

She was unsteady and sat back down to collect herself. She stood again but the objects in the restaurant were bobbing up and down. She sat down again and the waiter came to her assistance. "May I help you, madam? Should I call a taxi?" he asked.

"Yes, thank you," mumbled Sheridan.

***

Meanwhile, at 7:30 p.m. Jamie was sure that Sheridan had not gotten the message, so he had called again with the same result. He was a little worried. He was not too familiar with Sheridan's evening routine, but for most people who lived in the capital, the norm was to go home, freshen up and go out again, if so desired. Why hadn't she gone home after work?

Then Jamie felt guilty. Why was he calling Sheridan and not Ruth? Now he was angry with himself. Why should he feel guilty? Of course he loved Ruth. Had lover her all his life, it seemed to him. But she needed to learn the meaning of compromise. Why should she have things her way? No one would manipulate him. Not Ruth. Not his father. Ruth could call him when she was ready to think about him and not only about herself. Jamie couldn't wait on Sheridan any longer. He would go down to Dan's where there was always a steady supply of willing women.

***

When Ruth passed the police headquarters, she stopped at the bottom of Hillsboro Street and looked up at Mount St. Andrew. She always did this if she wasn't in a hurry. It was a spectacular view. There it was with its peak shrouded in fog, majestically towering above the capital with a number of small villages nestling at its base. The panorama had not escaped the tourists because there were a number of cameras clicking about her. That view always humbled her. And now she felt especially enchanted as the mellow sweet sounds of a steel band drifted to her ears. The bandsmen were probably entertaining the tourists at the war memorial.

She moved on. A short distance a fisherwoman approached her. "Come, miss, come and see. I have some fresh fish, fresh fish. Come buy some for your parents," she pleaded.

Ruth looked at the basket of robin. They were fresh. Her father delighted in fresh robin boiled with ochro, cabbage and green banana. She and her mother loved them highly seasoned with chive, garlic and pepper, fried dry. "Yes. I will have some," she said to the fisherwoman.

"How much?"

"Three pounds," answered Ruth.

It was the housekeeper's job to buy fish and stuff, but today was the last day of fourteen years of education that her parents had given to her; she could buy them some fish in spite of her elegant dress. Anyways, she did not have to walk far with some smelly fish in her hand. The bus terminal was twenty metres away.

Ruth did not like riding in the minibuses. People were packed like sardines and the music was always too loud and vulgar. Her parents wouldn't buy her a car, claiming that ladies must be driven, not drive. What galled Ruth was that her parents did not use public transport themselves. If her father couldn't drive them for one reason or another, he would call a taxi.

***

Alma, Judy and Sally left the library and were on their way home. They had just passed the bar where Sally had had a drink with Tony. When Tony, who was still sitting where Sally had left him, saw Sally going by, he rushed out.

"Sally!" he called. All three girls stopped and turned. Alma and Judy looked from Tony to Sally.

"He is the man I told you upset Ruth," explained Sally. Tony came towards them.

"Sally, could I have your number, please?" he begged.

"What do we have to talk about?" asked Sally matter of factly. Tony looked embarrassed.

"I am deeply sorry if I offended you in any way Sally. I humbly apologise. Please, could I have your number?" implored Tony. Sally melted and gave him the number. He wrote it down in his pocketbook then looked up straight into Alma's eyes. She had been staring at him. He was the most handsome black man that she had seen for some time; those eyes that nose, those perfect lips. Wow!

Their eyes locked. Alma did not look away. Then he sized her up. She was copper coloured right through: her long wavy hair, her sharp almond shaped eyes, and her skin. He had never seen that before. She had a pert nose and full, well shaped lips with the upper lip dark and lower lip rose pink. She was wearing a stretch knit maroon dress, with elbow length sleeves that clung to her, showing off her 36-25-38 figure.

"God!" he breathed. "You are beautiful, as beautiful as Ruth."

Alma frowned and looked away. She was a Christian and did not support the calling of God's name in vain. And why did he have to compare her to Ruth? She did not consider it a compliment. Ruth was white, she was black. Was she supposed to feel honoured to be compared to a white woman? No, thanks. She could hold her own being black. She didn't feel second to anyone because, regardless of rank or possession, everyone eats, sleeps, shits and will one day die.

Sally, too, was once again annoyed. Tony had not even hinted a compliment about her but here he was drooling over Alma. Judy felt invisible and was ready to move on. As if by a signal, all three girls turned in disgust and continued their journey.

Tony felt insulted and to save face, he went back into the bar. He was puzzled. What had he done wrong this time?

Chapter 6

Ruth poked her head inside her parents shop and called, "hi mom, hi dad. I've brought some fresh fish. Should I ask Martha to do the usual?" Mr. and Mrs. Sandison responded in the affirmative and Ruth was off to the house. She ran up the back steps and found Martha in the kitchen taking freshly baked rolls from the oven. "Hi, Miss Ruth," greeted Martha. "You have some fresh fish I see. I had seasoned some chicken for supper."

"That's alright, Martha you can still bake them, but Mom and Dad would like the usual fresh fish special also," responded Ruth, putting the bag of fish in the sink. "How was your day, Martha?" she asked kindly.

"Oh, it was alright, I suppose. I went by the school to look for me grandchildren carried some snacks for them, too, "Martha replied cheerily.

"I suppose that the children are all well?" questioned Ruth with interest.

"Yes, they be quite well, miss Ruth. Your father quite nicely gives me the weekend off to go spend with me daughter. I'm much obliges." Martha couldn't hide her pleasure.

"I'm glad for you, Martha. Now, if you'll excuse me."

Ruth headed for the dining room on her way to her bedroom. She passed the large, turned leg, mahogany stained rectangular dining room table with eight high backed chairs, slid her hand along a decorate sideboard and quickly turned into the hallway and up a gold plated banister curving stairway, down another corridor and into her room.

The jasmine-scented room was comforting. The walls and furnishing were all baby pink in colour and the furniture, including the walk to wardrobe were all white. The ceiling and beams were also white.

Ruth placed her shoes and purse on their stand and unplugged her telephone. She stripped down to her underwear and went into her en suite bathroom and prepared her bath.

She slumped into a sofa and waited for the bath to fill. Through the drawn curtains of the upper panes of her window, she could see that the sun was setting. The clouds were tinged orange.

It was late June and the days were longer now. She could also hear the tweet, tweet of the birds in the mango trees below the house. They always seemed so happy. She wished that she was a bird. Then she would be happy and not have to worry about Jamie. She dug her toes into thick carpet. Jamie. Had he caught up with that girl after she had left?

Ruth got up and went into the bathroom. She took off her knickers and bra and threw them into the laundry basket and turned and looked at herself in the full-length mirror. Her 36-24-36 frame was a beauty to behold. Her moss green eyes looked wistfully back at her and her firm rounded pink nipple breast seemed impudent. Her navel had healed well into a taut, flat tummy and the chestnut patch of hair between her thighs was like honeycomb between two graceful tapering columns. Her lips trembled. She hugged herself, exposing her curves, then turned away and turned off the bath taps. She lowered herself into the warm suds, placing her arm under her head for support.

The bath was soothing and Ruth relaxed. Then she sighed. What did Jamie want? As if in response, her free hand began to stroke her genitalia. Then she nibbled her clitoris with her fingertips, exciting herself. Jaime would probably like to do this, and go even further deep into me, exploring me. Why should he do it before he marries? Suppose I let him do it and then we break up? What's wrong with valuing chastity?

***

Jamie sat in the section of the bar where the lights were dimmed and coloured. He sipped his drink slowly. He always waited for a woman to slip in next to him. He wondered what had happened to Sheridan. Ruth. Suppose he gave her distance and some other guy got interested in her? She was so damn beautiful. She belonged to him. He had loved her since she was a child. But he was twenty-one, why should he get married just to have sex? That didn't seem right to him. God must be old fashioned or out of touch with modernity. Most people wouldn't get married but most people need to have sex. It is a physiological need. The Bible and his parents were outdated. But Ruth was not a Christian. What was her point?

"Is this seat taken?" a buxom young lady with cheap smelling perfume was standing there. Jamie did not like her perfume but it looked like he could find some comfort between those large, soft breasts. "No," he said, "I won't mind your company."

"I don't come cheap," replied the woman.

"I can pay," coaxed Jamie.

"Well, let's go," she finished, pulling back her chair.

***

Ruth stood on the bath mat and towel dried herself, then she went to her washstand and cleansed her face with moisturizing lotion. She dressed quickly, putting on a slip on house dress with a frill and matching slippers. She was all in blue. Then she gave her hair a quick brush and hurried down the stairway. She would call Sally later.

Ruth had not eaten since lunch. She was starved. As she entered the dining room, the pungent aroma of highly seasoned baking chicken whetted her appetite but her taste buds were screaming for fried fish. Martha was preparing the ingredients for the boilin.

She neither saw nor smelled fried fish. "Where is the fish, Martha?" Ruth asked.

"I've seasoned them and left them to marinade a while."

"Can I help you fry them?" asked Ruth eagerly. She could not wait until Martha was done with the boilin.

"Suit yourself missy. Just do them properly," cautioned Martha with a smile.

'Oh, Martha," pleaded Ruth. "I am depending on you to help me."

Martha instructed Ruth every inch of the way. Place a half cup of plain flour on a platter. Add two shakes of turmeric and two shakes of garlic power in the flour and mix well. Place the frying pan on the burner filled one third full of vegetable oil. Turn the burner to medium heat and allow the oil to turn sizzling hot. While the oil is heating, dip the fish one at a time into flour mixture on both sides and lay aside until oil is hot. When the oil is hot, place as many fish as the pan can comfortably hold and allow them to fry on each side for three minutes. Remove them from the pan when completed and drain on paper towel.

Ruth followed the instructions meticulously. She was determined to learn a little from Martha so that she could cook for her husband sometimes. Soon she was seated at the kitchen table, tucking into rolls, fried fish, tomatoes and hot milo with milk. The boilin was still cooking and would be ready long before Mr. Sandison closed up his shop at 8pm.

Chapter 7

It was Saturday morning, the day after. The sun was streaming through her window and the birds were chirping in the trees. Those birds were a lifeline. They gave her hope every morning. They were always so happy. It was a sound that she would never forget and none would ever better.

Ruth stretched and rolled over her eye caught the telephone line, still plugged out. She was horrified. How could she have forgotten? Oh no! Oh no! Sally must have called, perhaps Judy, too. Oh no. she wondered if Jamie had called. It was 7am, too early to call anyone but she got up and re-plugged the phone and went back to bed.

For Ruth today was not just Saturday, but yesterday was the last of college, in fact, the last day of school. She had been going to school since she was four plus years. Now she was eighteen. She was going to miss her friends and so on. But she was ready to get married and have a family.

Ruth had already sent her application to the Ministry of Education for a position of primary school teacher. She had already figured out that that position was the most convenient for a working mother, because of the nine to three work day. That would give her more time with the children in the morning and they could leave home together when their time came to go to school.

All other jobs were either seven to three or eight to half past four. Even secondary school began at eight. When the children were in secondary school, she would do a BA degree and apply for a secondary position. All of her friends were heading for university in one year's time, but she was heading for marriage, and happy about it. She had her life all planned. But there was one problem, Jamie. He was not fitting well with her plan. It was causing a bother to her and a rift in the relationship.

***

Jamie was thinking about her too. Last night he had had an experience that he would never forget and he was wondering how Ruth would compare. He had awoken early as was his habit, but today was his Saturday off. There wasn't enough work for two junior accountants on a half day. Usually, he would stay in bed, read papers, eat all sorts of crisps and drink malt. But today, he was thinking of the night before and Ruth.

The woman had gone home with Jamie. He had taken her straight to his bedroom since that was where he kept a small refrigerator with drinks, on the top of which was a tray filled with a variety of crisps. Jamie advised her to help herself while he stripped down to his briefs and lay on the bed, watching her, getting warm in anticipation.

The woman had taken a seat in a small armchair and had taken forever to drink a ginseng. When she was finished, she took off all her clothes, and poured herself a glass of wine. She then struck a provocative pose on the bed, next to his feet, her large breasts drooping temptingly, and now it did seem as if she really meant to take the whole night to drink her wine. Jamie decided that she was going too far and got up. He dropped his briefs and found a condom in his bedside table. His penis had shot out at a ninety degree angle as straight as a rod. It was a manageable size. He put on the condom and came around behind her. Then he put both hands around her waist and gently grabbed her breasts. Bending over her, he placed his face between both breasts and, as it were, massaged his cheeks with them. Then he sucked first one then the other, back and forth. She began to breathe heavily and he took the glass from her hand and put it out of the way.

Now Jamie came around to the side of the bed. With one hand behind her neck and the other at her bottom, he put her on her back. Then he put both of her legs, one on each of his shoulders, and feeling for her passage with his index finger, he penetrated her, deeply.

As if in a hurry, he drove in and out of her, now left, now right, now centre. The woman had a big pussy and the flesh was soft, so it gave him room to manoeuvre.

He loved it. Unlike the last time that he had brought a girl home; she had been so tight and dry that he could only go in and out centrally, and even with a condom, he felt bruised in the end.

Within three minutes, the woman began to moan, "No, no, no, noo, nooo!" Jamie was coming too, and he accelerated. Finally she screamed a 'no' that had no end and they came together.

After savouring the moment, Jamie got up and went to the bathroom. He cleaned himself and put on a new condom. This time, he was in no hurry. He turned that woman into every position that he could recall from his porn magazines. She had several orgasms but Jamie restrained himself, trying to make it last as long as possible. Finally he ejaculated again and a few seconds later, the woman came again. He rolled away from her tired.

They lay there for a while. He was just about to tell her that it was time for her to go when she reached over and held his penis. "One more time," she said.

"I'm drained," Jamie replied.

"No problem," she said. "Just enter me and I will do the work."

Jamie got up and cleaned himself again and changed the condom. The woman lay on her back and spread her legs wide. Jamie entered her supporting his weight on his elbows. He waited.

The woman held his buttocks with both hands and then, slowly, rhythmically, she turned her hips elliptically, round and round as if she was stirring a glass of juice, only that her pussy was the glass of juice and Jamie's penis was the juice stirrer. Jamie was mesmerized. He had placed that woman into every conceivable position earlier, but nothing was as cataclysmic as this. He was going ballistic, writhing, and gritting his teeth, beating the bed, wanting to scream like her.

God! He thought. The tip of his penis was being massaged by the woman's movements. The stem of his rod was being caressed simultaneously by her gently clinging flesh. It was the best sex that he had ever had. Ruth might be able to equal it but he didn't believe that she could exceed it. It could not get better than this. Finally he went up on both palms, said "No!" hit the bed, and then fell and rolled away from her; ecstatically exhausted she didn't come again.

Then she touched him. "Pay me before you fall asleep," she said knowingly. She was right. Jamie was almost already far away in the land of nod.

"Oh yeah sure." He reached for his pants and took out his wallet. "How much?" he asked.

"How much do I deserve?" she asked. Jamie switched on the bedside lamp and counted out ten twenty dollar notes and gave them to her. She was the eighth woman that he had brought home. The most he had paid before was fifty dollars. This woman, whose name he had not asked, deserved four times that. It was the most that the woman had ever gotten, but she hid her surprise.

The woman dressed quickly, but she was out of the door, Jamie was fast asleep. If she had not been honest, she could have robbed him. As she closed the door behind her, she thought that if she could meet a few more men like that young stallion, she would be able to open her gift shop sooner than she had planned.

As Jamie sipped his malt, he was re-living the last seven minutes of his encounter with that woman the night before and thinking of Ruth. What type of vagina did Ruth have? Small and slippery or big and loose? Medium and watery? Or was it medium and damp like Sheridan's?

Oh God! He thought. He wanted so much to go into Ruth and go into her and never stop going. But she wouldn't let him. How could she love him yet punish him? He had never kissed any other woman but her. He had never loved anyone else. Why should he marry at age twenty-one and give up his Saturday morning off to go to the shop or market? Not even for Ruth. Neither was he ready to give up those mornings to look after bothersome kids while his wife went shopping. He wasn't ready. Was that a crime?

Chapter 8

The phone rang. Ruth looked at the clock on her set of drawers. It was 8.45 am. Who was calling her this early, she thought as she reached for the telephone. Sally's voice was on the line. "Ruth, girl, are you alright?"

"Why?" responded Ruth lazily.

"I tried to reach you all night and could not. What was wrong?" asked Sally with concern. Ruth was touched.

"I plugged out the phone when I was going into the bath and forgot to re-plug it when I was finished," said Ruth guiltily. Sally was relieved. "What's up?" continued Ruth.

"Well, we were thinking that since school is now over, we could stop going to the library from our Saturday itinerary and go to the beach instead," Sally finished expectantly. Ruth laughed.

"Girl, we don't even have to shop on Saturdays anymore. We are on holiday. I wasn't planning to get out of bed today, but the beach sounds nice and inviting."

"OK then," Sally concluded, "Let's have a conference call and hear what the girls think."

The girls agreed to drop the shopping and meet at Alma's for lunch at 1:00pm and then go to the beach. Alma's parent's kitchen operated as a restaurant, with all facilities resembling a restaurant, and containing eight tables with four chairs each.

That settled, Ruth rolled over and snuggled up again. She wondered if Jamie had tried to reach her also. She felt that the onus was now on her to call him, just in case. She looked at the phone as if seeking its advice. The phone seemed to say to her, 'he will be up, reading his paper. Today is his half day off.'

Ruth did not pick up the phone. She was still hurt, feeling rebuffed. She had hurried from her exam yesterday, forgetting her friends, just to see and speak to him and he had picked a quarrel. They had not seen each other all week and she had thought that he would be as excited as she was at seeing him.

But, in spite of her wounded pride, after a night of sulking and feeling sorry for herself, she now itched to call him. Even his voice excited her. She loved him. Really loved him, and he knew it. He loved her too, and she knew it. Which of them should have the pre-eminence?

Ruth looked at the phone again and seemed to be gazing into Jamie's eyes. She lowered her eyes to his arrogant nose and then yearned to kiss his full soft mouth. She reached for the phone and dialled his number. Her heart throbbed and her eyes clouded with emotion at his throaty, "hellos?"

"Hi, Jay, it's me," she said, trying to sound at ease.

"Oh, Ruth," he replied as if surprised. Ruth was a little ruffled. Was he expecting someone else or didn't he expect her to call?

"Were you expecting someone else?" Ruth asked.

"No, no no no," said Jamie quickly, almost guiltily.

"Did you call me last night?" asked Ruth hopefully.

"No," Silence. Ruth felt awkward. Usually, Saturday was Ruth and Jamie's day off from each other, but because of the small quarrel, she had called today. It did not seem a good idea. "Well... have a nice day," said Ruth and hung up.

Ruth was puzzled. She and Jamie had had many quarrels, but whenever one called, they would forgive, forget and make up. Jamie was clearly in no mood to make up. He was cold and for the first time in their relationship, Ruth did not know what to do. She felt threatened, remembering the girl that she had seen talking to Jamie the afternoon before. She wanted to call Sally but decided against it. She lay back in thought.

**

Jamie was sorry that he had given Ruth the cold shoulder. It was because at the moment when Ruth had called, Jamie was engaged in thought, wondering what type of vagina Ruth had. And to hear her voice on the phone was like being caught red-handed. He wanted to call her back and apologise but then decided against it.

Perhaps, he thought, if I put her under some pressure, she would be more willing to let me stop wondering and instead discover what lies between her legs. He smiled.

***

There was a knock on the door. "Come," called Ruth. Mrs. Sandison pushed her head around the door. "You alright, sweetheart?" she asked.

Ruth answered in the affirmative and her mother inquired if she would need anything since they were on their way to town. This time Ruth's reply was negative. Ruth just wanted to be left alone to put more thought on Jamie before she met with the girls.

Mrs Sandison closed the door and began to hum a happy tune, which annoyed Ruth. The Sandisons usually closed their shop at 1:00pm on Saturdays to go shopping for themselves. Before this, they would have gone to the beach between 5:00 – 5:30 am for an early morning swim which senior citizens claimed is therapeutic. It usually energized the Sandisons. They would have met many more people in their age group on the beach.

None of the senior citizens could persuade their children to leave their beds so early in the day. The young people claiming that the senior citizens chose the darkest hour of the day to go to the beach because they wanted to hide their sags, bags and creases. The senior citizen hit back, stating the type of lifestyle wouldn't live to reach their thirties and forties, so they wouldn't get sags and creases.

The generation gap quarrel had even spilled onto the bus terminals with senior citizens refusing to ride with any bus whose conductor referred to them as either granny or granddad. An over enthusiastic conductor would run to an approaching senior citizen and say, "Granny, let me help you with your bags," in order to travel with his bus.

One senior citizen was overheard to reply, "Out of place! Out of place! That's what you are. Who are you calling granny? I'm not old, I'm just 73!"

Mrs. Sandison was still humming as she went down the stairway; the sea bath had been rather invigorating that morning. She could hear her husband whistling as he warned the car's engine. She almost down when a thought hit her. Hmmm, she thought. Ruth not wanting anything today? No bridal catalogue, no novels, no magazine, no perfumes, nothing. That's not Ruth. Come to think of it, she was a little dismissive. Something was wrong with her baby. She turned around and climbed the stairs again. She knocked on Ruth's door and asked to come in. Ruth told her to come.

Mrs. Sandison looked down at her daughter. She was indeed subdued. "Are you sure that you are alright, darling?"

"Yes, Mom," said Ruth without conviction and not looking at her mother.

Mrs. Sandison sat down on the edge of the bed and cradled one of Ruth's feet. Looking straight into her daughter's face she said, "Well, you do not sound alright to me. Is that Christian boy bothering you?" Ruth did not answer and her face crumpled as if she was going to cry. Her mother moved fast dropping her foot to put her arms about her daughter, cradling her. She was not pleased with that Jamie.

"Listen sweetheart. You are young and beautiful. You don't have to take shit from anybody, least of all that Christian boy. Didn't I warn you about them Christians, those hypocrites? You just drop him and find somebody, black, white or yellow who not only claims to love you, but respects you. You understand me?"

Ruth nodded, and her mother kissed her forehead; and gently rested her back on the pillow and went her way. Ruth felt comforted by her mother but she knew that her advice was hard to follow. She loved Jamie. Her mom just had a prejudice against Christians. But she did agree that Jamie was far from being an exemplary Christian. But, Ruth loved him and did not want anyone else.

Chapter 9

Ruth dug her toes in the sand and looked up at the sky. The sun was not directly overhead but it was still hot. It was almost half past four. She glanced lingeringly at the horizon. It was a scene that never ceased to warm her and arouse celestial thoughts; where the sky seemed to touch the sea and passing clouds appear to dissolve in the water. The world must be round, she always concluded.

Ruth was relaxed and Jamie seemed miles away for the moment. The gentle breeze swayed the coconut trees this way and that, playfully. White gallings pondered one leggedly about their next move. The faint murmur of the ocean and the sky break of the waves just below her feet were not only poetic but therapeutic for Ruth. This was what she liked most about a visit to the beach.

***

Earlier, she and her friends had one some resistant running along the beach, a few aerobic exercise and then had gone swimming. They were now sitting on the sand, next to each other, lost in their own thoughts, enjoying the ambiance. At this point, a black man stopped in front of Alma and said, "girl, you are really pretty, and like to have a good ass too. I would really like to f—k you." Alma spat contemptuously near to his foot. He reached over and slapped her, hard.

Alma grabbed her cheek and opened her mouth as if to scream, horror all over her face, but no words or sound came. Before Alma could close her mouth, her cousin, Dinah, and her friend Chloe, were on the scene. Dinah stood in front of the man and Chloe behind.

"Why did you slap my cousin?" Dinah asked him.

"Since when I have to answer to you?" was his insolent reply. With that Chloe hooked both of his hands from behind and locked them in his back. Then she locked one of his legs with one of her so that he was virtually standing on one leg. Simultaneously, Dinah slapped him again and again, right and left handedly, hard. Not being able to free himself from Chloe's grip, he spat in Dinah's face. Both women saw red.

Chloe let go of his foot and kicked him in the butt with her knee. Dinah wheeled twice, flew into the air, martial arts style, and hit him by his jaw with her foot. He fell and landed towards the incoming waves, which washed over him. A man from the small crowd that had gathered pulled him to safety.

After a while, he sat up groggily. His face was swelling and blood was dripping from the side of his mouth. He still tried to glare at the women and recalling the spit that she had forgotten to wash from her face,

57

Dinah spat into his face and went to the sea and washed her face.

After Dinah had spat into the offender's face, the man who had pulled him out of the water said, "That's enough, woman. Don't get me angry today!"

"Really?" responded Chloe, and with that she kicked him hard in the groin. As if seeing stars, his face contorted with pain, the man grabbed his crotch and fell to the ground.

Dinah and Chloe stood side by side, looking challengingly at the crowd, their attitude asking, 'Who's next?' But no one took up the challenge and they all went back to what they were doing, as if nothing had happened.

Ruth stood up. "Girls," she said, "let's go. Alma you are probably too shaken do drive, so I'll drive."

"I'm alright, now, Ruth. But thanks," replied Alma as if just waking up.

"OK," continued Ruth, "then Dinah and Chloe will go with you, and Sally and I will go with Judy. Fine everybody?" Everyone nodded and set off without a backward glance, just picking up their towels and stopping at the boot of Alma's car to pull on their T-Shirts.

Dinah's mother, Mona, was sister to Alma's father, Rupert Sangue. She had a diploma in food and nutrition, so he had made her head of his kitchen/ restaurant, but Alma had asked her aunt to give Dinah and Chloe leave to go to the beach with her. She used them as her bodyguards to ward off unwanted attention on the beach where a number of men believe that anything goes.

Dinah was five foot eight, slim and versed in martial arts. Chloe was five foot five, medium build and as strong as a horse. Both of them had never lost a fight.

The girls dropped Dinah and Chloe off and then drove on to Judy's house and easily a mansion; with her, and only child and her parents as occupiers. Mrs. Dembar did not like servants because they could never cook well enough or clean well enough to please her. So she did her chores herself and opened her gift shop at 10:00am when all other shops opened at 8:00am. The mansion contained a beauty salon with two professionals on call at any one time. Alma would need make-up in order to hide the slightly visible fingerprints of the beach offender on her face. The girls went out every Saturday night.

Judy hardly used the salon except to get her hair washed and cut. She wore her hair like Elizabeth Taylor, being of the same colour, and she had the same amber coloured eyes also. But she lacked Elizabeth's confidence and it showed. Being too slim in St. Vincent is not so favourable. The same height as Ruth, Judy measured 34-24-34. Not bad, but being the smallest of the four girls did not sit comfortably with her and she covered herself with big jeans and big shirts. She wore no make-up and no jewelry.

Mr. Dembar, who owned acres and acres of banana fields, was eager for Judy to get married and give him a grandson, since his wife would not agree to have another child. But Judy proclaimed that men were boring so Mr. Dembar was fearing and wondering if his daughter was gay. Of course, he would love her, but who would give him grandchildren?

Chapter 10

It was after 7:00pm and the girls were getting ready to go out. They were near done, all dressed like Judy tonight except that the other girls were wearing close fitting tops. The make-up artist was putting finishing touches on Alma's make-up and she was fussing a lot because she did not really like make-up. Ruth wandered off and found herself in one of the back porches. Her heart wasn't on going out tonight. She wanted things to be alright with her and Jamie and until they were, deep down, she couldn't take in much. The beach though was fantastic.

Judy's house was on a hill west of the capital. From the back of the house, one could see the capital and the harbour, the hills east of the capital, and the villages between.

It was twilight and the lights were on. The view was spectacularly breathtaking.

"Ah," thought Ruth. "This view is worth more than this house, for sure." It was refreshing and uplifting and she went back in to see if the others were ready.

They were, but Sally couldn't make up her mind as to what of Judy's bracelet to borrow. Mrs. Dembar sold mainly jewelry and perfumes, and she showered Judy with all sorts of tempting gifts to encourage her to dress more feminine. But thus far, her efforts had failed. Sally finally decided on a diamond encrusted gold bracelet. She wanted to wear the matching earrings, but the other girls advised that it would appear too formal and so she finished off with pink costume jewelry to match her top.

The girls decided to use one car for the night. So Alma locked up hers and they piled into Judy's. They were both Mercedes and they both were silver blue. As the girls drove along, the headlamps spotted several dogs along the way. Finally Sally asked, "Why do dogs roam so much at night?"

"I suppose it is because they sleep so much during the day," suggested Alma.

"Nah," said Sally. "I think it is because they are going to look for sex if they don't have a bitch at home, just like men." The girls laughed.

"Since you know everything," giggled Judy, "tell me where to park."

"Where are we going?" asked Sally.

"Didn't we agree to hang out at Kentucky tonight?" Judy responded.

"Who are you talking about? I thought that we were going to talent on the move."

"I couldn't take that today," put in Ruth.

"Oh, so you decided for the rest of us. Since when did you become dictator of this clique?" asked Sally playfully stern. They drove around the block and saw no

62

space to park. "I will just have to park at the market," concluded Judy.

"In that case, we may as well park at my home. It's almost the same distance," said Alma.

They all agreed and so they drove up to Alma's, parked and walked about 1000 metres back to Kentucky Fried Chicken. The ground floor was filled. They made their orders, waited for them and went upstairs. They were still unoccupied. They made their choice and sat down where they could see most of the coming and goings.

Tony had indeed called Sally the night before but he was only interested in talking about Ruth so she had hung up on him. She had not mentioned this to Ruth, of course. Sally was not interested in a steady boyfriend right now. They were possessive and made too many demands. More-so, she was off to London in a year's time to study law and couldn't be bothered with commitment now. But she liked Tony and she had heard that black men had large penises and she really wouldn't have minded testing the rumor with Tony. He was handsome. And she liked sex.

**

Sheridan, on the other hand had slept the night away. When she found out the next morning that Jamie had called, she decided to pay him a visit after work. She had never visited him uninvited before, but now she had to take the bull by the horns and make sure she did not lose him

***

The girls were about halfway through their chicken when Sally said, "Don't turn around girls, but that black man, Tony, has just come up the steps and is looking right at me. Is he tracking us? I swear..." Then Sally's jaw dropped and a look of horror crossed her face as she looked past Tony. Instinctively the girls, as well as Tony turned and saw about three metres behind him, Jamie with a tray of chicken and a girl, Sheridan hanging on to his arm.

All of the girls mirrored Sally's expression, but as Tony faced them again, it was very obvious which of the girls had the most stakes in the incident. Ruth was not only horrified, but she was also shocked, stunned, ruffled, embarrassed and humiliated. It was as if time was suspended for a moment and without meaning to, Tony stood, watching the drama unfold.

Jamie just nodded casually at them and found a seat with his back to their table. Upon this, Tony came to himself, a little embarrassed at having witnessed it in full view of the girls, and, feeling their pain, he found a seat that allowed him to watch Jamie fully and the girls covertly. He had intended to greet them before the incident but afterwards he deemed it would have been insensitive so he passed without acknowledging them.

So that was her man, the one she was waiting for yesterday, thought Tony. He looked at Jamie. Yeah, he was good looking, but so was Ruth. Tony wondered how the man could treat a beautiful girl like Ruth so callously. Was it a coincidence? But if it were, he would have looked surprised. Instead, he was as cool as a cucumber. Tony smiled inwardly. It must be Ruth was not giving him sex and that ugly one was or the ugly one's sex was better.

Tony was very much attracted to Ruth and therefore chose to believe that it was because Ruth wasn't giving this man sex that he was giving her horrors with an ugly woman. Tony smiled again but quickly creased the smile, feeling Ruth's pain. A woman must feel insulted when her man horns her with someone below her standard. Now Tony was angry with the man. How could he treat Ruth this way?

Tony glanced at Ruth. She was still in shock and had gone very pink in colour. Her friends were looking everywhere but at her. No one was eating. He wanted to cradle her in his arms or else strangle that man. He glared at Jamie and continued to do so until Jamie felt the stare and looked up to meet his eyes. Jamie turned his face away but Tony continued to glare at him. Jamie did not know this man who was glaring at him and figured that it was a case of mistaken identity and so did not look the man's way again.

All of the girls were uncomfortable. Finally, Sally said, "Let's go. Let's go to my place." They all agreed without fuss and left, their chicken forgotten. Sally lived on the same block as Kentucky, almost at the opposite end, save one building. Her parents were pharmacists and operated a pharmacy on the front of the ground floor of their building. They rented offices to other businesses in the back and the family lived upstairs in a large three bedroom flat.

Donald, Sally's twenty-year-old brother completed the family. He used to date Judy when she was sixteen and he was eighteen. When they had sex, it was the first for both of them but he did not wish her to know that he was still a virgin at eighteen. The whole affair was bungled. Judy was disappointed and the second attempt wasn't much better, so she gave up on him, more-so because he hinted that she needed to gain weight. Judy had never dated after that.

Tony was angrier that the man was ignoring him, treating him with indifference. He pushed back his chair and went over to Jamie, and stood next to him. He touched Jamie on the shoulder. Jamie turned an inquiring face to him. Eyeballing Jamie, Tony asked, "Why did you embarrass Ruth in front of this ugly woman of yours?"

"Why don't you mind your own business, nigger?", before Jamie could turn his face away, quick as a flash, Tony, a boxing enthusiast, had landed a right punch to Jamie's left eye and a left jab to his right jaw. Jamie went flying to the floor, Sheridan began screaming and Tony went back to his chicken.

Three security guards came running. Jamie's eye was swollen shut and blood was dripping from his cut brow. Two of his teeth were near to him on the floor and blood was running from his mouth. One of the guards turned back to call the ambulance and the police and the other two tried to calm Sheridan. On ascertaining that Tony was the troublemaker, the guards assayed to escort him out but he insisted that he was not leaving until he had finished his chicken, and he took his time. The police arrived in ten minutes and the ambulance in fifteen. Tony was arrested and taken to the police station.

Ruth explained to her friends that she and Jamie had had a little quarrel the day before, but she insisted, it was only a little quarrel. But again, she admitted, those little quarrels were becoming more frequent lately but they always made up. What happened at Kentucky was totally unexpected. How did it happen? Jamie passed her with just a nod of the head as if they were no longer lovers and he was just saying hello. She hadn't seen him all week but that was because of exams.

"Girls," she asked, "how did this happen so suddenly?"

"Perhaps it was happening and you did not notice," suggested Sally.

"Jamie want us to have sex, blurted out Ruth.

"But Ruth, the man is normal. What do you want him to do, wank every night when there are so many willing partners around?" asked Sally remonstratively.

"We can get married. I am ready," yearned Ruth.

"Perhaps he is not," reminded Sally.

"That is why I don't date because I am not ready for sex and that is all that men want these days. They don't want to get married, put in Alma.

"Why are you two so hung up on sex before marriage? I was hanky-pankying since I was twelve. When Donald's friends used to come for weekends, they used to sneak into my room," confessed Sally. "And I am going to continue to have sex, married or not," she finished.

"Can't you talk about something more interesting than sex?" pleaded Judy. Sally laughed.

"What is more interesting than sex, chemistry, anthropology? Sex is fun. It's exciting. You are allowing two experimental sessions with my brother to bias your concept of sex. You don't know what you are missing girl," exuded Sally, eyes shining.

"I want to find out. That's why I want to get married," said Ruth.

"And if you don't get married?" challenged Sally.

"Come on, girls. This conversation is boring. Ruth is not going to change her values, neither is Sally. Every man to his own order, change the topic," yawned Alma.

"What am I going to do about Jamie?" asked Ruth.

"Jamie visits you every Sunday after evening service. Why not wait and see what happens tomorrow and not jump to conclusion?" suggested Alma.

"I suspect that Tony knows that Jamie is dating one of us," ventured Judy. "He was looking at Jamie and the girl, the same time we did and then he just stood there, looking at us."

"Yeah, he was definitely coming our way when Jamie turned up," added Sally. The phone rang. All of the girls were sprawled on Sally's queen-size bed. She was in the corner. She climbed over the others and reached for the phone from the bedside table.

"Hello," answered Sally.

"Sally, this is Tony." Talk about the devil, thought Sally.

"Hi Tony, what's up?" replied Sally.

"Sally, are you eighteen? He asked.

"I am. Why?"

"I got into a fight with that guy that you all were looking at and I have been arrested. If no one bails me tonight, I have to spend the night here which i am not keen to do. My parents and circle are all in Biabou and won't get a bus into town this late at night. Will you bail me, please? I will owe you," he begged.

Sally envisioned herself in bed with him. She smiled.

"Yeah, as long as you remember those last three words I can bail you," she blackmailed.

"Yes, I know. I owe you."

"Ok, I'll be there," said Sally, and hung up.

Expressionless, Sally turned and faced the girls. As cool as if she had just been discussing a shopping trip, she related the matter to them. They were shocked. Ruth was frantic.

"A fight? Is Jamie hurt, where is Jamie?" she asked.

"I don't know if you were listening, Ruth, but we didn't discuss Jamie. I'm going around to the police station," Sally replied, assertively.

"I'm coming with you," said Alma.

"We are all coming," said Ruth. She had to ask Tony about Jamie. Of course she was going with Sally.

It was only three minute walk to the station. As soon as the sentry let them in, they went up two steps, into a room, and there was Tony sitting on a bench. Sally approached the station sergeant and Ruth approached Tony. As soon as she learned that Jamie was hurt and was probably in the hospital, she asked for an excuse and spoke to Sally.

"Do you mind if I leave now, please? Jamie is probably in the hospital."

"Sure," encouraged Sally. "Girls, go to the hospital with Ruth. I'm close to home and this might take a while." The girls left and Sally threw Tony a knowing look. Tony read her.

Ruth and Alma took a taxi to the hospital and Judy took one to Alma's home to retrieve her car and when meet the girls at the hospital. Jamie had recovered before he had gone to the hospital but he was still dazed and the A&E decided to keep him overnight for observation. The cut on his brow was sutured but they could do nothing about his missing teeth.

Mr. and Mrs. McKenzie were already by his side and his mother was fraught with worry. His father was calm. His son was alive. God had taken care of him. Why worry? The McKenzie's gave way to Ruth and Alma and later Alma gave Ruth and Jamie some privacy.

As soon as they were left alone, Jamie said, "That man who beat me up knew your name and was defending your honour. What's up, Ruth?"

"I met him or he met me while I was waiting for you yesterday. I told him that I have a boyfriend. Coincidentally, he was at Kentucky tonight and saw everything. But am I not the one who should ask what's up? You passed me with a woman on your arm and just barely nodded at me. What's up, Jamie?"

"Not now, Ruth."

***

Transaction over, Sally and Tony emerged from the police station side by side. "Where are you staying?" asked Sally.

"At my aunt's in Villa, he replied.

"Then why didn't you call her?" asked Sally.

"Call my goody goody aunt and tell her that I'm arrested! Are you crazy? When will I hear the end of it?"

"I live upstairs over the Clarke's pharmacy. Would you care for a drink?"

"Yes, thanks. I would like that," responded Tony, meeting Sally's eyes. They set off. "I can't thank you enough for what you just did there." He put his arm around her and squeezed her shoulder, drawing her to him. "Thanks."

Soon they turned into the alley along the Clarke's building and walked the length of it. Then up the steps, searched for the keys, opened the door and entered the hallway. Took off their shoes and placed them in a shoe pocket and then entered the white carpeted drawing room. Tony felt his feet sinking about three inches into the sponge-based carpet. The room was affluently furnished with plush dark brown sofas, wall paintings and sculptures.

A golden bowl of fresh anthurim lilies sat grandly on a huge floor television. Mr. and Mrs. Clarke were watching TV. "Hi, mom, hi dad," Sally kissed them both.

"How was your day, dear?" asked Mrs. Clarke.

"Fine, Mom." Mr. Clarke looked at Tony. A black man, he thought.

"Dad, Mom," said Sally, "Tony has come for a drink; we will have it in my room." Tony shook hands with the Clarke's then followed Sally into the kitchen to collect the drinks. He took a stout and Sally chose a sweet drink. Tony noted that everything was posh as he followed Sally down the corridor and into her cream-coloured bedroom.

"Why do you need such a big bed?" he asked.

"I had to get it to accommodate the girls when we have a sleep over. They have extra rooms in their homes. We have only three bedrooms," explained Sally.

***

The nurse popped in and told Ruth that it was time to leave. She kissed Jamie goodnight. Mrs McKenzie wanted to sit all night with Jamie but he and the nurse convinced her that it wasn't necessary. She left reluctantly. Ruth joined Alma and Judy who were keeping each other company in the waiting room. Judy had not gone in to see Jamie. Judy dropped Alma off to collect her car and then drove Ruth home, each occupied with her own thoughts after a long day.

***

Tony was sitting in a soft, single-seater sofa. Sally was sitting on the arm of the same sofa wth her arm draped across the back of the sofa. They sipped their drinks in silence. Every now and again Sally would bend over and kiss Tony's forehead or his nose. Tony sipped his drink. Then she got up in a hurry as if she'd forgotten something and switched on her hi-fi to a jazz her mind and then she put on the TV and went back to her place on the sofa's arm. She had put down her drink. She did not take it up again.

Now Sally draped her arm over Tony's shoulder and slipped her other hand down his shirt and began to caress his hairy chest and play with his nipples. She got up again and turned the lights right down. On returning, she took Tony's drink from his hand.

"I love Ruth," he said cautioningly.

"And I love you," she replied kissing his lips.

"So we understand each other?" Sally replied. "Business."

"Well, then let's make ourselves more comfortable," said Tony and he got up and stripped down to his briefs and Sally did the same they both fell into bed.

Sally and Tony made love to each other, caressing, touching, fondling, kissing, and sucking. When Sally slipped one of his testicles in her mouth and gentle twirled it around, moving from one to the other in quick succession and at the same time gently massaging his penis, paying attention to the tip, he experienced a new ecstasy and exploded, ejaculating on her back. They went into the shower to clean up and made love there too.

They finally showered and when they fell back into bed, Tony parted her tights and penetrated her. Then kneeling over her, he lifted her buttocks up toward him and pumped and pumped.

"Oh glory!" he said. "You have a great pussy: tight but pliable and juicy. Hmmmmm!"

"Your penis exceeds my expectation too," confessed Sally.

Tony rested Sally back down and turned her on her side, then on her tummy, then on her other side and finally, on her back again. Sally came twice before he ejaculated for the second time, depositing on the bed to avoid getting her pregnant. He had not planned this and was caught without condoms. They were at it again before the night was over and he didn't bother to go home at all that night.

In between her love sessions, Sally made a conference call to the girls and learnt that Jamie was alright.

Chapter 12

Ruth couldn't sleep that night, neither Mrs. McKenzie, but Ruth had more to worry about. Imagine, Jamie had the audacity to ask her what was going on? After one quarrel on Friday, he had walked into Kentucky on Saturday with a woman on his arms and still asked her, what was going on? Perhaps Sally was right. Perhaps it did not happen overnight. It just boiled over overnight. Perhaps Jamie was unfaithful to her.

And Tony, why had he hit Jamie on her behalf? Was he trying to attract her attention, ingratiate himself to her? By beating up the man she loved? The man must be a fool. She was not racist, but she firmly believed that people should keep relationship inside their race, handsome or not. More-so, how could Sally bail him after what he had done to Jamie? She had paid more attention to the bailing of that man than to Jamie's welfare.

Ruth dozed on and off. She did not sleep well. Finally, she reached for the remote and switched on the TV. Then she switched it off. Nothing else could interest her now. She checked the time and was surprised to find that it was already 5:00am she had better call the hospital to find out if Jamie was alright and if he would be discharged today. She reached for the phone and decided that it would be better to wait until 6:30 or 7:00 am.

Sally was up at five too. Her parents would be up at 5: to get ready to go to church for 7:00 am. They all went to church. They were Anglicans. Tony had to leave before her parents were up. She could bring her male friends but they were not allowed to sleep over. In St. Vincent children stay at home until they get married. If they never marry, and they are not crowded for space, then they never leave home.

Sally had a little problem. Buses were not readily available on Sunday mornings, and certainly not before 9:00 am. Not even taxis were available this early. She kissed Tony on his cheek and rolled off the bed. She went around to her brother's room and knocked.

"Come in," he mumbled. He was watching a porn video. "What now?" he knew that she wanted a favour.

"Could you drop my friend Tony to Villa please?"

"I have to get ready for church," he hedged.

"I know that, Donald. If you hurry, with very little traffic so early, you'll be back in time," she begged.

"Fifty dollars," said Donald.

"What?" replied Sally in shock.

"Fifty dollars," replied her brother determinedly unruffled.

"The car is mine too, you know," reminded Sally annoyed.

"I know. There are the keys," responded Donald, still unmoved.

Sally had never bothered to learn to drive. Why should she? She lived right in the centre of town. Her parents, brother and two best friends could drive. Why should she bother? She was sorry now.

"OK," she conceded, having no choice. "Fifty dollars."

"You have to pay me up front," said Donald. Sally looked at him.

"You don't expect me to trust you to pay me mission completed, do you? I know you Sally."

"Sally went back to her room to get the money or write her brother a cheque. Tony was dressed and sitting on the sofa.

"Good morning," he said with a smile. Sally kissed him on his cheek.

"Good morning," she replied, also smiling.

"I'm negotiating a ride for you. If you look in the bathroom chest, you'll find a new toothbrush. Freshen up."

"Yes, I'll freshen up, but forget the ride. I'll hitchhike," he said proudly. "You have done enough for me already."

"Drop that stance, Tony. You'll take the ride. No arguments. Hurry up." And Sally gave him a gentle push towards the bathroom.

As soon as he left, Sally wrote her brother a cheque and handed it to him reluctantly. Tony kissed Sally and met Donald for the first time. They nodded at each other and went down the corridor.

***

Ruth kept checking the time. It was still not six o'clock. Frustrated she went around to her parents' room and knocked. It was their sleep-in morning, but she needed to speak to someone. Her mother's voice invited her in. As soon as she opened the door she began to apologise for waking them so early.

"Hush, sweetheart," said her mother. "Call us anytime. Come."

Ruth went around to her mother's side of the bed. Her mother made room for her. Ruth lay next to her mother.

"You alright, baby?" asked her father. Ruth opened her mouth to answer and began to cry instead. Her mother put her arm about her but her father flung himself off the bed and hastened to his daughter's side. This was his baby. Six years younger than his last daughter. After the two girls, he was hoping for a son, but he loved Ruth nevertheless. He picked her up in his arms as if she was weightless and sat down in the sofa with her cradled to his breast. He let her cry, heart-rending sobs as if she wanted to dump all of her burdens. Mr. Sandison could never bear to see his children cry. He always wished he could take their pain.

Mrs. Sandison sat at her husband's feet on the floor, holding onto Ruth also. They didn't tell her to stop crying. They just waited patiently for her to stop, each wanting to cry too. Finally, after what seemed like hours, although it was only twenty minutes, Ruth stopped crying. Her mother handed her a handful of facial tissues.

"What's up, baby?" her father asked gently.

"Don't be afraid to tell us everything," added her mother. She did tell them everything.

"I am now waiting to call the hospital to see how he is doing, or if he is going to discharged. I am wondering if I'm losing him and worse, I am wondering if all of this just happened suddenly or if he was cheating on me all this time," finished Ruth. Her father squeezed her. Her mother sighed and looked at her husband, waiting for him to speak.

"First of all, baby, I want to meet this black man to thank him for doing what I would have done myself, if I were there," said Mr. Sandison.

"I don't love him, Dad. And I don't want him. I want Jamie," protested Ruth.

"Baby, I'm not asking you to invite him to ask for your hand in marriage. I want to meet this gallant man. What he did was wrong. You can't go around beating up people who do things that you don't like. But I am your father. I will break the law for you if this man did it, I want to say thanks. You will see that I meet him."

"Yes, Dad," submitted Ruth. Mr Sandison continued, "secondly, people don't turn up with people on their arms overnight, whether they be lovers or friends, it takes time. I believe that your Jamie has not been faithful but for your sake, I hope that you don't lose him. But, if you do, it's not the end of the world," he squeezed his daughter. Mr Sandison looked at his wife.

"Now, sweetheart," she began. "Let me get this straight. When Jamie came in with the girl, did he see you?"

"Yes mom. That's what humiliated me so much. He saw us and just nodded causally to me because his hands were full. Then he sat with his back to us. We were all so shocked and ashamed, and people could see our embarrassment so we just got up and left. Perhaps that is why the black man, by the way his name is Tony, got vexed and beat him up," explained Ruth still smarting from the experience. The Sandisons were angry.

"Really!" they said together.

"See what I'm saying?" continued Mrs. Sandison. "If you run after him after treating you with such scant respect, he will do you worse. He will never respect you. I say to drop him. Cry all you want, but leave him. You are too young and beautiful to take shit like that."

"Your mother has a point, baby. If you don't respect yourself, who will respect you?" added Mr. Sandison.

"But I need to know how he is doing, at least," begged Ruth.

"Yes, find out about his welfare and so on. Even visit him he is not well, but no more," Mrs. Sandison advised. It was almost seven o'clock. Ruth thanked her parents for their love and support and went off to call the hospital.

***

Mrs. McKenzie did not sleep well. She prayed for her son every waking moment. At 5:00 am as usual, she got up and did her devotions then she prepared breakfast. At exactly 5:30 she woke her husband and he did his devotions too and then she brought him his breakfast. She sat on the edge of the bed.

"Dear," she began, "we have to leave about 6:15 to go the hospital to get Jamie."

"Why do you have to go? Aren't you cooking before you go to church today?"

"Of course, I must cook but I'm going to get my son."

"Since he has left home I have been collecting him every Sunday morning and you've never offered to come along."

"This time you are collecting him from the hospital and I'm coming with you," replied Mrs. McKenzie firmly.

"Suit yourself," said he husband, not pleased.

"Hurry up, dear," busied Mrs. McKenzie.

"I have time. I'm leaving at 7:30."

"7:30!" exclaimed his wife.

"7:30," repeated her husband firmly.

***

When Ruth called the hospital, the nurse told her that all of Jamie's tests were alright so he would be released but he had to be seen by the doctor and that would take place between seven and eight o'clock. Ruth then asked her father if he would mind taking her to the hospital and both parents agreed to accompany her. They arrived at the hospital about 7:40am, five minutes before the McKenzie's. They had to wait because the doctors were making their rounds. When the McKenzie saw the Sandisons in the waiting room, Mrs. McKenzie said:

"What are you all coming to visit my son for? That little slut of yours make her black man beat up my son and you still have the bold facedness to make me see you? I told him a long time ago to drop that heathen bitch and look for a nice Christian girl."

Both Mr. Sandison and Ruth were shocked, and their jaws dropped open in surprise. Even Mr. McKenzie was horrified. But Mrs. Sandison was equal to her retorted;

"Are you going to church this morning?"

"And hear the nastiness that is coming out of your mouth? I don't trust Christians, but at least the true ones certainly don't talk like you. That two timing, promiscuous, no-good, hypocritical, scoundrel of yours is no Christian and now I can see why. Like mother like son. He is not good enough for my daughter. I told her long time ago to drop him and look for a good man."

Mrs. McKenzie was squaring up to reply when her husband said, "That's enough, Ethel!" in a voice that she dared not disobey. But it was time for Mr. Sandison to have his say, having recovered from his initial shock.

"Mrs. McKenzie, did you refer to my daughter as a slut?"

"You heard me, didn't you?" she answered unapologetically.

"You would take it back, Mrs. McKenzie," said Mr. Sandison menacingly.

"Or else?" asked Mrs. McKenzie. Mr. Sandison was angry.

"If you were a man, I'd clean up your mouth with my fist. But I can't hit a woman. I'll sue you for defamation of my daughter's character," he finished.

"We don't have time or money to waste on this hypocrite, I'll clean her mouth for her," said Mrs. Sandison. And before anyone could stop her, she slapped Mrs. McKenzie hard across her mouth and said, "Turn the other cheek, Christian!" Stepping back she threatened, "Sue me now, you bitch and as soon as I get the warrant, I'll come straight and beat you up. "I'll go to jail for my daughter."

Ruth stood rooted to the spot. She wanted to run away but her legs felt like lead. She just stared into nothingness, pretending that she wasn't there bathed in shame.

One side of Mrs. McKenzie's mouth was swollen and one of the lips was probably cut because there was a little trickle of blood.

"We won't be suing you, Mrs. Sandison," said Mr. McKenzie in a forced calm. "Christians do make mistakes but we try not to render evil for evil. I do not believe that your daughter is a slut and I apologize on behalf of my wife. But I do not believe that my son is any of those things you called him either," he finished.

"She started the name calling!" rejoined Mrs. Sandison, still angry.

"I know," conceded Mr. McKenzie," and I'm sorry."

"I'm sorry too," returned Mrs. Sandison, but still casting murderous glances Mrs. McKenzie's way.

Mr. McKenzie stepped forward and shook hands with Mr. Sandison.

"I'm sorry," he said again. "May I take this opportunity to invite you and your family to our church. You are welcome, any time."

"Thank you, for everything," replied Mr. Sandison.

Chapter 13

So Jamie had a Sunday off from church and so did his mother. Neither of them wished to expose their swollen body parts. The doctor gave Jamie ten days sick leave to allow his eye and jaw to heal. He would miss work but he appreciated the time to think. There was much to think about: Ruth, Sheridan, the damaged relationship between both parents and that black man.

Jamie now realized that he should have revealed his extracurricular activities with women more gradually to Ruth, instead of dropping it on her so suddenly yesterday at Kentucky. He had suspected that she and her friends would be there. But he hadn't really planned it that way.

Sheridan had followed up on her intention to visit him after work. When she had arrived he was just in the process of getting ready to go for a swim. He had told her that, but she had indicated that she would not mind staying and do some household chores for him while he was gone. On hearing her intentions, Jamie had invited her in, sat her down and told her that Ruth was his girlfriend. Why then had he come into her life, she had wanted to know.

Jamie explained to her that at that time, Ruth was proving to be difficult and that he had been considering moving on to someone else and so he had turned to her, Sheridan. But now, he had gone on to explain, he was sure that he did not wish to leave Ruth.

Sheridan had not been convinced. She accused him of wanting to use her and have her as a sideshow, as players do. Her heart could not be turned on and off like a tap when it suited his fancy. Jamie had tried to apologise explaining that he thought it would be better for them to end the relationship instead of going deeper, which would be harder for her, since he had no intention of leaving Ruth. But she had insisted that she was going nowhere. Since he wasn't married, he was hers too.

Jamie was getting a little angry. What did she mean that she wasn't leaving him, he thought? That wasn't her choice. He just had to tell her to get out and not come back, plus stop calling her, stop talking to her. Then what could she do? He thought. But he had reconsidered; after all, he did not have to pay her for sex so he could save that money towards a car. If she wanted to stay, it was her choice.

Out loud, he had assured her that he did not wish her to go; he just did not want her to get any illusions. She in turn had assured him that she knew what she was doing and he had left her and gone for a swim. As soon as he had gone, Sheridan set to work, sorting clothes, hanging, laundering and ironing, then cleaning, vacuuming, and so on. Jamie must think I'm stupid, she thought. I didn't take my pill this morning, and I'm not taking anymore. I'm going to get pregnant. Then how will he get rid of me? Married or not married, me and that child will always be around. Tired of taking shit from men, she had finished. When Jamie came back, very late, and she was still there, they had gone to Kentucky.

***

Mrs. McKenzie stood in front of the full-length mirror on her wardrobe. Nearly fifty, she looked great, same blue eyes and blonde hair as Jamie. She had mischievous eyes and usually a small medium mouth. But today, after that slap, half of her mouth was swollen and twisted to one side. Now she had two grudges against Ruth Sandison: her black man beat up her son and her mother slapped and threatened her. She would do anything to keep her son from her.

Mrs. McKenzie loved the Lord and her good works and charitable deeds around the community had kept her size between 12-14. But she couldn't understand how the good Lord could ask her to love her enemies, do good to them that hate you and pray for them that despitefully use you. That was not fair. It was not possible to love people like Doreen Sandison. And she, Ethel McKenzie, wasn't going to try. God must understand human limitations.

***

"Fancy Pastor McKenzie inviting us to his church, eh?" said Mrs. Sandison. She and her husband had gone back to bed after returning from the hospital in order to catch up on their Sunday morning sleep.

"Ah, he was just trying to make peace, he knows that we don't go to church," replied her husband lazily.

"Someone would have to pay me handsomely to sit in church, the same church, with Ethel McKenzie," responded his wife. "Because she is so skinny, she thinks that she is a model. Calling my daughter a slut. I swear.."

"Quite, Doreen. Get your rest," interrupted her husband.

***

Ruth felt shattered. Her career and marriage plan was in tatters and she was sure that she wasn't going to get out of bed for many weeks to come. She felt like she had fallen down a deep hole and no one knew that she was there and so would not be able to find her. She couldn't assimilate how on Friday afternoon, she had been a happy young woman hurrying after an exam to see he boyfriend, and by Sunday morning her whole life had turned upside down. No. She was dreaming. So she was going to sleep and when she woke up, everything would be alright.

***

When Mr. and Mrs. Sandison emerged from their rest, it was almost 11:30. In earlier times when the children were small, Sunday was a family day. After they had slept late, Martha would have brunch (half breakfast, half lunch) ready, and then the family would go riding, picnicking, hiking, or to a community fair or something. Sometimes, Martha used to go along to help to look after the children, especially if they were going to the beach. But after the girls got to their late teens, it was every man to his own order.

Now, they still had brunch but afterwards, Mr. and Mrs. Sandison would take themselves off to anywhere that suited their fancy. Today, since Martha had the weekend off, they were going to brunch at a hotel. Usually, Ruth would stay at home, poring over bridal catalogues, longing, dreaming and planning, reading magazines and newspapers and have Martha serve her dinner in bed. Then, she would get up and get ready for about eight o'clock; Jamie would arrive to spend the evening with her.

But today, Ruth was in no mood to read anything. She wanted to sleep but her demons would not suffer her to do so. She dozed and tossed, on and off. Mr. Sandison knocked on her door and was invited in.

"Baby, you do remember that Martha is not here today? And do you remember that you do not like to

90

prepare your own meals? I would be grateful if you could accompany us to brunch at Villa Lodge, which goes until four o'clock and then there is a play at the Memorial Hall at seven o'clock."

"Thanks, Dad, but I don't feel like leaving my bed today."

"I know, baby, that's why I want to take you under my wings today. I won't enjoy myself knowing that you are at home and unhappy. Please?" begged Mr. Sandison, standing over his daughter. She could never say no to her father when he begged like that, so she got up.

"OK, Dad, I'll be ready in five minutes," Ruth conceded.

Ruth washed her face and patted it dry. Then she quickly brushed her hair and held it together with a scrunchie. She opened her wardrobe and looked at the rows of clothes hanging there. She closed it again. She did not feel like dressing up. Instead she pulled out a drawer, took out the diamante breasted, black cat suit and slipped it on. Then she went to the shoes stand and took out a pair of black, diamante topped medium high slippers and put them on. She was ready, no make-up, no earrings, no bracelet, no perfume, nothing. She was just going with dad. But she still looked stunning. The suit accentuated her perfectly shaped figure and curves and she had a youthful glow that was usually hidden by the make-up, only this time, it was somber tinged.

It was a lovely day, there was no fog shrouding the top of Mount St. Andrew today and the birds were having a feast time. There was certainly no hint of rain because the cumulus clouds were a perfect white.

Ruth got into the back of the white Toyota Corolla and lay down, using her fists as a pillow. Her parents looked at each other and said nothing. On the way, they stopped at a coconut vendor but Ruth did not feel any enthusiasm for coconut milk then, so her parents had one each and asked the vendor to trim one dozen coconuts and place them in the car boot. They paid and were on their way, tooting the horn to acquaintances on their way from church. They passed through the capital which was now mainly deserted except for a few vagrants still sleeping under galleries and two entries at the court house and post office respectively. Ruth saw none of this and was not interested either.

The traffic was usually mild on a Sunday morning and so motorist could gamble a bit and speed when they ought not. Very shortly, villa Lodge loomed ahead and in less than a minute, Mr. Sandison turned in at the gate. Ruth got up reluctantly. The car was locked up and the family went to reception to pay for their entry pass. The entertainment hall was comfortable crowded. Groups of people were everywhere, around tables, the pond, a few palms, at the bar, drinking, eating and talking. They were heading towards the food when someone said:

"Hi Ruth, you're with your parents today?" her parents stopped as Ruth turned. She knew that voice.

Sure enough, it was her past head teacher Mrs. Martin. Mrs. Martin noticed her discomfort and asked:

"Ruth, dear, are you alright?"

Ruth mumbled.

"Yes...er...yes."

On hearing Mrs. Martin's concerned question to Ruth, her parents flew to her side, both with their arm around her. Both asked, "Are you alright, baby sweetheart?"

Ruth collected herself a little and said bravely, "Yes, I'm OK."

Then Tony, who himself was surprised but pleased, said: "It's because of me, aunt, I met and introduced myself to Ruth on Friday but she told me that she has a boyfriend. We met again yesterday in circumstances I prefer not to mention and I am sure she have preferred not to see me here," he finished.

"Is that so, baby?" asked Mr. Sandison.

"Yes, dad. Since Friday afternoon I can't seem to get rid of him. I was just a little shocked to see him here,: said Ruth helplessly.

"A little shocked?" responded Mrs. Martin. "You looked as if you'd seen a ghost. Tony is my nephew. He is staying with me until he finds a place in town. He'll be working at the TV station soon."

Without asking, Mr. and Mrs. Sandison knew that Tony was the black man who had beaten up Jamie and Mr. Sandison planned to get acquainted with him before he left or before Tony left. The Sandison chatted with

Mrs. Martin a while and then went to get some food. They had not eaten all day.

There was a wide variety of food available, viz, potato pudding, doucana, fried bakes, saltfish cakes, pizza, conch salad, fried prawns and fried fish, roasted breadfruit and bowl jowl, roti, chicken and chips, crayfish and calaloo, and much more. Ruth was sad but now hungry and filled her plate with fried prawns, coconut homemade bread and potato pudding, accompanied with a medium glass of guava drink. Her parents were happy to see her eat. Mr. and Mrs. Sandison sampled just about everything then took a table at the far end of the pond.

They were almost through their meal when Tony deliberately passed their way on his way to the bar. On his return, Mr. Sandison invited him to join their table for a while. He gladly accepted.

"Those men over there and those at the bar are all interested in your daughter, Mr. Sandison," said Tony ingratiatingly, "and so am I but she wouldn't give ne the light of day," he finished looking straight at Ruth. Ruth looked straight back at him as if she wasn't seeing him and continued eating.

"Well, there isn't anything that I can do about that," responded Mr. Sandison. "I can't choose for Ruth, but I sure do thank you for defending her honour yesterday. I don't recommend it though, but it is just something I would have done myself, and I appreciate it," said Mr. Sandison as if he was preaching.

"I didn't go over to hit him," confessed Tony. "But he was impudent and on top of that, he called me nigger, and then I couldn't stop my hand."

At that Ruth looked at him scowling. Couldn't stop his hands indeed, she thought. Because of him Jamie was hurt and will most likely not be visiting her later, especially after what had happened between their parents at the hospital. It was all this man's fault. Then she stopped herself. It was Jamie who had brought that girl with him and chosen to ignore her.

This man saw it all and thought that Jamie was wrong. She switched again.

"Why are you scowling at me?" asked Tony. But Ruth ignored him and sipped her drink.

"Aw, don't bother with Ruth," said Mr. Sandison, trying to rescue the situation, although he felt that Ruth was rude to his guest. "You come to my shop and pay me a visit anytime you want to," encouraged Mr. Sandison, instructing Tony on how to find his home.

Ruth looked at her father as if to ask, 'are you crazy, inviting him to our home!' He looked back at Ruth as if to say, 'well, it's your fault. If you weren't so rude to him, I would not have had to over extend myself.'

Tony was delighted at the invitation but tried to sound as casual as he could when he replied, "thank you for the invitation. I'll be sure to drop in on you sometimes." He looked at Ruth triumphantly and she scowled even darker.

Chapter 14

Ruth was sprawled on the three-seater sofa in her drawing room, her eyes glued to the clock on the wall. She had been looking at the clock since 7:45 pm, Jamie usually arrived around 8:00 pm. Earlier, her parents had unsuccessfully tried to convince her that in the light of all that had transpired, it was unlikely that Jamie would keep his usual date with her. More-so, Mrs. Sandison had insisted, 'that Ethel McKenzie would not let her son go out tonight.' But Ruth would not budge. She must stay, just in case. Suppose Jamie came and she wasn't there? How could she enjoy the show while worrying if Jamie had come? She must stay at home for her own peace of mind, so her parents had gone to the play without her.

Ruth paid no attention to the clean, rich, red carpet on the floor. The expensive paintings and carvings on the walls did not interest her, neither was she delighted by the mass of flowers around the room. Her attention was on that rectangular, brass, ornamental clock on the wall. It was now 8:10pm. Jamie should have been here by now. The kitchen door slammed. Ruth froze. Who was that? Her mind went wild. Horrible images barraged her. Footsteps were coming through the dining room. She turned terrified eyes towards the dining room's exit. It was Martha, Ruth almost fainted with relief.

"Miss Ruth, you alright?" Martha had expected to see Ruth and Jamie on the sofa. Instead, she was met by Ruth's petrified stare and then, to Martha, Ruth had seemed to collapse. Martha immediately rushed to her side, praying:

"Lord Jesus, please, kum by yah."

In response, Ruth gasped, "I'm alright, Martha. I thought it was a burglar or rapist."

"You didn't expect me?" asked Martha disappointingly.

"I had forgotten, Martha. I was on the lookout for Jamie," Ruth apologized Martha looked relieved.

"I'm sorry that I scared you, Miss Ruth. Really sorry," apologized Martha contritely.

"It's not your fault, Martha. I should have remembered. Could you bring me some water, please?"

Martha was glad to be of service and hustled quickly to fetch the water. "Here you are, Miss Ruth." Ruth drank slowly and felt revived, then she remembered and her eyes reverted to the clock. Her heart sank. It was 8:20 pm Jamie was never late. Handing the glass back to Martha, she said:

"Thank you, Martha. And how was your weekend?"

97

"I was great, church was great. Everybody was great," smiled Martha, relieved that the crisis was over.

"I'm glad to hear that, Martha. Thanks again," said Ruth dismissively. Martha said goodnight, picked up her bag she had dropped on beholding Ruth's calamity, and trotted off to her quarters.

Ruth kept her eyes on the clock. In a strange way, she was finding solace from it, while at the same time, daring it to turn back its hands to 8:00pm so that she could hope again. With its hands nearing 8:30pm, Ruth knew for sure that Jamie was not coming and she did not seem to have the strength to climb the stairs to go to her room. Then a thought hit her. 'No way,' she said to herself. She could not let her parents come home and meet her there. It would be too much for them to either empathize or sympathize with her. She should have listened to them. She gave one last glance of the clock and pulled herself out of the sofa, crossed the room and crawled up the stairs, she eventually got to her room and, without changing her clothes, she went straight to her bed.

After about five minutes, she got up. Now she was angry. Why should she sulk? Didn't her mother say that she was young and beautiful? Why should she break her heart over a man who was cheating on her and flaunting it in front of her face? She fell back on the bed again. She loved him. She loved him. Then the words of a love song came to her: 'why do I keep fooling myself, when I know she loves someone else, only a fool breaks his own heart…' Was she a fool? No, of course not! How could she be wrong to grieve over her boyfriend, when just two days ago everything was alright, or so it seemed? She couldn't forget about him already.

She got up and went to her magazine stand and took up two bridal catalogues. She couldn't call any of her clique now. Judy would be out with her parents. Alma would be in church. Sally would be out somewhere.

***

In fact, Sally had gone to the play. Although her parents were there, she had not gone with them. Just as she was about to turn into the hall, she had run into Tony. He had come with his aunt and her family. He excused himself and he and Sally had forgotten about the play in their eagerness to repeat Saturday night's rendezvous. Once again he had told her how great her pussy was and she had responded that it was because he was so well endowed, pussy and penis fitted like a glove.

"We belong," she had whispered but he could not respond because they both climaxed together. She went into the ninth heaven with a high pitched, suppressed moan and he had beaten the bed with his fist as her vagina convulsed around his penis. After five minutes, they went into the second round and at the moment when Ruth was thinking of Sally, she and tony had just left her home on their way back to see the final act of the play.

Life couldn't get any better for Tony, except for one thing. He longed for Ruth to talk to him. He didn't mind if she cursed or abused him, as long as it was her voice. He wondered if Sally would give him Ruth's phone number. They were walking along in silence when he asked Sally for Ruth's number.

Sally remembered their agreement, but she was still hurt. They had had sex without a condom again and this time he had not withdrawn. She was worried. Suppose she got pregnant? And all he could think about was Ruth. But she gave him the number. He had not pretended to her.

***

Tony was happy, but Jamie was not. He missed Ruth. Every Sunday evening for the past year, Ruth and he had spent the night wrapped in each other's arms on that sofa. He wondered if she had waited for him and longed to feel her body and kiss her. That black man was right to defend her. He had done her wrong. Since 7:45pm he had gone downstairs to call Ruth to inform her that he would be there and had met his mother sitting next to the phone with her Bible on her lap looking meditative. He had not wanted to disturb her or indeed rub salt in her wounds by calling Ruth in front of her. How many times had she reminded him that she had a swollen lip because of Ruth's mother? Or that she had missed church for the first time in years because of Ruth's mother?

No, Jamie decided. He was not spending his ten days sick leave with his parents as they had suggested. That guilt trip of his mother was a humbug. Come Monday, he was going home, back to his apartment. He had not called Sheridan either. If he couldn't call Ruth, why should he call her? If she wanted to know where he was she should have come early to the hospital before he had left. Anyway, how did he know that she had come at all? She had said that she would.

***

When Mr. and Mrs. Sandison came home at ten o'clock, they knew that Jamie had not come or else he would still have been there. They knocked on Martha's quarters and said goodnight and then went up to their daughter. They decided not to go in and told her goodnight from outside the door, affirmed their love and added that they had seen Tony and Sally at the play.

Ruth picked up her phone and called Sally. It rang six times then Sally answered.

"Why are you taking so long to answer?" asked Ruth, pretending annoyance.

"Girl, I was just coming in when I heard the phone and I couldn't find my key for a while," Sally answered.

"Why do you lock your bedroom?"

"To stop my brother helping himself to my money when his allowance runs out before the next one is due," Sally explained.

"Don't your parents pay Donald a salary?"

"They pay him a monthly salary, but still give him a weekly allowance. He doesn't spend his salary. That is to build himself a mansion."

"Mom told me that you and Tony were at the play," Ruth continued accusingly. After all, it was Tony who had caused all of this mess. Why was Sally siding with him?

"Yeah, I met him there. He came with his aunt and her family. He asked and I gave him your number," confessed Sally sensing Ruth's silent accusation.

"You didn't!" exploded Ruth.

"I'm afraid I did," affirmed Sally coolly. "He begged so much, I didn't have the guts to refuse him."

"Sally, that man has caused all of the mess that I'm now in and you gave him my number?" asked Ruth in disbelief.

"How is Jamie, still cool?" asked Sally ignoring Ruth's anger.

"I don't know! I haven't spoken to him since I last saw him in the hospital, thanks to Tony!" shouted Ruth. Sally yawned.

"Ruth, dear, we'll talk tomorrow. I'm tired. Goodnight." And she hung up. Ruth stared at the handset in her hand. Had Sally really hung up on her? She wondered if she should call her back. How dare

Sally hang up on her! But in spite of her annoyance, she decided against it and replaced the handset.

Two minutes later, the phone rang.

"Hello," Ruth answered.

"Hello, Ruth," the person replied. Ruth suspected that it was Tony and her anger flared but she kept her cool.

"Who is this?" she asked warily.

"Tony."

"What do you want?" her voice was tinged with anger.

"Why are you angry?" he asked placatingly.

"You hurt Jamie and so I missed seeing him tonight, all because of you," she finished.

"I'm sorry; he said contritely, "I honestly did not mean to hurt him. Please Ruth, forgive me." Ruth was taken aback.

He seemed genuinely sorry. It would be childish for her to maintain a grudge. Now, what should she say? She would be gracious. She changed her attitude.

"I'm sorry I was harsh, Tony. It wasn't all your fault. I suppose that I am just lashing out like a wounded animal. Please, forgive me." Now it was Tony's turn to be amazed. She was gracious. His heart warmed.

"You don't have to apologize," Tony returned kindly, "I understand how you feel. I just wish…"

"Wish what?" asked Ruth.

"That you would cry on my shoulder and dump your frustrations on me. I'll take anything to be near to you." He was going too far.

"No, thanks, Tony. I'll continue to cry on my pillow for the time being. But, thanks for calling. Goodnight." And she hung up, like Sally.

Like Ruth, Tony looked at the handset in his hand and wondered if he should call back. Like Ruth, he decided against it and he too, hang up. At least, he smiled; self assuredly, she had spoken civilly to him. That was a good start. Also, he had not beat about the bush. He had made his intension clear. He wanted to be there for her.

Ruth's phone rang again. This time it was her sister Megan, calling from England to find out how well Ruth had performed in her exams. Ruth assured her that she had prepared well and therefore believed that she had done well. They chatted a while and then her other sister, Dawne, who was visiting with Megan, took the phone from Megan to ask Ruth if she was planning to come to England to study. Ruth laughed. She reaffirmed to her sister that she had not changed her plans. She was going to get married, enter the teaching profession, and when her children entered Secondary school, she would get herself a degree.

Dawne asked Ruth if her plans sat well with Jamie. Ruth responded that she was sure that she was going to get married, but at that moment, she wasn't sure if it would be to Jamie. Her sisters promised to provide the best bridal gown for her whenever she was ready and then said their goodbyes.

Ruth replaced the handset and then changed into her night wear. Then she turned the lights off. She decided then and there from now on, she would begin to respond more positively to the volume of attention that she received. Who knows? There could be someone out there just as good as or even better than Jamie. She did love him, but there was no denying that what he had done to her yesterday was near unforgivable.

He had embarrassed her in front of that woman. Put that woman above her, passed her as if he did not know her, in front of her friends and Tony. Yet he still had the audacity to ask her what was going on. Things were going to change, thought Ruth as the bells of slumber chimed in the distance.

Chapter 15

It was Monday morning and Ruth's entire clique was still in bed at seven o'clock. They did not envy the people who still had to contend with the morning rush and traffic. For Ruth, it would just be about ten weeks' vacation since she was hoping to enter the teaching profession in September. But for the others, it would be one whole year before they went off to university. They were all along the same train of thought.

So Alma called Judy, Judy called Ruth, Ruth called Sally. Sally suggested that they should use the time to get more familiar with St. Vincent. They had visited all the islands of the Caribbean, as well as London, New York and Paris but they had not yet visited the other eight islands that make up St. Vincent and the Grenadines. As a matter of fact, none of them had visited all of the historic or beauty sites on St. Vincent. Therefore they decided to explore St. Vincent during their holidays.

Then Alma asked, "By the way, how is Jamie?" Ruth paused and the atmosphere changed. The girls waited, empathetically. Ruth told them of the verbal physical confrontation between her mother and Mrs.

McKenzie, her meeting with Tony at the brunch, how Martha frightened her, how Jamie had not come and finally that Tony had called. They all chorused, "Wow!" then Alma added.

"Girl, you've been to hell and back. What can we do to cheer you up?"

"Call Jamie at his parents' house and find out how he is doing and when he will be going back to his apartment," Ruth answered quickly.

"Your wish is my command," agreed Alma.

"Anything else?" Judy asked.

"Not that I can think of right now," replied Ruth.

"Why don't we go shopping today?" this from Sally. They all agreed to go shopping and Alma promised to call Jamie around nine o'clock. They hung up.

***

Sheridan had gone to the hospital around nine o'clock on Sunday, only to be told that Jamie had just left. Then she had gone to his apartment and found it locked. She suspected that he was with his parents, and not knowing where his parents lived, had called every McKenzie in the directory until she had found the residence of Jamie McKenzie, but his mother, not too nicely, told her that Jamie must not be disturbed. She was not deterred. She prayed that Jamie would return to his apartment the next day and promised to visit him straight after work.

***

At exactly nine o'clock, Alma called the McKenzie's home. Mrs. McKenzie answered.

"Hello Sis. McKenzie, how are you?" said Alma.

"Who is this?" she asked.

"This is Alma Sangue. May I speak to Jamie, please?"

"Alma Sangue? Bro. Kenneth Sangue's daughter?" she wanted to make sure.

"Yes, I'm proud to be," answered Alma.

"Oh, how are you, dear?" crooned Mrs. McKenzie. "so you'd like to speak to my son?"

"if you'd let me," chuckled Alma.

"Sure, sure. Come Jamie. Someone wishes to speak to you," and she handed the phone to Jamie who was sprawled on the sofa and left the room.

Jamie and Alma exchanged greetings and then Alma told him that Ruth had delegated to her to find out how he was doing and when he would be returning to his apartment. Jamie wanted to know why Ruth had not called herself. Alma asked him why he had not called Ruth on Sunday night. Not willing to give her an explanation, he conceded and affirmed that both his jaw and eye were still sore, he was on antibiotics, but he would be returning to town after lunch. They said their goodbyes and hung up.

Immediately after, Alma called Ruth. Ruth was expecting the call and picked up right away. Alma conveyed the information but did not tell her that Jamie had questioned Ruth's delegation.

Ruth's parents dropped in before going down to breakfast and then to the shop. While they chatted, Ruth Said:

"Mom, Dad, what a difference a weekend makes, eh?"

"Not a weekend, my dear, a day. Why?" asked her mother.

"All of my marriage plans seem to be in shambles now. Nothing is sure," replied Ruth.

"Not even life is sure, darling. But why are you stressing yourself about marriage? I'm not ready for you to leave home, neither is your father. More-so, you are eighteen, not twenty eight. Why the rush?"

"Good things come to those who wait, the old folk say," put in Mrs. Sandison.

"And hurry birds don't build good nests," added her mother.

"My friends and I are going shopping today," said Ruth, changing the topic.

"Have enough money?" asked her father.

Ruth replied that she hadn't and he left the room and came back with five hundred dollars for her. After they had affirmed their love, they wished her a good day and left.

At 11:00am, Ruth was standing at the gap near to her house that adjoined the leeward highway, waiting for a bus. Then a car stopped and the driver asked:

"Want a ride?"

Ruth smiled, shook her head and said, "No, thanks. I don't take rides from strangers." Then she heard a familiar, female voice.

"It's alright Ruth. I'm here." She stooped a little and looked into the car. It was one of her recent tutors. She smiled again and crossed the road. The tutor opened the door and she stepped in.

"God morning, ma'am, sir. I didn't mean to be rude. But I don't take rides from strangers" she explained apologetically.

It's alright Ruth. You don't have to explain. It's better to be safe than sorry. If more young girls did like you, they wouldn't get raped and killed," the tutor finished. Then she asked:

"Where are you off to on the first day of your end of school?"

"I'm going to Alma's for lunch and then we are going shopping," said Ruth laughing.

"Well, enjoy your day," said Mrs. John. Ruth thanked her.

It was a lovely day, bathed with radiant sunshine and hardly a cloud in the sky. The vegetation was lush and didn't seem to mind the sun at all, especially the cedars, whose sturdy, glossy leaves reflected the rays brilliantly.

Ruth asked the driver to drop her off at the court house. After thanking them, she walked a few metres, crossed the pedestrian crossing turned right, another twenty footsteps and left into the alley and up to Sally's apartment. Sally was not quite ready and so Ruth waited in the drawing room, admiring the paintings to pass time.

After about ten minutes, Sally was ready. They were both dressed in jeans, Sally with a black and red checked shirt and Ruth with a green and white striped shirt and both in high heels. They decided to walk to Alma's since they were not in a hurry and it was not really far. But when they were almost there, Judy's Mercedes pulled up at their feet so they go in.

"You are all dressed like me today," she giggled. "Except for those heels, of course." Judy wore Clark's male shoes.

"No way!" laughed Sally with Ruth joining in.

"Our clothes are not as big as yours. You are the smallest, but wear the biggest clothes." They all laughed again.

"Great day isn't it?" said Judy.

"Couldn't be better," responded Ruth with Sally agreeing with a vigorous nod.

***

When Jamie told his mother that he was leaving after lunch, she could not hide her disappointment. She had been hoping to pamper him for ten days. If there had been a telephone in his room, Jamie would have stayed but there was only one phone and now that he had tasted real privacy, his mother's pampering was not enough to keep him.

He could have had a phone installed since he had begun to work, but for one reason or another, his mother did not like the idea. He went out to the shed to ask his father to transport him since he did not like the idea of standing on the highway with a patch over his eye, waiting for a bus.

***

Alma had ordered curried goat with rice and green pigeon peas, a side order of sliced sweet potatoes, ripe plantains, yam and fresh salad of lettuce and grated carrots. The girls would choose their own deserts. Alma's two younger sisters, Marcia and Marsha, as well as her oldest brother, Winston, were having friends in for lunch also. Mona and her staff were very busy.

The girls talked about everything and everyone: the warning parents, Jamie and Sheridan, Tony – although Sally did not say much here, Ruth talked of the ride from Mrs. John and fashion. Judy did not fancy the current trend of gathered skirts with suspenders. They were to girly for her, but she liked the striped shirts. Except for Judy, everyone wanted new jewelry. They agreed to visit Jamie after shopping.

Soon lunch was over and they freshened up. Since they planned to start shopping from uptown and work their way down, they decided to take the car and park it on Bonadie's Street. Alma took her car because Judy said that she was in no mood to contend with uptown traffic. The girls bought their clothes from boutiques and their shoes from stores, since most of the boutiques did not sell shoes. They decided to visit only boutiques that day and return another day to buy shoes.

After they had parked, they began at Velma's boutique and worked their way down, window shopping and greeting friends along the way, having not yet seen anything that excited them enough to warrant a purchase. Then they got to Egmont Street, and went up to Y.Delima where there were several boutiques. It was there that they began to shop. These shops had the latest trend. They bought a little of everything: underwear, nightwear, swimwear and shorts, shirts and trousers and the latest skirts.

They were so laden down with bags that they decided to take them back to the car and so they walked back uptown and put the shopping into the car boot. Then they drove the car to Bay Street, opposite the police headquarters and parked.

From Bay Street, they walked to Back Street, passing many street vendors coaxing them to buy their wares. The girls obliged, purchase little things such as fancy combs and hair clasps and clips, handkerchiefs, magazines and for Ruth, another bridal catalogue. They went into Clarke's Pharmacy and bought a lot of cosmetics including creams, moisturizers, lotion and so on. These were heavy and once again they walked back to the car and put them into the boot.

"Girls, let's go check out the jewelry by Mrs. Dembar and then call it a day. It's already four o'clock," said Ruth.

***

Tony had taken Sally's advice and had checked out the real estate pages in the newspapers. He was now scheduled to view an apartment in Kingstown Park at 4:30pm; Tony was relatively pleased with life at the moment. He had fallen in love at first sight with Ruth; into his lap had dropped Sally, who was meeting his sexual needs and on Monday 5th June, 1985, exactly one week away, he was going to begin his new job with GrenTV.

He spent the morning traipsing from one furniture shop to the next, comparing prices, since he was going to rent an unfurnished apartment. A lot of women gave him unabashed admiration and female clerks waited on him like royalty. He was that handsome. But Tony had had enough of running around even before he had gone to university at age twenty-two there used to be a cold war among women he ran with and those who wanted him.

There were a few verbal confrontations. But things had really come to a head one night in a bar restaurant when two of his women came to blows in front of him and in front of his friends. They accused him of running with trash, which was not true. All of his women were respectable, middle class girls, but as the Bible says, 'wrath is cruel, anger is outrageous, but who is able to stand against envy?' And so he had dropped all of his women and soon after, had gone off to university where he had gone for three years without sex. Sally was the first since he had returned and he wasn't planning on rocking his own boat.

***

The girls entered Mrs. Dembar's gift shop. There were three other attendants, but Mrs. Dembar waited on them herself. They were looking at jewelry, and except for Judy who couldn't hide her boredom, they exclaimed over everything that Mrs. Dembar showed them. The three of them finally settled on a pair of bracelets each. Alma's was gold, engraved beautifully, Sally's was gold with ruby stones and Ruth's was gold with sapphire stones. Mrs. Dembar was advised to send the bills to the girls' parents.

Finally, Mrs. Dembar turned to her daughter. "Sweetheart, don't you want anything at all?" she asked as if in despair. Mrs. Dembar wished her daughter was a girlie as her friends so that she could lavish gifts on her.

"Oh, mom, you know that I have enough," wailed Judy. The other girls laughed as they waited for Judy and her mother to finish this usual encounter. Mrs. Dembar looked disappointed. Judy felt guilty but on the other hand, thought that her mother must learn to accept her. Anyway, to humour her mother, she asked, "do you have any new watches?" Judy didn't mind a watch. She liked to keep up with time.

Mrs. Dembar's face lit up, "oh yes," she said busying herself to show them to her daughter. "I have one that you'll love." She opened the box and showed it to Judy. It was quartz gold with blue face, no numbers and golden hands. There was a diamond in the twelve position. So Judy removed her sports watch and her mother gladly placed the new watch on her hand. Then Judy leaned over and kissed her mother and with many thanks, the girls left.

Alma drove a little way past the apartment building where Jamie lived, stopped and then reversed into oncoming traffic. She was just a few feet from the spot where she intended to park when a taxi pulled into it. She waited patiently. Taxis are usually just dropping clients and do not stay long. As she waited, out of the taxi stepped Tony looking wistfully at his watch.

Instinctively, Alma looked at hers also, it was 4:35pm Tony crossed the road quickly and then turned towards the girls as if he had heard someone call.

Perhaps he felt watched, and there were all the girls peering at him from the car. He waved and hurried towards the ground floor of the building and knocked on a door. A gentleman opened quickly and looked at his watch as if to indicate to Tony that he was late.

The girls were paying so much attention to Tony that they had not assimilate that the taxi had gone. It was Judy who said, "Alma, are you waiting for another taxi to take your space?" They all laughed and Alma reversed into the space.

"What is Tony up to?" asked Ruth. "Can't we go somewhere without him turning up?" the girls rocked with laughter. "No, seriously," continued Ruth, "since Friday when that man met me waiting for Jamie, I've not gone anywhere without him turning up."

"He's looking for an apartment," Sally informed them. "He asked me to help him but I told him to check the papers."

"And he has found one two floors below Jamie!" exclaimed Ruth.

"What kind of coincidence is that?" that man has a dog's nose, tracking me or anything associated with me. I don't like this," Ruth finished warily.

"Ruth, it is just a coincidence. I can bet my last dollar that Tony does not know that Jamie is on the second floor. But even if he knew, what difference would it make?"

"Drop it, girls. We are here to see Jamie. Come out of the car let me lock it up," said Alma.

"Does Jamie know that we are coming?" Sally asked.

"No," answered Ruth, "But he should suspect that I would come," she said hopefully, now wondering if she should habe called first.

Ruth led the way uncertainly. Judy commented that Ruth did not appear to know where she was going. "I've never been here before but I've been given the directions several times. Come through the door on the left side of the building. Climb the steps to the second floor, and it's the first door that opens into the porch. Here is that first door." So they all went in and up the steps.

Jamie was probably expecting them because second after the knock, the door opened and he smiled, or tried to, since his jaw was still clearly swollen. The smile revealed about one third of the space which one of his premolars had previously occupied. The patch over his eye gave him a comical appearance and the girls had no trouble returning his smile.

Jamie invited the girls in and closed the door behind them. He then welcomed them and asked if they would like some drinks. They all did. They drank and chatted for a while and then Jamie asked if the girls would mind if he and Ruth went into the bedroom for a private chat. No one minded.

As soon as they were out of sight of the others, Jamie put his arm about Ruth and drew her close. "I can't tell you how much I've missed you. It's two

Sundays ago since I held you," he said, rubbing his chin in her hair.

Ruth was surprised by this attitude of his. Hadn't he passed her as if he didn't know her at Kentucky's?

Out loud, she said, "so shy didn't you call me last night? I waited and waited," looking accusingly up at him.

He kissed her forehead. "Every time I assayed to use the phone, mother was sitting next to it, so I gave up and decided to return to town today." Ruth believed him. Her mother had warned her that Mrs. McKenzie would do anything to stop Jamie from visiting her and who knows, perhaps from calling her too.

They stood there, Jamie feeling the curves of Ruth's body and she reveling in his presence with her head on his chest. Finally he asked, "who was that black man?" Ruth told him everything. Then she apologized that he had got hurt on her hehalf. She was very sorry. He laughed and told her that perhaps he did deserve it because he had done her wrong.

Now, it was her turn. "What is going on between you and the girl that you were with on Saturday, the same one who came out of the store with you on Friday?" Jamie hesitated. Ruth waited.

"I began to notice her about two months ago after you were adamant about no sex before marriage. Now you can say that she is my main sex partner."

Ruth's had shot up as quickly as a bullet. "Main, you mean that there are others?" she asked as if in shock.

Jamie looked at her forehead instead of her eyes and said, "She is my only sex partner." He reconciled to himself that the others were all one night stands; he did not consider them his partners.

Ruth's heart sank and her face was crestfallen. She loosened her hold on him and looked away. Tears, for whatever reason, threatened. Here she was waiting to get married to the man she loved before having sex. And he had circumvented her, put her on a shelf and found a way to meet his needs. When would he even think of getting married? No wonder he by passed her in Kentucky. She couldn't meet his needs.

"Ruth? What's wrong?" Jamie asked.

"Nothing," she lied. She disentangled herself from his arm and feeling drained was about to take a seat on the sofa when there was a knock on the front door. She looked at Jamie. He looked scared. Her heart stopped as they waited for someone to answer the door.

The door opened and she heard Sally say, "Yes?" then someone asked, "I take it that Jamie is in, right?"

"So?" answered Sally challengingly, recognizing her as the Kentucky girl.

"Then I'll wait outside," the girl replied unfazed.

"Why don't you get lost and go find a man for yourself, woman?" Sally was menacing.

"Why should I? Jamie isn't married you know." And with that she took a seat on the porch chair ignoring Sally's sour glances.

Ruth turned to leave. Jamie grabbed her on her arm and said, "wait," pleadingly, desperately trying to figure out the situation.

"Wait for what? To be second fiddle?" and she pulled away from him and walked into the living room as bravely as she could. "Let's go, girls," she said without stopping, heading for the door. The girls got up quickly and followed. No one looked at Sheridan who was wearing a smirk. They filed down the steps silently. It was raining on their friend and they felt helpless.

As soon as they exited the building they were not all pleased to see Tony leaning on the car, obviously waiting for them. They were feeling Ruth's pain and there was no room for outsider.

They were crossing the road, Ruth leading the way, when unable to contain herself any longer, she broke sobbing, "ohhhhh," holding her chest with both hands. Her knees buckled. Quick as a flash, Tony swept her into his arms as if she was weightless. As Ruth sobbed, "Oh, oh, oh," the girls, all with moistened eyes, gathered around crying, "Oh Ruth, oh Ruth." Then Tony took charge of the situation.

"Open the car, Alma."

Alma sped around to the driver's side and opened the door and Tony, still cradling the sobbing Ruth, crawled with some difficulty into the back seat. It was an awkward situation. They looked at each other. Then Judy said, "Alma, you take Ruth home, Sally and I will walk. We'll find out later what Ruth wants us to do." They all agreed and Alma slid behind the wheel. She wished though, that the girls could have been there to help her bear the burden of Ruth's heart-rending sobs. Now she wondered if she should ever fall in love.

Ruth was wondering if the other girl had seen her moment of weakness and the shame of it added to her pain and she hid her face on Tony's chest and tried to cry the pain away. She felt useless to Jamie. She felt discarded. She felt deeply wounded.

Tony just held her, not understanding her pain. He did not know that Jamie lived on the second floor. But somehow he suspects that these tears had something to do with Jamie. He wondered if someone had given Ruth some bad news about Jamie. He speculated all sorts of thing as she wet his shirt with her tears. He was glad to have been there to catch her before she hit the ground, but he had not the faintest idea how to stop the teas and it was eating his heart out. He held her closer, not knowing what else to do and decided it would be better if he just let her cry until she couldn't cry anymore. At least she'd feel emptied, refreshed and with new resolve.

Ruth felt Tony's effort to comfort her and she sensed more shame because moments before she had broken, she had nothing but contempt for this man. Now here she was in his arms. "Oh, oh," she started up again.

***

Of course Sheridan had seen Ruth break. She wouldn't have missed it for the world. "Take that, you bitch!" she had hissed. "Plenty more like that to come," she had threatened. She had wisely not knocked on Jamie's door again. He knew she was out there and when he was ready, he would open the door for her. She was patient.

Jamie was devastated. His plan had backfired. He was hoping that if he let it be known that other women were willing to meet his sexual needs then Ruth would free up in order to keep him out of arms of those women. She didn't seem game. Oh Lord, what had he done? He mustn't lose Ruth. He had watched and waited for her all of his life and as far as he was concerned, she was his. Oh no. Suppose that black man got wind of this and tried to take Ruth from him? Anyway, he comforted himself; Ruth wouldn't date a black man.

Nevertheless, Jamie knew that he had messed up big time. He should have listened to older men who knew more about women. Didn't they say that he had messed up big time? Didn't they say that a man always lie to a woman in order to keep her happy? Why hadn't he told Ruth that Sheridan was just a friendly co-worker who he sometimes unburdened to? Now he got angry. That line would have blown up in his face after Sheridan's behavior at the door. He would have to continue to pay for sex and get rid of her if she began to act as if she owned him.

Ah, thought Jamie. It's not fair. If a man lies to his woman and she finds out, he may lose her. On the other hand, if he tells her the truth, he may still lose her. The man can't win. He just can't win. He stuped his teeth. But we men do give ourselves problems. We put ourselves in compromising situation and expect the women to adapt to it. But then he argued, the wisest man who ever lived had 700 wives and 1000 concubines. So if Solomon was so wise and yet he said that the eyes of men are never satisfied, why do our women expect us to stick to one woman for the rest of our lives? But then, if he had stuck only to Ruth, he would not be having this trouble now and Solomon himself said, 'All is vanity and vexation.' Real vexation was what he was having now and Sheridan could sit out there for all she was worth because he was in no mood to see or speak to her right now.

***

Judy and Sally walked to the Clarke's home. On the way they had discussed Ruth, deciding that if she'd prefer to be left alone for the night, well. But if she wanted company, they would all go to her and have a slumber party.

Donald was at home so Sally asked him to take Judy home. Judy declined stating that she would take a taxi.

"Nonsense girl," said Donald emphatically, "what's wrong with you? I don't bite you know. I'm taking you home," and got up to get his keys. After he left the room, Judy asked, "But Sally, why don't you learn to drive?"

"Laziness or complacency, I suppose," answered Sally.

"Come, Judy," said Donald jingling his key in a business like fashion as he led the way out.

"We'll talk later Sally," said Judy, following Donald without protest.

"Sure," replied Sally.

Ruth did not wish her parents to see her in the state that she was in, so she asked Alma to drive right up to the front door and then go tell her parents that Tony was with her and he would pay his respects to them later. On Alma's return, she told her to go home and get some rest and she would call her and the others later.

With his arm about her, Tony escorted Ruth to the front door. She took out her keys and opened the door and then turned and wave to Alma. Then Alma remembered the shopping in the boot. Nah, she thought. Now wasn't the time to think about shopping. She reversed into the road, drove forward a little, stopped and went back to close the gate. Then she was on her way home. In her heart, she said a silent prayer for Ruth.

As soon as Donald found a space to slip into the traffic, he said to Judy:

"I am much better in bed now, Judy. I've had a lot of practice."

"Why do you think that I need to know that? Judy asked in a tone that Donald couldn't decipher.

"Well, we could make a new start, ain't it?" he said.

"And who are you planning to give the drop in order to make way for me?" she asked, almost with a sneer.

"I don't have any special girl, I just move around." She looked at him unbelievingly.

"Honest," he said. "I'm waiting for you. You do know that I still love you?" he confessed taking his eyes off the road for a second to look at her.

"Don't ever do that!" she screamed.

"Do what?" he asked in surprise at her reaction.

"Take your eyes off the road for even a second, especially in traffic. Don't you know that it takes only a second to produce an accident?" she was angry. "You must be more careful," she remonstrated.

"OK, OK, I'm sorry. Please fix your face," he begged.

Judy had a smile. "Yes," she said, picking up where they had left off, "if you still love me, how is it you didn't call me or invite me out or anything for the last two years? What kind of love is that?"

"Because you are arrogant and unapproachable, Judy. You always seem to be sneering at someone and because I flopped two years ago, I always believe that it is me that you are sneering at," said Donald heatedly, recriminatingly.

Judy knew that he was right to some extent. She had never dated since and was not interested because that first experience with Donald had turned her off. But she realized now that she could have dated other guys without having sex.

She looked at Donald. He was pulling up her gate. He looked just like Sally, except for the nose. He had his mother's perfect nose: straight, right size, right curves, right amount of flesh. He was handsome, she concluded.

"Well, Donald," she said as he opened the door for her, "call me some time if you wish. I am not as unapproachable as you think."

His face lit up. "Shall I call you tonight?" he asked excited.

"I'm not sure what the girls are doing tonight, but you can try."

"Talk to you later then," said Donald, greatly relieved.

"Thanks for the ride," said Judy going down the few steps to her door.

"At your service, ma'am," laughed Donald.

***

Ruth closed the door behind them and welcomed Tony to her home. Then she guided him to the large sofa and invited him to sit with her. She instinctively looked up at the clock, that clock that had been there for years, but now held a new significance for her. Last Sunday night as she had waited for Jamie, she had watched the clock more than she had ever watched it before and in a strange way, it had become her friend, carrying her secret as it beheld her pain and disappointment.

Now she looked at Tony. "Do you mind if I lean on you? I feel drained, it makes me almost weak."

Tony smiled and opened his arms. "Always at your service, ma'am."

Ruth lay back in his arms and cuddle up to him. Her father had spoilt her with cuddles every time she had shed a tear and unconsciously she had inculcated that in times of pain, a cuddle would give comfort. She did not wish her parents to know that Jamie had caused her pain for the second time in as many days because they would, especially her mother, insist that she never speak to Jamie again, but she needed time to get herself sorted out. Hence, she accepted solace in Tony's ready arms, a man she had met three days earlier but with whom so much had transpired that it seemed like years.

"Would you like something to drink, eat, Tony?" Ruth asked suddenly remembering manners of hospitality practised in their home.

Tony would have of course. He hadn't eaten since lunch and it was now 6:00pm, but he had no desire to let her go, so he said, "not now, thanks."

"Fine," said Ruth. "When you are ready let me know and Martha will get it for you."

"Who is Martha?"

"The housekeeper." And as if Martha was eavesdropping she emerged from the dining room into the corridor that led to her quarters. She pretended not to see them but on her way back she would have to acknowledge them or be completely blind.

"Tony," Ruth began, "how long were you standing by the car before we emerged from the building this afternoon?" Tony thought for a while. "About fifteen minutes or so, why?"

"Do you remember that girl who came in on Jamie's arm at Kentucky's on Saturday?"

"Remember her? I don't forget people that easily. In fact, believe it or not, she passed while I was standing at the car, scowling menacingly as if she was trying to intimidate me, which of course, she failed to do, and went into that same building a few minutes before you girls came out. She probably lives in one of the apartments because she was obviously coming from work," Tony concluded.

Ruth giggled in spite of everything. Tony was glad he'd made her laugh, but couldn't see the joke.

"No, Tony. She doesn't live there, Jamie does and she was visiting him. She met us there and so I left,"

129

finished Ruth, no longer giggling but choking up as the memory flooded back.

Tony was in disbelief. Jamie lived in the same building that he was about to move into! And again, he had let Ruth down, made her feel second to that woman. Tony was angry.

"If I'd known, I'd have stopped her from going in," he said. "I wouldn't have touched her. Just stood at the door, anything to protect you," he finished, looking tenderly down at her. Now he understood the tears. Her heart must be in turbulence, he surmised.

Chapter 16

Donald and Judy were on the telephone until about 4:00 am on Tuesday morning, catching up on lost time. Among other things, Donald apologized for telling Judy that she needed more weight. He now claimed that she looked fine and should wear whatever she fancied. They argued a little bit, though. Donald wanted Judy to accompany him to an 'On the Move' calypso tent show that Tuesday night. Judy countered that she and the girls had already decided to attend a few tents shows that week since they had never gone before, because they were either studying for exams or having exams in May and June, when the tents were in action.

Donald said that all of the girls were now young women, and sooner or later, the group would have to take second place to individual interests, and he wasn't taking no for an answer. They agreed a compromise, that Saturday night should remain strictly for the girls and Judy decided to sleep for most of the day, in order to be fit for her first tent show which had a bad reputation for never starting on time thus ending very late. Donald knew that he would surely be very late for work that Tuesday morning.

***

Esther Dowers busied herself, no, not cleaning her house or preparing her husband's meals. They could wait. They always had to. Esther was the self-appointed, unofficial reporter for Pastor McKenzie's church. She had to get to the bottom of every rumour and report the truth to every member's house. She was a good Christian, she did not gossip in church or on her way from church.

This Tuesday morning, with the sun shining brightly and the world at peace, she was about to walk three quarters of a mile, and pass many other shops just to visit the Sandisons' shop in cocoa village, a small area in Lowmans Hill community. It was just yesterday that she had learned from her neighbor, that it was an assault by Mrs. Sandison that had kept Sis. McKenzie from church last Sunday. The neighbour's daughter was a nurse, who just happened to be working in A&E that Sunday morning. It was the juiciest news that Esther had heard for a long time and she would outsmart Doreen Sandison in getting her to verify it for her.

Now most people, including Esther, did not like Doreen Sandison. True, she was beautiful to look at, but when she looked at a person, her dark, sharp, bold eye swept him or her a measuring glance that told clearly that the person did not measure up to her. It left the lowly esteemed feeling like crap and the self-confident feeling a strong urge to give her a slap. But no one ever did. She had been a fighter during her school days, and because of her size, no one was willing to test her. But they all concluded that she was a snob.

Esther couldn't understand what a nice man like Mr. Sandison was doing with Doreen. When he looked at a person, he gave him or her, his full attention, making them feel special and in most cases, she was tempted to call for another item just to get a little more of his attention. So he sold in the general shop and Doreen sold in the snackette where persons tended not to linger.

But what Esther did not know, was that everyone who knew her, wondered why a kind, good man like Dan, her husband, stayed with her. He always had a smile for everyone, and everyone returned his smile because he seemed in need of some tender loving care; he looked mauger and hungry. After all, Esther never seemed to have the time to cook a proper meal for him. When she deigned to, he gave most of it to the dog and cooked a small pot for himself.

Certainly, Esther was a good cook, but her culinary arts were preserved for special occasions, such as when she did not feel like walking from door to door, she would get on the phone, and invite everyone to dinner. They would all turn up, knowing that after a well prepared three-or four-course dinner, there would be the most juiciest news and gossip. Everyone who did not get an invitation was slaughtered. Many felt that the good Lord knew what he was going by not giving Esther any children.

Esther peered out of the window to ascertain what the weather was like. There were no threatening clouds and Mount St. Andrew was clear. It was a lovely day. She did not have to take her umbrella. She hurried to the front door and was soon closing it behind her, her shopping bag hanging loosely on her arm, smartly dressed with an essence of haste. She had to be back in time to bake a cake. She and Sister Arlene were paying a visit to Sister McKenzie about tea time. They really wanted to see the extent of her injury themselves, even though it should be almost healed by this time.

Sis. Arlene had closely befriended Esther because she was attracted to Dan and used any excuse possible to come to their home. But Dan did not notice Arlene. He was not even aware that he was supposed to notice her. Neither was he aware of what people thought of him. In himself, he was happy. He had been given a good education; was now a highly paid surveyor, had accepted Jesus as his Saviour, built a house and then married a woman to meet his sexual needs. Whatever anyone said of Esther, she had never denied her husband sex during their fifteen years of marriage. What else could a man ask for? Hence, Dan's smile and Arlene's futile attempts to attract him.

It was after nine o'clock, but Esther was not surprise to meet Lark and Junkie only now on their way to school. She suspected that today would be another

134

day when the school would not be blessed by their presence. Everyone knew Lark and Junkie and they were not easily missed in a crowd. Lark was as black as tar and Junkie was very fair, but next to Lark, he looked white. Both boys were aged seven and both had family problems. Lark's mother had spoilt him rotten and now could no longer control him, so he did whatever he wished, but it did not include going to school regularly or early. Junkie's mother suffered from depression and his big sister tried her best but there was a limit to her success.

There were a number of women on the way to their farms though, with a crocus bag slung over their left shoulders, and cutlass in their right hands and all wearing tall water boots. They were always late in getting to their farms because they had to see their children off to school before setting off. Most of them kept animals and since they did not own enough land to allow the animals to roam and forage for themselves, they had to tether them and so had to go and changed their positions every day and bring them buckets of water. Esther did not stop to chat with anyone. It was close to tea time and she have to bake.

Esther's pulse raced with excitement as she stepped into the Sandison's shop. She waved cheerily with a wide smile at Mr. Sandison and continued on purposefully with a nervous grin to Mrs. Sandison's corner. Mrs. Sandison wondered what had brought this rumour mongering Christian into their shop and asked, "what brings you, Esther?"

"I need some eggs, and there is none up the road," replied Esther. Of course, Esther had not checked.

"So you've walked all this way to get some eggs?" asked Mrs. Sandison suspiciously. Esther was riled.

"I need to make a cake for Sister McKenzie by tea time. It was your fault why she did not come to church on Sunday, wasn't it?" she finished accusingly.

"If she was a good Christian, a little slap on the mouth wouldn't keep her from church, now would it?" taunted Mrs. Sandison. Secretly, Esther did not mind that Sister McKenzie had been taken down to peg or two – she was sometimes a little too much with her airs and style and all that, but not by this heathen, Doreen Sandison.

"Look here," she retorted, "Sis Mckenzie is not your child so you have no right to hit her," Mrs. Sandison put both hands on her hips and leaned over the counter into Esther's face.

"That bitch called my daughter a slut! I should have boxed her teeth down her throat. How dare you tell me that I shouldn't hit her?" finished Mrs. Sandison now with a finger pointing dangerously too near to Esther's nose, causing her to take a few steps backwards. Mr. Sandison heard his wife's raised angry voice and called cautioningly, "Doreen?"

Esther had gotten what she had come for and so did not bother to respond to Mrs. Sandison. She dared not, anyway. She turned and went over to the general shop and procured the items for the cake, demurely accepting an apology from Mr. Sandison on behalf of his wife.

Esther was happy. She had a smile on her face. Oh, she thought. So Sister McKenzie called Ruth a slut. That nice girl. Esther hadn't heard any bad thing about Ruth, so she was alright. Sister McKenzie was wrong, but so was Doreen Sandison. Then her thoughts shifted as she saw Lark's mother standing at the bus stop at Shop Rock. She went up to her.

"Kara, you need to go to the welfare to get help for Lark and talk to them about Junkie, too."

"That's exactly where I am going," replied Kara. "I am tired of complaints. When adults try to admonish them, they use all sorts of vulgarity on them."

"They should be put into foster homes because you can't handle Lark," advised Esther.

"Foster home! Not my child. I just want some advice," said Kara, turning away from Esther. Esther took her cue and moved on.

***

Donald was indeed late for work and his mother was not pleased. He was not an example to the other workers; neither was he learning to be responsible. How could he succeed them? Did he want to ruin the business? His mother wanted no excuses, no matter how plausible they were, so he apologized and promised solemnly to do better.

***

It was about 10:30am when Judy called Alma. Ruth had not called Alma. She had not called anyone. They all assumed that Tony had done a good job of comforting her. But Sally had no peace. She was struggling with an emotional dichotomy, her loyalty to Ruth and her growing desire for Tony. She was fearing something that she had never experience before: jealousy of Ruth.

In fact, Sally never had any reason to be jealous of Ruth. True, Ruth was very beautiful, but Sally knew that she could hold her own. Plus, they were both intelligent and both had wealthy parents. Sally was the one who was regularly dating but was not ready for the commitment of going steady, so she engaged in casual sex and dumped the men at her pleasure. But now, she had had sex twice with Tony and instead of discarding him as usual, she wanted him more, much more. She wondered if it was because she did not really have the prerogative to dump him, why it was she wanted him. People are strange. Was she, for the first time falling in love? Or was it just human nature to want something that one can't have? Tony loved Ruth. Sally had no answer, only confusion. But she really meant it when she told Judy that after all the shopping and excitement of yesterday, she couldn't do it again today and Alma felt the same.

So Judy called her mom. She did not want to go shopping alone and she and Donald were going out later. She needed something girlie to wear. She asked her mom to pick up something for her. The request sounded like music to Mrs. Dembar's ears. How she longed for her daughter to be more feminine. She wondered if she was hearing right but was afraid to ask lest Judy should recant. Hence, Mrs. Dembar called Right Stuff boutique, gave them Judy's statistics and asked them to send a collection of elegantly casual wear to her home and then to send her the bill.

Chapter 17

There was a rap on the door. Jamie looked at his watch, 8:05. That must be Jason, he thought. Jamie sighed wearily. He wondered if being a good neighbour meant that he had to supply Jason with all of the little things that he constantly ran out of, morning and evening, almost every day. He had a suspicion that his mother was partly to blame because Jason probably witnessed the huge stack of groceries that she insisted on giving to him each Sunday evening when they dropped him home. Whatever the reason, he was tired of hearing, "I'm sorry to bother you, but could I borrow two eggs, please?" or "could I have a few spoonfuls of sugar, please?" or "you don't happen to have any sardines, would you?" What he didn't ask for, the grocer did not sell and he never returned anything.

Jason rapped again, louder and longer this time. Jamie rolled off his bed reluctantly.

"What do you want, Jason?" asked Jamie as he pushed the door open.

"Aw, man. Why do you think I need something, man?" I don't need nothing, man. I just want to tell you that since this afternoon when I came home, this young

140

lady was sitting in the porch, and now I am going out again, she's still here. So I decided to rap and wake you up."

Jamie put his head around the door and sure enough, there was Sheridan sitting, still in her work outfit.

"Thanks man," said Jamie giving Jason a fist.

"Anytime," replied Jason, feeling vindicated. And he went on his way.

Now Jamie's anger returned and with one hand on the door handle he just stood there, tall and handsome looking down at her feeling no need for words. Whatever feeling he had had for her, it was all gone now. He almost despised her. This woman had caused thing to get messy between him and Ruth and he would never forgive her. He turned and went back inside, leaving the door open. After a little hesitation, Sheridan followed.

Sheridan felt awkward. Perhaps she should go home. He had not spoken to her and he was clearly angry. It was because of that bitch, she thought angrily. I'll get him. He wants sex, and I'm off the pill. I'll get him, she thought again, comforting herself.

She went into the bedroom and stripped down to her underwear. Then she poured herself a glass of wine and sat on the edge of the bed, sipping it. Jamie was lying on his back but he was not looking at her, he was thinking of Ruth and how she must have felt when confronted by Sheridan that afternoon. Jamie felt rotten and even angrier with Sheridan. Still, they had not spoken to each other.

Suddenly, Jamie hurled himself up, swung off the bed and went purposefully around to Sheridan. He took the glass from her and placed it on the fridge. Then he pushed her onto her back and ripped her knickers off. Supporting his weight on one elbow, he pushed her thighs apart with the other hand and drove into her. He had not put on a condom; he had not even taken off his boxers, just slipped out his penis, unwittingly stating that he was not making love to her, just having a quick release, treating her like a thing, a dispenser.

Jamie didn't take long to ejaculate. It was almost three days since he had last had sex and his testicles were full again. He deposited deep into her, and then withdrew feeling relieved, his anger abated but his scorn still rife.

He got up and went into the bathroom. He took off the boxer and threw them into the laundry basket. Then he turned on the tap to run himself a bath, hoping that by the time he was through, Sheridan would be gone. He hoped he was fertile because she was. But she was hopeful too. She had lain still after he was finished with her, prayerfully urging the sperms up her cervix and into her fallopian tube. Her hope had borne fruit too, although it would be three weeks before she would know, because that night fertilization had taken place.

Ruth felt comforted in Tony's arms, but she felt a twinge of guilt too. She would have bet her last dollar

142

that she would never let this black man, who had hurt Jamie, touch her. Thing were moving too fast for her. So much had happened within three days that it was unbelievable. She pinched herself to make sure that she wasn't dreaming. That in fact, she and Jamie had been sharing an intimate moment when they were rudely interrupted by that woman's knock on the door and the subsequent events had catapulted her into this man's arms. She looked up at him.

"I'm taking advantage of you," she whispered dismally.

"No such thing," Tony hastened to assure her. "I want you to take advantage of me."

She smiled.

"I love Jamie, Tony. That's why I feel rotten lying here in your arms, and I was really angry with you."

Once again Tony reassured Ruth that he did not mind whatever it took to have her lying in his arms, and suddenly it dawned on him that he meant it. He felt wicked and devious because he knew that if it meant that Jamie must continue to be a foolish cad in order for Ruth to fall into his arms to stay.

Ruth glanced at the clock and noted that it was 7:30pm. Her parents would soon be up. She excused herself and went to her room and freshened up. Then she took Tony down to the shop for the drink that her father had promised him.

***

Jamie decided not to call Ruth although his heart bled for her. What could he say? They had not yet resolved the conflict which had resulted from the Kentucky incident, and two days later, here was the same woman, knocking at his door, just when Ruth wanted answers. What could he tell her that would even smell credible? Perhaps he should tell Ruth that he would never speak to Sheridan again. But suppose he did that and Sheridan turned up uninvited again? That would spell disaster. Well, probably he should consider marriage after all. That would solve all the problems. No. No. No. He was not ready for that.

At twenty-one, he just had a job and a couple of thousands in his account. Before he got married, he needed a house, a car and a generous amount of money in order to give him the security for marriage. Too many people rushed into marriage and got burdened down with rent and everything else and financial problems sabotaged their marriage. He would take his time.

But again, if he didn't marry now, and Ruth did not agree to give him sex, he would have to continue to have those sideshows affairs to meet his sexual needs. Oh Lord, he thought, I am going around in circles. I'm getting nowhere with this problem and thus, he fell asleep.

Chapter 18

Jamie's phone rang. It was 9 o'clock on Tuesday morning. It was his mother. She wanted to know how he was doing and if he was remembering to take his antibiotics. He assured her that he was doing well and she shouldn't worry. They assured their love for each other and hung up.

Then Jamie turned his attention to Ruth. Perhaps, he should call her. Ager yesterday, he did owe her an apology, even if he couldn't supply a plausible explanation. He called Ruth's number. She stretched for the handset groggily.

"Hello," she whispered sleepily. The tone of her voice excited Jamie and he got a hard on. He cleared his throat to steady himself.

"Ruth, darling, I must apologize for yesterday," he began. Ruth waited.

"I am really sorry that I embarrassed you again yesterday. I can now see why you had no desire to come by my place. From now on, I will visit you. You wouldn't have to come here again. It is not my wish to hurt and it won't happen again."

"Yeah," replied Ruth, all sleepiness having dissipated. "All of a sudden, you no longer wish me to come by because you do not want me to mess up your extracurricular affairs. Isn't that it Jamie?" she asked hotly.

"I just want us to have an understanding relationship, Ruth. I don't want to lose you."

"Yes, I quite understand. You want to have your cake and eat it too," she finished.

Jamie was angry.

"Talk about kettle telling pot its bottom is black. You want to have me as your lover but keep your virginity. Who the hell do you think I am a eunuch? Think again, woman!" Then he slammed the phone down. That's it, thought Jamie. Ruth and I need a holiday from each other and when she leaves the Garden of Eden, we will talk again. He flung his pillow as if it had offended him and went to get some breakfast.

Ruth had intended to call her friends but right then she did not feel like talking to anyone so she did not replace the handset but went to see if Martha had her breakfast ready.

***

When Esther returned to her home, there was Arlene waiting on the porch for her. Esther beamed a greeting and Sister Arlene knew that Esther had good news. They gossiped and worked and the cake quickly took shape.

At ten past four, both of them presented themselves, well decked out, at the McKenzie's residence.

When Pastor McKenzie answered the door, they were kindly told that Sister McKenzie was indisposed and was not receiving visitors. Esther wished that the earth would swallow her. Then she was angry. All of that work for nothing. She still stood there, wishing that she could take back her cake, even if for her own consolation.

Pastor McKenzie gave Esther a queer look. Why was she still standing there? Hadn't she heard what he had said? He cleared his throat.

Taking the cue, Arlene said, "Let's go Esther. We'll visit some other time."

"Indeed!" chorused both Esther and Pastor McKenzie. The one meant, never again! The other at last!

***

When Daniel arrived at Judy's home that afternoon, it was just a little past six and the show was to start at 8:30. Judy led him to her bedroom after he had exchanged greetings with her pleased parents. There was a pleasant mild fragrance and all of the colours were either pea green, white or like the curtains, a combination of both colours. Except for the bed which was still strewn with the abundance of new clothes that the boutique had sent, everything else was in order. Plus, there was a soft music flowing, seemingly from all of the walls and roof and Donald was romantically stimulated.

He drew Judy close and began to kiss all over her face: her forehead, noise, cheeks, chin. When he got to her lips, he decided to go deep and he wanted more, more. He then let go of her and made some space for both of them on the bed. Then, as if in one moment, he stripped down to his boxers and lifted her up, gently placing her on the bed and lying next to her.

Now he began to kiss her passionately and his hand slipped under her loose house dress and he caressed her slender body. With this, Judy assisted him by slipping the dress over her head. He then turned his attention to her neat, firm breast and sucked then alternatively, then moving to her navel as his hand caressed her thighs. As his hand moved onto her pubic area, Judy slipped off her knickers and his boxers.

When he felt the wetness between her thighs, he parted the hair gently. He made love to her as if he was savouring a delicacy. He had learnt that driving into a woman as if he were a fire engine brought him a quick release but robbed him of real pleasure. This way he could actually feel Judy's flesh enveloping his penis in a warm, caressing embrace. He wondered if it was because he loved Judy so much, but her vagina seemed to him, the nicest. He felt as if he were in heaven.

***

Tony was busy all day Tuesday with moving in and putting his apartment in order. By the end of the day he was very tired and decided to take a long, warm bath then call for pizza since he had no intention of going out again.

Tony hadn't called Sally. Having held Ruth in his arms the night before, he just wanted Ruth and no one else. He just couldn't play this running around thing again. He had found what he wanted but she loved that scoundrel, Jamie. Tony wondered what he could do. He realized that he would just have to try to be there to catch her when Jamie pushed her down, and one day she might just get tired of Jamie and turn to him.

After the bath, Tony was eating and watching TV when he saw someone like Ruth's double in an ad and so he decided to call her. But her line was busy. She was talking to Sally. Except for Judy, none of them had left home for the day.

***

The wise old sage says, 'When it rains, it pours'. Nearly four weeks later, rocking news circulated Ruth's camp and changed everything. Sally, Judy and Sheridan were all pregnant.

The Dembars were over the moon with joy, that is, except Judy. Mr. Dembar announced his retirement immediately. His nephew would take over the running of the plantation. Mr. Dembar felt he would need to watch over his grandson. Of course, it would be a boy.

Mrs. Dembar was already planning a wedding but Judy stubbornly insisted that she was on her way to university and not ready for marriage. More-so, she would never get married as a result of pregnancy. Mrs. Dembar was so heartbroken that Donald had to intervene, counseling Judy that he was not going anywhere and whether they married now or later, it was no difference to him and advised her to do it for her mother's happiness.

Judy agreed on the condition that her mother did all of the preparations, everything, and did not bother her with anything. Judy would just turn up on the day. That pleased Mrs. Dembar immeasurably.

***

Ruth was devastated. She couldn't believe that Judy was getting married before her. She was the one who talked, dreamed and thought of marriage consistently. Judy was the least interested. Her parents had even been wondering if she was gay and now she was getting married! Ruth couldn't take it in.

The girls, without Judy, had gone to the few remaining calypso tent shows but they had all gone to the major shows and the two final days' parade. The Wednesday after Mardi Gras when they were all exhausted from two days of jigging, jumping and dancing, they decided to go to the beach to relax.

They were lying on towels, side by side, absorbed with their own thoughts and allowing themselves to be bathed by the therapeutic ambiance of the surroundings when Alma interrupted with, "By the way, Judy, how are things with you and Donald?"

"Oh, girls, you wouldn't believe how Donald has grown up. We had sex before going on our first date for two years and he was so smooth and professional, I was impressed."

"How can you tell how good he is if you haven't been around?" asked Sally.

"You don't have to be around to know these things. They are instinctive, especially if you watch a lot of TV," replied Judy.

Rudy was surprised to hear Judy's confession. She sat up so that she could look Judy in the eye.

"You and Donald are having sex?" she asked incredulously.

Now it was Judy's turn to be surprised. She returned Ruth's stare with the expression, 'are you for real?' Then out loud she had asked, "And what is wrong with that? You know I tried it two years ago. I am not a virgin like you," she said snidely. Ruth's anger flared.

"And what's wrong with being a virgin?" she asked hotly.

"You haven't told me what's wrong with having sex," replied Judy coolly.

"I'm sorry, Judy," relented Ruth. "It's just that you have been so boyish, reserved, not wanting to do girlie stuff, that I didn't put sex and you together."

"But can't you see that I have changed since Donald and I are dating again?" asked Judy in surprise.

"Yes, but preconceived ideas, I suppose. I said that I am sorry," Ruth reminded Judy.

"I'm sorry that I asked Judy about her affairs, because it almost started a quarrel," added Alma. Just then Dinah and Chloe sauntered up.

"Sally, every minute I see you spitting and spitting, are you pregnant?" asked Dinah. There was a shocked silence.

Then Ruth said, "Dinah, Sally has developed a bad habit, we have spoken to her about it already."

"Bad habit, my foot. She either breed or she has worms," said Chloe. This aroused Sally.

"My parents are pharmacists. I certainly do not have worms. I've missed my periods, though, so perhaps I am pregnant."

Now even Dinah and Chloe were shocked. Before they could recover, Judy put in, "But I have missed my period too, but I don't spit every five minutes. Except ….. Lord have mercy! There is a change. I can no longer tolerate the smell of frying bacon in the morning. It make me sick," finished innocently.

"Judy!" from Alma.

"Oh Lord," from Chloe.

"Oh Jesus," from Dinah.

Ruth jumped up and began to run around in circles, muttering insanely, "Oh my God! O my God!"

Everyone forgot about herself and went to Ruth's assistance, all talking at once and trying to comfort her. Pull yourself together, what's wrong with pregnancy? It's not your problem, let's talk about this, and so on.

Finally Ruth sat down and put her face in her hands. No, no, no. She thought. Girls of their class did not get pregnant out of marriage. What's worse, they belonged to her clique. How could she bear this?

They talked about the situation and advised Sally and Judy to attend the doctor to ascertain their condition. But something was niggling Ruth and she was hesitant to ask in front of everyone lest she triggered another row. She would call Sally as soon as they got home and upon this she suggested that they leave the beach.

The sky was almost clear except for a few cirrus clouds. Ruth preferred cumulus clouds because they were so bubbly and unshapely that she could imagine them to be all sorts of things. But she couldn't help noticing that the mango trees were laden with fruits, and the summer rain and sun were making them juicy and golden and everywhere the birds were having a party. She looked at Sally. They had both gone with Judy.

"What?" asked Sally.

"Can't I look at you? Replied Ruth frowning.

"We were best friends since we were five. Don't you think that by now I can read your mind? Your eyes, expression, mannerism; come on, ask me."

"I'll give you a call when I get home," Ruth conceded.

"Really, what is it that you don't want me to hear, Ruth?" asked Judy annoyed.

"I just don't want another row," Ruth apologized.

"Ask me," persisted Sally again. Ruth shrugged and said:

"Since you haven't told me of your latest date, and I haven't seen anyone around, I can't figure out who you've been sleeping with," she unloaded. Ruth was quite taken aback by Sally's answer.

"Tony."

Ruth was sure that Sally had not said Tony, but to be certain she asked:

"You did not say Tony, did you?" Sally scanned Ruth's face wickedly before answering.

"I did say Tony. Anything wrong with my sleeping with him?" she challenged. Judy kept her eyes on the road. She too, was a little surprised.

"You slut!" hissed Ruth, centimetres from Sally's nose. Sally recoiled and spat back:

"You wicked bitch!"

"Tony loves me!" retorted Ruth, flushing red. Thankfully Judy pulled up at Ruth's gate but she made no move to get out and Judy put her hands in her lap and waited. She would listen this one out.

"And I love him," rejoined Sally, bristling.

"Why don't you go find yourself a man?" Ruth asked nastily.

"And why can't you keep your man out of another woman's arms?" said Sally cutting Ruth to her bones. "Tony is not yours."

Ruth was stumped for a moment, then she said determinedly as she opened the car door, looking Sally straight in the eye, "We'll see about that, Sally. We'll see about that. Later Judy."

And with that she walked proudly to her front door. Judy was stunned. She closed the door that Ruth had left open and said to Sally, "you were both nasty."

"She started it. She asked for it, but we'll survive. Don't worry."

Judy drove off.

***

Jamie had not gone to the street parties and parades of the two last days of the carnival but he had gone to several after parties held by the nightclubs. He loved the wide variety of hot food that The Pumpkin had and so he had chosen to patronize it. Sheridan went with him or better put, Sheridan invited herself and he resigned himself to her presence. He notice Donald and his gang and they exchanged nods. But Donald noticed that the girl clinging possessively to him was not Sally's friend, Ruth.

Two days earlier, that girl had come to the pharmacy to purchase a pregnancy test kit, and the very next day, had returned to ask for supplements for pregnant women. Anyway, thought Donald, she was probably running an errand for someone who was too scared to do it herself, so he dropped the thought.

Sheridan was cognizant that Donald was looking at her. He had attended to her two consecutive days in the pharmacy and he had not forgotten her. She felt uneasy. She asked Jamie if he was acquainted with the dark haired, straight-nosed man in the plaid shirt. Jamie replied that their relationship was merely casual and that he was the brother of Ruth's best friend. That information gave Sheridan no comfort. She began to suppose.

Suppose he told his sister that he had sold her pregnancy test kit to her. Suppose his sister told Ruth. Suppose Ruth asked Jamie and Jamie asked her. Sheridan didn't want it to happen that way. She wanted to tell Jamie when she thought that the time was right. Now she supposed that she was in a fix.

"Are you all right?" Jamie asked Sheridan with genuine concern for there was worry and panic all over her face and eyes.

"Er,er..er.. yeah," she stumbled in reply, having gone off into her own world of thoughts. Jamie was not convinced and suggested that she drink some brandy and coconut water, setting off to get it for her. Instinctively she said, grabbing his sleeve, "No, no, I can't drink alcoholic drinks now," and flushed pink, realizing that she had said too much.

Sheridan looked Donald's way but he was not minding her now. A little alcohol can't harm, she thought.

"Oh, nothing, nothing. Get me the drink," she replied looking at everyone but at Jamie. Jamie was not convinced but went to get her the drink and himself another beer.

Jamie did not venture into the dance hall because he did not wish to dance with Sheridan. He had not ordered any food lest it should appear that he had taken her to dinner. He would encourage her to go home since she was not well. He would call a taxi. Surprisingly, Sheridan agreed to go home.

Alma chided Dinah and Chloe for meddling in Sally's affairs. They were not Sally's friends, so they had gone too far. Dinah defended their action by stating that she and Chloe had merely expressed an observation. They had not forced a confession out of Sally. Anyway, they continued, couldn't Alma see that Sally was grateful to get if off her chest?

***

Ruth pushed her head into the shop door and waved kisses to her parents. Then she walked to the back of the house and up the kitchen steps. After greeting Martha, she asked her to get some fish from the freezer and fry them for her supper, and with that done, she went to her room and flung herself onto her bed.

Now the anger returned in full. How could Sally have sex with Tony, knowing that it was her that he was interested in? How could Tony tell her that he loved her, hold her in his arms, then go and make love to Sally, knowing that she and Sally were friends? She could never understand men. Perhaps they were really ruled by their dicks. Anyway, she thought, that wasn't fair. Her father wasn't ruled by his dick. All men were not the same.

But Sally had challenged her. After all of these years, Sally should realize that she couldn't challenge her and win without a fight or struggle. Now, the fight was on. She had said, "Tony is not yours." That was true. Ruth was not even sure of Jamie. But from today, Ruth was determined to get one of those men, preferably, Tony, just to show Sally.

***

As soon as Judy got home she was grateful that her mother had not gone to work that day and had gone straight to her.

"Mom," she had asked. "If a woman suddenly develops a spitting habit or gets sick in the morning at the smell of frying bacon that never troubled her before, does that mean that she is pregnant?"

Her mother had replied that neither case was necessarily so, but in a lot of cases they are. She had continued with those things that science couldn't explain and had to asked Judy if any of those symptoms were hers. Judy had laughed and told her, yes, and thus the discussion on marriage had ensued.

***

Sheridan had decided that she wanted to be doubly sure before telling Jamie and so, the first Friday after carnival, she, Sally and Judy had found themselves in the same doctor's office. Ruth's friends and Sheridan eyed each other belligerently while they waited, but the expression on either side was asking, 'what are you doing here, are you pregnant too?" a week later, all of the results were positive and Sheridan decided to walk home with Jamie after work. She dared not risk anyone hinting it to him before she did.

When they got to Jamie's apartment, she quickly rustled up a cucumber and lettuce sandwich with cheese for him. Then cleaned the bath and ran it for him. While the bath was filling, she sat and watched while he relaxed, finishing off his drink and snack.

"Aren't you hungry too?" asked Jamie.

"No, I'm alright," Sheridan answered. Jamie sat up and faced her.

"Since that night at the Pumpkin, you have been acting strangely. You have something to tell me. Come on. Say it."

Without hesitation, just as if she had to say it before she changed her mind, she blurted out, "I'm pregnant."

Jamie turned rigid and his hand drew tighter and tighter about the bottle of malt his knuckles were white and so was his face. His jaw twitched.

"Pregnant?" he asked dazed. "You, you told me that you were on the pill," he finished weakly and unbelievingly.

"Perhaps I missed a day or two and perhaps we had sex on those days," she lied, trying to sound absentminded.

"Could....could you leave me alone, please? I need time to think," begged Jamie, still dazed.

"I'll turn off the tap," Sheridan tried to be causal. After she closed the tap in the bath, she left promising to see him on the weekend.

Although Jamie was lying down, he felt weak at the knees. Oh no he thought. Oh dear Lord, no. not my father. Not my father. How was Pastor McKenzie to face his congregation and tell them how to live, when he couldn't even control his own son? How was he going to tell his father that he was fathering an illegitimate child? His father had encouraged him to follow his brother's example and get married. He had rebelled and left home and was about to bring shame on his father.

Jamie had not yet spared a thought for his mother. With her, he could do anything and she would find a plausible excuse for him. His thoughts had not yet meandered around to Ruth, only his father. He loved and respected him; it was never his intention to tarnish his father's ministry or image.

Jamie felt literally sick and staggered into the bathroom trying to puke but nothing came and forgetting all about his bath, he flung himself upon his bed with a broken heart. The prospect of having to tell his father was overwhelming. It was like, father, I have let you down. And he was to hurry or else as soon as the co-workers found out that Sheridan was pregnant, someone would be sure to call and ask Pastor McKenzie if he was aware that he was having another grandchild.

Jamie wished that he could flog himself; at least he would feel better. Why had he been so foolish? Sheridan told him that she was on the pill and he had relaxed his vigilance. Sometimes he used condoms, sometimes he did not. One moment out of step, and look at what he was facing. Oh Lord. Oh God. No, no, no, no! Now another thought hit him, hard. His father would tell him to that the honourable thing to do was to marry Sheridan. But he couldn't do that. Not even for his father. Even if there was no Ruth; Ruth, Ruth. How was she to be blamed for this? He was not the run around type. If she had agreed to let them have sex, he would not have had to turn to other women.

161

Now was no time for blame and recriminations. He would have to tell Ruth too, before she heard it on the street. But Ruth was the lesser of two evils right then. On Sunday morning his father would be there to pick him up and go to church and spend the day with them. It would be better if he told him no so he could have a day to mull over the situation before facing his congregation on Sunday.

***

When Judy called Ruth, it was not just to tell her that both she and Sally had had positive results, but that her mother and Donald had forced her into an agreement for an imminent marriage as a result of her pregnancy.

It was like a treble blow for Ruth and she literally could not speak. Realizing that she had dealt Ruth a hard blow, Judy told her that they would talk later, hung up and called Sally.

"No," said Sally. She had not yet told her parents because they were not too pleased that Donald, their heir, was getting married, having not yet gone to university or build himself a house. They did not like it. But they understood the Dembars' position; they would not like their daughter to get pregnant out of marriage either. At least the Dembars were wealthy.

Having heard her parents' perspective, where did it leave Sally? How could she face them now? It would be like a double blow for them, and Sally was more concerned for them than herself. She was considering an abortion. Tony wouldn't marry her.

Judy admitted that it was a very complicated situation, especially as the child was fathered by a black man. Sally stopped her there. She did not at all mind having a child for a black man, especially one like Tony. The problem was that she was pregnant for a man who was in love with someone else. More-so, since that day when Tony and Alma had taken Ruth home after encountering Sheridan at Jamie's place, Tony had not called her. She did not even have a man to present to her parents. As far as she was concerned, abortion was her only option.

But Judy could not agree with Sally. Why worry about her parents? The child was the innocent party here. Her parents would get over their disappointment. Anyway, parents were wrong to have false expectations of their children instead of supporting them along the path that fate led them. Judy sounded wise and sensible. After all, Sally did love Tony, and wouldn't mind having a child. She would stop thinking about abortion and go with the flow. Give her parents some time, then tell them. Then the girls talked about Ruth. Sally and Ruth were not on speaking terms and this was adversely affecting the group. Was this the end of their group, especially with two of them soon to become mothers?

Chapter 19

Tony had completed two weeks of training and for the past week, he had been a regular feature on Nightline News. All of the patrons on radio call in shows were raving about him. At last, they said, GrenTV had some sense to get a young man on the evening news, a breath of fresh air, and so handsome. It was Alma who called Ruth to tell her that Tony was on TV because Ruth was into music and not a TV fan. So she had gone down to the drawing room to watch him, and had done so every evening for the past week. He was growing on her, those eyes, those lips – he really was handsome. But he was black and in spite of everything she loved Jamie.

But Ruth didn't understand why she loved Jamie. She just loved him. Perhaps it was because he was her first love. He claimed to love her too, but why didn't she agree to have sex outside of marriage? Did loving someone mean that you had to submit to their every wish in the name of love? No way, she thought. It must be me. I am not going to lose myself for love because I could become a nobody, with low self-esteem, low self-confidence, low everything. I am not compromising.

She wondered whether, if she had had sex with Jamie and had become pregnant, Jamie would have married her. Donald was such a gentleman, she thought. Why wasn't Jamie like that? No wonder mom hates those Christians.

Jamie had not spoken to her for several weeks but she was not allowing herself to move on to anyone else. She and Jamie belonged and he would be back. In the meantime, she could play around with Tony. Just to show Sally, if for nothing else.

The phone rang. Who was calling the drawing room phone? She wondered. It was Jamie. He had tried reaching her in her room. He sounded tired. Ruth was not prepared for what he had to say.

"I've just given my father some news that he would have preferred not to hear, so I've decided to just get it over with and let you know also. That girl, who knocked on my door that evening when you and your friends were there, is now carrying my child. I'll talk to you some other time."

The phone went dead but Ruth continued to hold it to her ear, daring the voice to continue to speak, but words of comfort, but none came.

Slowly Ruth replaced the handset, and then got up as if she had the weight of the world on her back. She switched off the TV and somehow found her way to the room. She was in some state of shocked disbelief.

Ruth sat on the edge of the bed, her mind blank and dazed. She just stared and stared, looking at nothing in particular. Finally, she crawled into bed as if she was stealing a part of someone else's bed, put her clasped hands under her head and fell asleep.

The telephone rang and Ruth awoke but she thought that she was dreaming so she did not pick up the phone. As it continued to ring, she knew it was for real and stretched for it. When she heard Tony's voice, she broke down. After all, he had let her down too. Tony felt that urge to hold her wondering what was the matter.

"I'm going to get a taxi and come to you right now. Then you can tell me what's wrong," he said comfortingly.

"No, no. I don't want you to come. Jamie called me earlier and told me that that girl is carrying his child and he told me that he loved me. And you, yes you, are trying to convince me that you love me too and yet you went and got my best friend pregnant too."

Tony was shocked.

"Sally! Pregnant!" he exclaimed.

"Hasn't she told you?" asked Ruth between sobs.

"Sweetheart, since that first evening when I first held you in my arms, I couldn't go back to Sally and I didn't call her either,"

Ruth stopped crying. Oh no. Poor Sally. She probably felt alone. She would call her in the morning.

"Alright," said Ruth. "I believe you."

"Can I come to you now?" begged Tony.

"It's midnight. My parents are in bed," Ruth replied.

"But I work from 3-11 pm Monday to Friday. I would have to see you either late at night or early in the day. Which do you prefer?" Tony asked.

"A little of both, but for now late at night. I'll ask my parents if it's alright." She took his number and went knocking at her parents' door.

Mr. Sandison was just dozing off. "Is that you, pet?" he asked. Ruth responded and she was invited in. Mrs. Sandison sat up, asking if something was wrong. Ruth assured them that all was well but sat down and told them of all the pregnancies and finished by asking if Tony could come at that time. Mr. Sandison told her that if he wanted to come, then it was ok with him, providing that she did not allow anyone to get her pregnant outside of marriage. She assured her parents that she would take care of herself and kissed them goodnight and left.

She went back to her room and called Tony who answered on the first ring. She told him everything that her father told her.

"Babe," said Tony. "Even if I got you pregnant, which I have no intention of doing, I would marry you as soon as I found out."

"So how come you are not marrying Sally?" challenged Ruth.

"Sally and I had an arrangement, Ruth I am not in love with her. I never told her that I love her. I didn't fool her into false expectations. Ask her if you think I'm lying," gushed Tony.

"No, no. I believed you. Hurry up and get here."
Ruth was indeed looking forward to his comforting
arms. She could talk to Sally without even telling her
that she, Ruth, had won the challenge. But if Tony was
telling the truth, Sally must know that Tony was in
Ruth's grasp, not Sally's

Ruth went down to the drawing room to await
Tony's coming. Twenty minutes later, a taxi stopped at
their gate and soon there was a knock on the front door.

"Who is it?" asked Ruth.

"It's me, Tony," Tony replied.

Ruth opened the door with a smile. Ruth locked the
door behind Tony and he kissed her on her forehead.

"Let's go to my room," she invited. "I fell asleep
dirty after receiving the bad news and I badly need a
shower," she finished.

She had never invited Jamie to her room because
she felt that things could have gotten out of hand, and
loving him the way she did, she was afraid that she
might not have had the will to stop him if he had wanted
to go all the way. She was not in love with Tony. She
loved being loved by him.

Tony followed her up the stairs, nothing the
affluence of his surroundings. Tony's parents were into
banana cultivation just like the Dembars, although their
spread was about half the size of the Dembars, but it
afforded them a comfortable life and tertiary education
for him and all his siblings.

Tony savoured the femininity of the room and its pleasant fragrance.

"Have a seat," said Ruth. "Or if you are tired, you can stretch out on the bed. "I'll be back in a jiffy," and she went into the bathroom. She was indeed quick and come out in a white bathrobe and stood in front of her dressing table. Tony had stripped down to his boxers and was stretched out on the bed. She had thought that he would have taken the privilege fully dressed, except for his shoes, but she didn't bother to rebuke him.

Ruth chose a clean nightdress and knickers and return to the bathroom to put them on. Soon she was back and slid into bed and cuddle up to Tony. He turned onto his side and put his left hand under her body and with his right hand; he drew her closer so that she was wrapped up in both his arms. He kissed her face all over and then began to talk.

She related to him the problem that was creating the conflict between her and Jamie and that is seeking to meet his sexual needs, he had now gotten his girl pregnant. Not only that, Jamie had not spoken to her for several weeks, until that evening when he had called to tell her that Sheridan was carrying his child. Now Ruth felt unloved, discarded, and useless to Jamie. And it hurts. She choked up and stopped talking.

Tony held her closer. "And why are you holding on to him?" he asked patiently, kissing her forehead.

"I love him, but don't ask me why because I don't know. Perhaps I'm just a fighter and do not like losing to anyone. I don't want to lose to that girl."

"You have a negative perspective, darling. It's the wrong way to look at it. You are young and beautiful. Leaving a man doesn't mean that you are losing to anyone. It means that you are smart enough to know what you want and you are principled enough not to sell or compromise your values to get it."

"But I had him first, and she is winning," moaned Ruth.

"That is because you refused to compromise. If Jamie can't accept that, then let him go. Sweetheart, why don't you let me take care of you? Marry me, please," begged Tony. "Jamie doesn't deserve you."

"But I'm not in love with you, although I enjoy being with you. How can we marry?"

"But you'll learn to love me, given time. Love grows out of friendship."

"I don't know, Tony. Right now, I can't say. As you've said, give it time."

"OK," conceded Tony grudgingly.

Ruth told him how Judy had made an about turn that had surprised her and left her wondering if she really knew Judy. She elaborated how Judy had gone from being boyish and hating girly stuff to being a glamorous young woman and even more appalling, got into sex.

"Was she always like that, I mean, was she always boyish and so on? asked Tony.

"No," answered Ruth. "She began parading masculinity and hating femininity after two attempts at sex with Donald went wrong and he told her she needed to put on weight."

"Well, see that? She was just hiding behind masculinity because Donald made her feel that something was wrong with her femininity. It lowered her self-concept. Now that he has made things right again, she is blossoming again.

"So she didn't really hate girlie stuff then?" asked Ruth.

"No, she was just angry that she couldn't be the girl she wanted to be. Thanks to Donald," explained Tony.

"I didn't think about it that way. So she was really hurting inside. Poor Judy. Anyway, she is pregnant too and getting married. She doesn't need my sympathy. In fact, I'm a little jealous," finished Ruth.

"Jealous! Why?" asked Tony lifting his head to look into her face.

"I was the one who was hung up on marriage yet she is going before me."

"You know how to change that, sweetheart. I'm at your service," Tony whispered in her hair.

They talked till about 4:00am then Tony decided that it was time to leave. He dressed, and then called a taxi. They waited in the drawing room and when the taxi's horn tooted, he kissed her and left, promising to call later.

***

At 11:30 am, Sally's phone rang. She was in the kitchen just about to get herself a sandwich, but she placed a food cover over the ingredients and ran into her bedroom. It was Tony.

"Sally, can I come by?" he asked.

Sally paused. Then she said, "If you can still remember where I live after all of this time, I suppose you can."

"See you in a few minutes," Said Tony and hung up.

Sally recalled the first time that Tony had visited her home. That night she bailed him. He had been lucky. Jamie refused to press charges, claiming that Tony was like a hero for defending Ruth's honour. She didn't understand whys he had no intention of picking up that phone to tell him that she was pregnant.

By midday, Tony was at the door and Sally let him in. She asked him to take a seat and she sat opposite him.

"What brings you here?" she asked, business-like.

"Sally, I know that you feel abandoned, but I've been falling more in love with Ruth and it makes it impossible for me to keep up our arrangement. I'm sorry."

"So why are you here?" asked Sally, bitterly.

"Ruth told me, indirectly. And I want you to know that I'll stand by you and the baby."

"Meaning ?" queried Sally.

"Meaning that I'll be around. No one will have to wonder who is your child's father, and the child won't have to ask for his daddy."

"Sally was touched and had to open her eyes very wide to keep a tear from spilling. He had taken care of her concerns. It was embarrassing enough getting pregnant out of marriage for her status and class, worse if it was evident that there wasn't a man by your side.

"Thank you," she said gratefully, knowing that she had brought this on herself. "If you meant what you just said, I appreciate it very much. I can't tell you how much, and with that she broke and couldn't stop the tears.

Tony sat next to her, put both arms around her and kissed her forehead.

"Don't cry, Sally. It's my fault too. We are in this together. You are carrying my child and I'll tell them that we are not thinking about marriage as yet. We don't have to say why, and time will take care of everything. Agreed?" asked Tony tenderly. Sally nodded. Then she left to freshen up and await the arrival of her parents when they closed for 1:00pm.

***

Ethel McKenzie couldn't believe that her son, her baby, had fathered an illegitimate child. With a nobody at that. She had called Doreen Sandison's daughter a slut, but she knew that Ruth was no slut. She had class and her parents had money. She refused to believe it yet she began to cry.

"Stop your foolish crying and babbling, woman," said Pastor McKenzie to his wife. "If you had not spoilt him he would not have become derelict to responsibility and other Christian values. Instead, he would have followed his brother's footsteps and gotten married. But you couldn't stop calling him baby, so perhaps he has not yet become a man."

But his wife refused to dry her tears. How ashamed she was going to be. She Ethel McKenzie, pastor' wife, having an illegitimate grandchild. And she sobbed some more. Then she turned to her husband. It was his fault. If he hadn't nagged Jamie into getting married, he wouldn't have left home. He might have gotten Ruth pregnant instead, which would not have been so bad.

Pastor McKenzie was horrified at what his wife had just said and poked his head out the front door to make sure that no one had overheard this unprincipled woman. Then he turned on her.

"Illegitimacy is illegitimacy whether with Ruth or not. Sin is sin whether it is with rich or poor. You don't talk as if you know God, woman! Our son has done wrong, and the honourable thing for him to do, is marry the girl."

Ethel's sobs stopped immediately and her jaw dropped in horror.

"My baby, marry a nobody! Are you crazy, Pastor?" she finally blurted out.

Pastor McKenzie lifted his hand as if he was going to hit her then restrained himself and withdrew to his study to talk to God about the matter and to ask God why he gave him a wife like Ethel.

***

When the Clarkes came home, Tony and Sally were still seated together. After the greetings, Tony asked if he could speak to Mr. and Mrs. Clarke after they had had their lunch and a little rest.

Mr. Clarke looked at his wife. Mrs. Clarke looked from Tony to Sally, then at her husband and said, "This sounds serious. Lunch can wait."

She took a seat opposite the young couple and her husband sat next to her and said to Tony, "say on, son." Donald excused himself.

Tony winced and began. "Sir, Ma'am, it is not with pleasure that I tell you that Sally is pregnant with my child."

The Clarkes blanched with shock. He continued, "not that I am not pleased to be having a child, but we did not plan for it to happen this way, since we are not planning to get married because of this. But I'm not going anywhere. I'll be here for Sally and the baby. I'm sorry."

The Clarkes were now angry. "If you're not planning to marry my daughter, why did you ask to speak to us?" asked Mr. Clarke. "She could have told us herself," he finished.

"We're in this together," said Tony regretfully.

"No, you're not," said Mrs. Clarke angrily. "Please excuse us. I want to speak to my daughter in private."

Tony looked ruefully at Sally, then got up and took his leave, promising to call her. After the door closed behind Tony, Sally and her mother looked at each other while Mr. Clarke waited for his wife to speak.

"Why didn't you tell us, Sally?" she asked softly, with subdued anger.

"After the way you reacted with Donald and Judy, I just thought that it was too much for you to bear. I have not lived up to expectations," answered Sally self-deprecatingly. Her parents felt sorry for her and Mr. Clarke went and sat next to her with his arms about her and her mother's look softened.

"Sweetheart," she said. "No matter what you do or don't do, you are still our daughter; we are still your parents. The burden is lighter when shared and although parents don't ask for burdens, we don't run away from them. Understand?" she asked tenderly, sensing how ashamed and afraid her daughter must have been. She continued, "You've made me feel as if I'd let you down to have to lean on that man rather than on me or your father."

"It was he who suggested it when I told him that I had not revealed my condition to you," explained Sally.

"But since he's not going to marry you, he should not have come here. Who does he think he is?" raged Mr. Clarke. Mrs. Clarke looked at her husband. "We should send her away, don't you think, dear?" she asked, expecting an ally.

"Without question," he replied staunchly.

No one asked Sally's opinion. Her mother continued. I'm going to call my sister in England and tell her to expect you. Book your flight on Monday. You were going to study next year anyway; you're just going a little earlier. I would not have my daughter pushing belly without a ring on her finger where everyone knows us. No, sir. And put up the child for adoption," she finished.

At this, Sally found her voice.

"I won't do that, Mom. I love Tony, and I'm keeping the child. It's not his fault."

"Of course, it's his fault," Mrs. Clarke retorted. "If he's not ready for marriage, then he should use a condom. Not go around getting other people's daughter pregnant."

"Oh mom!" groaned Sally shaking her head woefully as she listened to her mother's tirade. Mrs. Clarke continued.

"Well, if you wish to keep it, fine. But make sure when you are ready to commence university, to bring the child to him. My sister can't help you babysit, and neither can I. More-so, I will have nothing to do with a black illegitimate grandchild," argued Mrs. Clarke heatedly.

"Mom!" screamed Sally in horror, holding her tummy. Mr. Clarke squeezed Sally's shoulder. "Come on, Betsy," he said to his wife.

"Whatever colour or class our grandchildren are, they are ours. Your attitude can't change that fact. Don't bother with your mother, honey, I'll pay someone to look after him or her," said Mr. Clarke Comfortingly.

"You will pay to look after that child, Darren, but not in this house. And that's the end of the conversation. Go and pack, Sally!" she ordered.

Mr. Clarke pecked Sally on her check as his wife sailed out of the drawing room. "Don't worry," he whispered. "I'll take care of your baby, even if I have to build a house for you and pay someone to look after him."

Reassured, Sally hugged and kissed her father and said, "Thanks, Dad. I love you so much." Then she set off to obey her mother's orders, not daring to tell her that she was no longer a little child.

***

Mrs. Clarke started at her reflection in the mirror. Donald looked like his mother. Sally had her father's nose. At 43 years old, Mrs. Clarke knew that she was still beautiful, but right then, she felt ugly. Her full lips trembled, and she bit the lower one. She had failed her children. She could not believe that Donald was getting married at twenty, before he had accomplished his goals. One month after 'A' levels Sally, eighteen, was pregnant. She must be seeing a movie or having a nightmare. She dropped down heavily on the stool in front of her dressing table. What kind of a parent was she? Where had she lapsed?

Mrs. Clarke had strongly suspected that Sally was into sex. She had always taken her male friends to her bedroom. She had wanted to tell her to keep condoms in her bedroom and in her purse, but she did not wish to be perceived as interfering or making suspicious or suggestive hints to her daughter. She would have been mortified if she had made unfounded suggestions and Sally had rejoined with, "Mom, I'm not into sex."

Now she wished that she had risked that mortification. It would have been better than how she was feeling now: a complete failure. She had hoped that her worldly-wise daughter knew how to take care of herself. Why are old sayings always right? An ounce of prevention is better than a pound of cure. Mrs. Clarke sighed. You know what, she thought. I did nothing to prevent the first ill-timed pregnancy, let me make an effort to prevent the second one. And with that she got up wearily and found her way to Sally's room.

***

Mr. Clarke was watching TV. He had forgotten to eat and was trying to avoid a discussion about Sally with his wife. He was a practical man and did not have tears to cry over spilt milk. He would look after the child, if he was forced to, and Sally would get on with her life. He really couldn't take any moaning from his wife, and he hoped that she would notice his attitude and refrain from the topic.

***

Sally was sprawled across her bed with a large empty suitcase beside her. Mrs. Clarke pushed the suitcase aside and sat next to her daughter.

"Sweetheart," she began. "I can't tell you how badly I feel for letting you down."

"It wasn't you fault, Mom." reassured Sally, squeezing her mother's hand.

"Yes, it was," continued Mrs. Clarke. "I should have told you about condoms, the pill, rhythm and contraceptives in general. I did a bad thing. I took it for granted that you knew, and I'm sorry."

Sally laughed in spite of the situation. Mrs. Clarke couldn't see the joke.

"Oh mom!" said Sally, still giggling. "I know all about those things. We learnt them in biology and social studies. And even if we hadn't, girls learn from each other, you know. I just ran out of condoms and got caught, mom. Don't blame yourself, please."

Now Mrs. Clarke felt stupid. What was she to say? Here was her daughter laughing at her. But Sally went on, "and mom, please don't hate Tony or the baby. I did ask for it. I wanted to see if black men were as well-endowed as is rumoured and to go further and experience it. I begged him to have sex with me although he told me that he loved someone else." Mrs. Clarke went pink, then white, and pink again.

"Sally," she said horrified. "Sally!" she repeated, recalling how she had insulted Tony when her daughter had most of the blame. "How could you?" she finished at last.

Sally reached for her mother's hand and squeezed it again. "I love him mom. I don't know why, but I love him."

"Oh, Sally," wailed Mrs. Clarke, "It is doomsday to be pregnant for a man that is not yours." She leaned down and hugged Sally.

"Worst thing have happened, Mom others in this situation may find themselves abandoned by their love ones, with no visible means of support. I am blessed. I am lucky. So don't worry, mom. Time will take care of everything and thanks for your support. It means the world to me. I love you, mom." And for the first time or a long time, Mrs. Clarke broke and cried, more with relief than with anything else. Sally's mature approach had lifted her mother's burden. Thank God that Sally was a lot like her father, thought Mrs. Clarke. Darren would be pleased to hear that Sally was not worrying.

Chapter 20

After the taxi had taken its leave, Ruth went back to her room: hoping to catch up on sleep. But sleep fled. She lay there thinking. What would her parents say now that Jamie's girl was pregnant? She could hear her mother saying, 'leave him.' She would not pre-empt them. Her thoughts went back to Tony.

She had enjoyed lying there next to him, being loved and comforted by him, no stress, no conflict. Why didn't she marry him? It was clear that he adored her. But she wanted Jamie, who had not called her for several weeks and when he did, said that he had made someone pregnant. Why did women gravitate towards men who treat them badly, and take for granted the ones who love them? Perhaps we like the challenge and the worries that come with it, thought Ruth. She wished that she did not still love Jamie because she preferred the comfort, not the worries. Oh well, she concluded, she would give it time. Hadn't Tony helped her through this difficult moment? Had she broken down with sobs as usual? No, she had not. So, she would give it time.

Then a thought hit her, so she got up and went over to her magazine rack and took up two bridal catalogues.

Then she went back to the bed and sprawled herself on it and began to turn the pages of the first one. She hovered over the gowns and drooled at the wedding bands and engagement rings. She still couldn't believe that Judy was getting married before her. She had said that she would be willing to wait for two years after leaving college before getting married, but with Judy soon to go, she wanted to marry soon too. Ah, she thought, life wasn't fair. Wasn't she the one who was planning and dreaming about marriage?

But who was getting married? Judy. She pushed the catalogue away with annoyance and rested her head on her arm. And thus, she fell asleep.

***

Alma's devotions that Saturday morning were tearful ones. As soon as she had begun to pray for her friends, the tears had come. They were so excited when they finished college and were looking forward to a year of fun before going off to university and Ruth to her first year as a teacher. Now, just one month after college, things were not the same among them. She knew that things had to changed, but she was overwhelmed by the swift flowing currents of events. She wondered if she was being childish, and felt a twinge of self-pity.

She got up from her knees and reached for her Bible, knowing that she would find comfort therein. She turned to Psalm 121 and read: 'I will lift up my eyes to the hills, from whence cometh my help, my help cometh from the Lord, who made heaven and earth.'

Yes, she said to herself, I will look up, not around, not down, not back, but up. She felt better and read on. After she had finished, she felt strengthened and encourage. She therefore decided to call the girls later to see if she could encourage them to go out that evening. They had not gone out for the past two Saturdays. As she went down to the kitchen/ restaurant, she was glad that she had decided to postpone dating for Post University. She did not envy her friends.

***

After prayerful meditation, Pastor McKenzie decided that it would be better if he and Jamie had a face to face discussion without his wife's presence. He would visit his son's home about two o'clock on Saturday afternoon, when he should be home from work. When someone knocked on his door at 2:00pm on Saturday, Jamie thought that it was Jason, and as usual, wondered what it was that he wanted this time. He was more than surprised when he opened the door to his father and was so lost for words that he could do no more than beckon him into his home by way of welcome.

When Sheridan saw Pastor McKenzie, she got up hastily to take her leave upon which Pastor McKenzie said, "I take it that this is the young lady who is carrying your child." No one answered. He continued, "sit down, sit down, dear."

Jamie looked menacingly at Sheridan and said to his father, "no, dad. She is leaving." So Sheridan took up her bag and excused herself.

Pastor McKenzie looked at his son with dismay. "That's rude," he said. "She could have stayed. We are going to talk about her," he continued seriously. Jamie could feel his bristles rising. This was why he had left home. His father just would not understand that he could no longer dictate to him. He always rebelled. How could a pastor not understand the powers of persuasion over coercion?

"Sheridan is my business, dad. I don't want to talk about her," said Jamie with veiled anger. "I told you about her condition to prevent you hearing it on the street. I did it out of respect for you. I would be grateful if you would respect me to handle my own affairs," he finished, looking at his father in the eye. But Pastor McKenzie did not waver.

"Son, the honourable thing for you to do is to marry this young lady. You do not wish to have children scattered all over the place. You want them under one roof so that they can get equal care, attention and the direction and influence of a father. Drop you stubbornness and think of the child."

Jamie finally took a seat opposite his father. "If I marry for the sake of a child, my marriage will be unhappy too. He may even thing that it is his fault.

Children are more sensitive than we credit them for. I will be there for this child but I will not marry Sheridan, period."

"Well, son, I will have to publicly administer a verbal discipline in church on Sunday, and you will have to sit in the back until you do get married," answered Pastor McKenzie with resignation. Then he added, dropping his confident stance.

"I must have let you down somehow, son. Your mother must be right. She claims that I drove you away from home. I'm sorry, son. I can't tell you how sorry I am," he finished trying hard to hold back his tears.

Jamie did not expect his father to crumble and his humility touched and softened him, making him feel ashamed of his actions that were causing his father grief. He knelt before his father and put his arms about him.

"I'm sorry, too, dad, I really did not mean to let you down or cause you shame. Please, forgive me." Then the two big men cried.

***

Alma waited until ten o'clock to call the girls. Sally wasn't sure if she wanted to go out and promised to call back later to let her know. Ruth was still broken from Jamie's news, and was in no mood to leave the house. Judy and Donald had agreed that Saturday evenings were for the girls. Or were things different now that they were getting married?

187

Alma stared at the handset in her hand but it had no answers. She shouldn't feel rejected, but she did. What a difference a month makes, she thought. Perhaps she should have dated. But she immediately rejected this thought. No way, she mused. She didn't have enough fingers to count the number of girls who had dropped out of school pregnant. Young divorces were on the increase. No, she wasn't missing anything. She would just have to go alone or take Chloe and Dinah with her. Things were better when shared, at least some things, she corrected herself; not willing to share a man when she did get one. Later for that, she thought, as she went in search of her new going out companions.

＊＊

After breakfast, Mr. and Mrs. Sandison decided to have a talk with Ruth. The night before they had given permission for Tony to visit late; but were too sleepy to indulge in a discussion. Ruth was still sleepy but welcomed her parents. They sat on her bed and wanted to hear again all she had told them last night. After all, they had been sleepy and just wanted to make sure.

Ruth told them of the pregnancies and impending marriage. Then she finished with, "Why am i not the one who is getting married, mom and dad? It isn't fair," she wailed resting her head on her father's thigh. He stroked her tangled hair. Both parents laughed in spite of the situation.

"I'm in no hurry to see you leave home, honey," said Mr. Sandison.

"But Ruth, you are just eighteen, why hurt your head over marriage?" asked her mother.

"Judy is eighteen too!" replied Ruth sulkily. The parents looked at each other.

"Ruth, dear," said Mr. Sandison, "you seem more concerned about not getting married, than about Jamie's extracurricular affairs. Am I right in this assertion?"

"No, Dad. It's just that my not getting married seems easier to talk about. Sally says it is because I can't keep Jamie that another woman got him and that hurts." Ruth choked up and her mother put her arm around her.

"Having sex with a man, is no guarantee that you would keep him dear. You do know that, don't you?" asked her mother tenderly.

"I know, Mom. That's why I'm saving myself for my husband. There is no guarantee that if I give Jamie what he wants that he will marry me. I don't want to bed hop," surmised Ruth.

"Don't let anyone make you change your principles, honey. If you don't know what you stand for, you will be like chaff, tossed to and fro by the wind. I am proud of you and your stand," Mr. Sandison assured her, seconded by Mrs. Sandison.

"Thanks, Mom, thanks Dad," replied Ruth, raising herself up and giving each a kiss and quick hug. Then she asked them to buy her some novels and newspapers during their shopping that Saturday.

Ruth was surprised and relieved that her mother did not tell her to leave Jamie. Perhaps her mother had at last realised that in some cases telling a young person not to do something is an indirect way of telling them to do it, and vice versa. Ruth wondered if that strategy was what is known as reverse psychology.

Anyway, she knew for sure that she loved Jamie, but she also now know that she was not prepared to wait forever for him. If someone else loved and treated her well, she could spend the rest of her life with him. If Jamie was honourable as Donald, he would have honoured her desire and married her. So why should she wait for him, she thought. Just a few hours before, Ruth had been sure that she was willing to wait for Jamie. Now, she was certain that she would marry someone else if Jamie delayed. Judy's impending marriage had definitely impacted heavily on Ruth's plans.

***

Dinah was peeling potatoes and Chloe washing up as Alma approached. They both turned at the sound of her footsteps.

"Dinah, Chloe," she began. "I really feel like going out later but none of my usual gang seems similarly inclined. Please, would you like to accompany me?" she asked engagingly.

"If you can pay to babysit our kids, it's alright." replied Dinah, with Chloe nodding in agreement.

"That's no problem," answered Alma gratefully. I'll ask Auntie Mona to give you an hour off to organize your baby-sitting," she said, adding, "thank you so much."

As Alma turned to leave, Chloe put in, "But how come your friends abandon you so?" Alma explained that they had not really abandoned her but the various pregnancies had complicated the friendships and individuals now had to priorities.

"I see," said Chloe. But as soon as Alma left the kitchen, Chloe turned to Dinah and said, "You would have thought that these rich people could afford to buy condoms to prevent pregnancy. We can't afford it."

"Aw, man! It ain't have nothing to do with money. We can get free condoms at the clinic or go on the pill, also for free. Rich or poor, people sometimes forget caution and all can get caught," was Dinah's astute reply.

"Yeah, that's true. But when we get caught, we have to bring it because we can't afford abortion," rallied Chloe.

"True, a lot of abortions take place, but a lot of people do bring their children. For one, you're not sure that you'll get married and two, if you throw away all your children, who will be there for you when you are old? So it's fifty-fifty," Dinah calculated.

"I wasn't ready for children," sulked Chloe. "Every time you want to go out at night, you have to worry about a baby sitter, and salaries are so small. So I can't live."

"I wasn't ready for children either, but now I wouldn't exchange my two for the world," said Dinah proudly.

Then Mona came in asked them why the dining area had not been cleaned after breakfast and neither the chicken or beef for lunch had yet been seasoned. How could Alma ask her to give them an hour off when they were working at this unacceptable pace? That reminder was the stimulus for speed and the girls dropped their chitchatting as they were going, they would finish way before the schedule.

***

After Jamie and his father had regained their composure, Jamie told his father that he had opted to stay away from church until he got married. He did not intend to sit in the back of the church to embarrass himself. His father agreed, prayed a blessing upon him and left.

Jamie breathed a sigh of relief. That was a burden taken care of. His father wouldn't have to face the unwelcome task of 'reading out' his own son. Now he looked at his watch. Nearly three o'clock. He was expecting Mrs. Sandison at four. He wondered why she had asked to come to his apartment to talk about his relationship with her daughter. He wondered if she would find the place. He went out onto the porch and looked around. He had given her correct instructions. No sensible person could miss the building he thought, and went back inside.

Mrs. Sandison's coming, preceded by his father's had clearly disorientated Jamie. He went into the kitchen and realized that he didn't want anything there. He went into the bathroom and noted that it was clean enough. He did not wish to lie on his bed. He shook his head in exasperation sat on the sofa and turned on the TV, but paid no attention to it.

He lay back on the sofa with both palms under his head. What did this woman want? he asked himself. Anyway, he reasoned, she is Ruth's mother. He determined that it must be pregnancy that had triggered this meeting. Jamie was uncomfortable, but was intractable in his desire to postpone marriage until he was ready. So he surmised, if Mrs. Sandison was coming to try to force his hand to marry her daughter, she could think again. With that he felt strengthened and went for malt and some newspaper to occupy his time until she came.

After half past four there was a knock on the door. Jamie's heart lurched with anticipation or was it trepidation? He dropped the paper and hurried to open the door.

Mrs. Sandison kicked Jamie viciously in his groin. He grabbed his crotch with both hands, doubled over and fell forward. Mrs. Sandison stepped out of his way as he fell, writhing in pain, with his face contorted. As he hit the porch with half of his body still inside the apartment, she grabbed his T-shirt and pulled him fully out, using both her hands. She tried kicking him in his groin again, but not getting proper leverage since his hands were still there, she began to kick into his chest, violently.

Finally, breathing heavily, and fixing her track suit and tying her laces, she turned and left. She had not said one word to him.

Earlier in the day while she and her husband were shopping, she had left him waiting outside where Jamie worked, telling him that she was just going to drop a message for a friend. When she had left home that afternoon, she had told her husband that she was going to the hairdresser.

Earlier that morning when she and her husband had discussed the various pregnancies with Ruth, Mrs. Sandison had said very little about Jamie or about his and Ruth's relationship. What's the use, she had thought. Ruth was not prepared to leave him and her husband went along with whatever Ruth wanted, so Mrs. Sandison had decided to take matters into her own hands and face the consequences. That was exactly what she was doing now. She was on her way to the police station. She felt no fear. The sun was high and there were only a few wispy cirrus clouds in the sky. Red hibiscus flowers waved pleasantly at her as she passed someone's fence, seeming to give her a nod of approval.

If Ruth wouldn't leave Jamie, then she, Doreen Sandison, would do whatever she had to do, to ensure that Jamie left Ruth. She wanted that man out of her daughter's life.

She reached the police station and was about to go past the sentry when he stopped her.

"Where are you going, Ma'am?" he asked

"To make a report," Mrs. Sandison replied, and he let her go.

Mrs. Sandison walked up the two steps into the station and addressed the station sergeant.

"Good day, Sir. My name is Doreen Sandison from Lowmans Hill. I've just finished giving one Jamie McKenzie a few kicks and left him laying on his porch. I don't know what condition he is in. He lives in the apartment block that borders the road to Kingstown Park, as well as the road to Level Gardens. First floor, first door in the porch."

"Are you serious, Ma'am?" asked the sergeant incredulously.

"You don't think I came in here to con a date with you, do you?" The sergeant stared at her still disbelievingly, so she continued.

"I don't date black men and secondly, I am happily married."

The sergeant shook his head and said, "OK Ma'am, I'll have to dispatch the CID and the ambulance to corroborate your story so you'll have to take a seat in the meantime."

195

Still shaking his head in disbelief at the audacity forthrightness of this woman, he went towards the phone and with her thanks expressed; Mrs. Sandison took a seat on the bench. A man who was sitting there and had heard everything, withdrew to the end of the bench to put distance between himself and Mrs. Sandison, whose fearless attitude had struck fear into his heart.

After her mother had left the room, Sally decided to call Alma before she forgot. Sally told her that she wasn't inclined to go out because her mother had, as it were, ordered her to go to England and she was in the process of packing. She promised that they would all get together before she left. Alma was sad at the news but wished her well.

Sally turned back to her bed and looked at the empty suitcase. What should she put in there? She would buy clothes when she got to England, after all, she didn't want to be out of style; tracksuits, jeans, underwear, nightwear and load of towels. She was at it for about two hours when she began to feel tired and threw herself across the bed.

Sally didn't want to go but she didn't want to stay either. If Tony had been all hers, she would have stayed. She wouldn't have minded at all. Having an illegitimate child was the least of her problems. Having a child for a man who was in love with another woman was another thing. She wondered if her casual attitude to relationships and backfired on her. She wondered if she was being punished and that was why she had fallen in love with Tony. She really had had no plans for a serious relationship right now, and now this! Anyway, Sally comforted herself; Ruth is a racist where men are concerned. She will never marry Tony and I will get him in the end. With this thought, she dozed off.

***

After about half an hour, the sergeant went over to Mrs. Sandison and told her that she was under arrest and read her rights. They had found Jamie right where she had left him. The ambulance had taken him to the hospital and an x-ray had determined that there were a number of fractured ribs. Mrs. Sandison could call her lawyer and someone to bail her if she did not wish to spend the night in the cells.

Mrs. Sandison called her husband after having spoken to her lawyer. She asked Mr. Sandison not to tell Ruth anything. He therefore dismissed his customers with humble apologies and closed the shop, telling Martha that he was going to see a matter and would be back soon.

Mr. Peters, the lawyer, arrived at the police station a few minutes before Mr. Sandison and asked to speak to his client in private before the sergeant took the statement. Mrs. Sandison told him what she had done and added that she had no regrets because Jamie had no respect for her daughter, and went on to tell him about Sheridan.

"Now," began Mr. Peters, "we are going to plead mental aggravation upon you by this young man. You are an aggrieved mother who was driven by an intrinsic, inherent desire to protect your offspring. Any parent could understand that, and we should plea leniency from the judge. Therefore, when you go to give your statement, you have to drop this bullshit attitude, and even if you have to pretend, begin to show remorse so that when the sergeant takes the witness stand in weeks to come, he can testify that you had begun to show remorse after being in the station for about one hour. Understand?" he asked seriously.

"Yes, I understand," said Mrs. Sandison, matter-of-factly. "But Mr. Peters, I don't know if I can pretend. I tell you, I have no regrets. That boy is abusing my daughter mentally."

"You leave me to tell that to the court and go in there before that sergeant and begin to learn to pretend or face three years in jail for grievous bodily harm. You can't go around breaking ribs and thinking you'll get away with it by saying that you have no regrets, understand?" asked Mr. Peters with a no nonsense expression on his face. Then he added, "Remember, if you go to jail, there is one less person to look out for Ruth. So start looking out for her now and go in there and say sorry in that statement." Those last words hit home and Mrs. Sandison's arrogance crumbled.

***

About 5:20pm when Mrs. McKenzie opened her door in response to a knock, she was very alarmed to see two police officers standing there and a cold wave of fear washed over her as she clutched her dress and whispered, "yes?"

"Good afternoon, Ma'am," one of the officers greeted Mrs. McKenzie. She nodded a reply, unable to speak. "Are you Jamie McKenzie's mother?" the officer continued.

At the mention of Jamie's name, Mrs. McKenzie fainted and the other officer shouted, "catch her!" as he himself caught her as she slumped forward. In his study, Mr. McKenzie heard the commotion and hurried to the door and saw the officers with his wife in their arms. He therefore told them to hold on while he opened the other side of the door.

They placed Mrs. McKenzie in the recovery position on the sofa and asked Mr. McKenzie to loosen any tight clothing that she may be wearing then fetch some smelling salts. This done, Mrs. McKenzie opened her eyes when the salts were placed under her nostrils. "Oh," she said, trying to sit up.

"Lie still for a while," cautioned one of the officers. Then he turned to Mr. McKenzie, "I suspect that you are the parents of one Jamie McKenzie?"

"Yes, we are," replied Mr. McKenzie, his expression seriously concerned.

"When I asked your wife a similar question, she fainted," said the officer in way of explanation.

"Shall we sit down?" asked the officer. They sat down.

"Jamie was severely kicked in his chest sometime after four this afternoon, by one Mrs. Doreen Sandison of Lowmans Hill, who herself reported the matter to the police also after four this afternoon. The matter was investigated and he was taken to the hospital and x-rayed. He has three fractured ribs. It is our duty to inform you. We sincerely regret this unfortunate incident and will be willing to help in whatever way we can. The matter, of course, will be taken to court in due time. We will take our leave now. Here is the department's card, and here is my card. Thanks for allowing us to do our job. We'll be in touch." The officers rose and bade goodbye to the McKenzie's. Mr. McKenzie saw them to the door with thanks of appreciation and promised to keep in touch. Then he returned to his wife, who was in a state of disbelief, now fully recovered and sitting up.

"I can't believe it," said Mr. McKenzie, shaking his head. "I just can't believe it." Mrs. McKenzie just kept staring blankly, still in shocked disbelief, saying nothing. "I can't believe it, but I can understand it," continued Mr. McKenzie.

This injected life into his wife who jumped up in a frenzy, waving her arms at him threateningly as he held his ground. "You can understand that that horrible woman kicked my son and broke his ribs. What's her justification, and what kind of father are you?" as she sobbed heart-rendingly.

Mr. McKenzie tried to comfort his wife. "Honey," putting an arm about her; "she must have heard that Jamie, who is supposed to be dating her daughter, has gotten another woman pregnant. It doesn't look good from her daughter's point of view. Think about it, honey. So she probably went berserk. That's why I've said that I understand it. I didn't say that she was right to take the law into her own hands. Come on, sweetheart, let's go visit our son."

"Yes, yes," agreed Mrs. McKenzie. "And I'm staying with him all night and tomorrow. I'll call Sister Arlene." And with that she collected a handful of tissues from the sideboard and dried her face then went to the telephone.

"Hello?" answered Sister Arlene.

"Oh Sister Arlene," began Mrs. McKenzie, and started to cry again.

"What's wrong, Sister McKenzie?" asked Arlene alarmed.

"Oh, that wicked woman Doreen Sandison kicked my son Jamie and broke his ribs. So you'll have to take charge of the Sunday school tomorrow because I'll be at my son's side," she finished haltingly between sobs.

Arlene expressed her sorrow at such sad news. She assured Mrs. McKenzie that all would be well at church and with her son, because they would make it a matter of prayer. She also told of how enraged she was about Mrs. Sandison's action. Someone should give that woman a taste of her own medicine.

As soon as Arlene replaced the phone, she hastily pulled on her outdoor shoes and almost ran all the way to Esther's to tell her the news. It was so momentous to express by telephone.

Arlene did not note that the sun was already lowering and soon the sky would be orange coloured, the sea bronze as the sun sets. The people of Burgin Hill had become accustomed to spectacular view of the setting sun. She also seemed not aware that there was a swift breeze and that it was a little chilly. More-so, she was completely oblivious that she would, at this time, be upsetting Esther's favourite pastime.

***

Indeed, Esther was in her back yard, sitting on a bench and keeping an eye on a coal pot in which she was roasting a breadfruit. She did this every Saturday afternoon. Esther believed that roast breadfruit with bowl jowl was the best dish ever. Bowl jowl was made with small pieces of dried cod, stewed with slices of tomatoes, cumbers, sweet peppers, onion and vegetable oil.

A number of Vincentians shunned breadfruit, claiming that it was brought by the colonist from the South Sea Islands to feed slaves and that they were no longer slaves. Esther countered that since she was no longer a slave, she was free to eat whatever she chose, and that was breadfruit and bowl jowl, her favourite dish.

Thus, when Esther did not answer Arlene's several raps on the door, Arlene stood crestfallen, wondering where Esther had gone. Then she recalled that it was Saturday afternoon, and Esther could only be at one place and she fled from the porch as if pursued by dogs, to the back of the house.

"Esther, Esther!" shouted Arlene calamitously. Esther shook with fear and almost burned her hands on the hot coals as she turned the breadfruit. "What now?" she asked as she stood to meet Arlene. "Woman!" she said, her voice rife with rebuke. "You calling me like if my mother dead or something. What happen now?"

"Sorry, sorry. I didn't mean to alarm you. Sorry."

"Alright," conceded Esther grudgingly but now eager to hear what all of the excitement was about. "Yes, tell me," she invited.

Now it was Arlene's turn to be displeased. What was wrong with Esther? Why did she have to give her such dressing down? Since when wasn't she excited to hear news, making her have to apologize and all!

"You don't look like you are in a good mood today, Esther. I'm going home. I didn't come here to beg you know!" with that Arlene turned on her heels.

"Oh, come on Arlene," said Esther placatingly. But Arlene ignored her. She followed Arlene. "Arleen, please."

"Forget it, Esther. You like to show yourself too much when you ready. I'm tired of your shit, making me have to apologise and all. Who the hell do you think you are?"

"You are too sensitive, Arlene. Every little thing offends you. Perhaps you need a husband."

Arlene stopped and faced her, surprise at this jibe. It hurt.

"Really?" asked Arlene in a low, angry voice. Well, she could be nasty too. "Well, if I had a husband, he would not be looking mauger like yours. Instead of walking from house to house minding people's business, I would be cleaning my home and cooking for my husband so that he could look respectable." With that Arlene turned on her heels again leaving Esther stumped for words.

Arlene turned towards home, still feeling slightly bruised. Yes, she would go to her home, her own home, where she could sit in comfort and talk to others on the phone without exposing herself to insults. Thank God she had her own home or else they would have treated her like shit. She used to be a sweeper of schools, and although the dust used to make her sick, she had persevered and saved her money along with the earnings that she made from her knitted and crocheted work, until she had given up the sweeping job. The house consisted of one bedroom, a drawing room and kitchen and a bathroom.

Nevertheless, the church folk still treated her like the least of the disciples because she didn't have a husband. This was an underlying problem that Arlene did not talk about. When she was younger, none of the few men in the church was interested in her because she was only a sweeper. They did not realize that half of her earnings came from her handiwork, of which she was justly proud. Now that the house had lifted her status, the few men were either married or occupied.

Arlene decided that she would really have to start praying specifically for a husband before she got too old to make children. She just need to ask God to bless her and expected to get a husband, but perhaps, she did need to tell God exactly what she needed. And if she still didn't get a husband, she was quite happy the way she was.

***

While Mrs. Sandison and her lawyer were having their discussion, Mr. Sandison was being enlightened about his wife's exploits that afternoon. Mr. Sandison was horrified and begged the sergeant not to release it to the news media. The sergeant told him that he would need to be persuaded to do him such a great favour.

"You could pass by my shop anytime," said Mr. Sandison.

"I don't drink," replied the sergeant.

"Should I write you a cheque then?" persisted Mr. Sandison.

"Cheques leave trails that can be followed, sir."

"Well, you tell me," conceded Mr. Sandison, and waited expectantly on the sergeant.

Finally, the sergeant said; "you know what, I'll pass for that drink. But I want it in cash. Monday afternoon."

"See you then," replied Mr. Sandison thankfully then stood aside to await the lawyer and his wife.

***

The Jamie/ Sandison affair was not mentioned on the evening news so Ruth did not get wind of it and her parents said nothing of it to her. The following Monday morning, soon after Mr. and Mrs. Sandison had had a little chat with Ruth before going down to the shop and Ruth was trying to fall back to sleep, she was jolted fully awake by a choir of voices chanting:

"Down with the Sandisons
Who they think they are
Go to another shop
See how they like it!"

What's that? Ruth asked herself, lifting her head to listen. But she heard it again and again, and it didn't stop. So she got up and went to her bedroom window and flung it open. There were about sixty or seventy-five adults with their backs to her, blocking the entrance to their shop as well as to their house. Most of them were carrying placards, which were turned away from her. And the chanting went on. what's this? Ruth wondered, troubled.

Thus, she changed hastily into white slacks and a vest, pushed her feet into her red slippers and went down to Martha. No, Martha did not know what this was all about. She was just about to rush out to her parents, when Mrs. Sandison came up the kitchen steps.

"Ruth, darling, we need to have a chat. We'll go to your room." Ruth followed her mother up the stairs. Mr. Sandison called the district police. The news had gotten around Burgin where most of Pastor McKenzie's church members lived. By Sunday morning after church, everyone knew of the Jamie/Sandison affair and decided to do something about it, led by the white people, whom Arlene and the other black people simply followed.

They were not going to cause any trouble. They would just block the entrance, chant and wave their placards. After all, Christians must stand up for each other. Doreen Sandison was not only a heathen, she was a snob.

Most children in St. Vincent run errand to shop for their parents, but that Monday morning, the children who attempted to patronize the Sandison's shop were intimidated by the close packed, chanting, placard-waving crowd who left them no space to get into the shop and so they went to another shop which was much farther away.

But Tommy, the village handyman, would not be intimated. He insisted that they make room for him to pass but no one budged and told him to go to another shop. But Tommy would not be persuaded. After all, it was the Sandisons who gave him credit when he didn't have money. Why should he now spend his money where he could get no credit? Who did these people from Burgin think they were?

Tommy tried to barge his way through, but when he was again pushed back, he lashed out and was straight away knocked to the ground. He got up groggily, having hit his head, stating that he would be back. By this time, the news of the disturbance was reaching other people because the intimidated children were explaining to their parents why they were so long in returning from their errands. So when Tommy came with a bump on his head, it was enough. Who did those people from Burgin think they were? Everyone rushed to find a weapon, bottles, stones, sticks and even a few cutlasses and leaving the children behind, almost the whole village went out to confront these people who were hindering their lives and hurting their friend Tommy.

The villagers stood on the other side of the road, facing the chanting Burgin Hillers. No one wanted to pass the first blow. Then Tommy came up with a bright idea and it was soon whispered around. So they set off, but not back to their home. They were going up the hill that bordered the very road on which they were standing. When everyone had gotten to the top of the hill, someone counted to three and then they rained bottles and stones on the chanting crowd relentlessly. In fewer than five minutes, they had dispersed, quite a few en route to the clinic, having sustained cut cheeks and foreheads and broken scalps.

At ten o'clock, the district police arrived. One policeman, was very exasperated when he did not see any crowd blocking the Sandison's entrance as they had reported and went into the shop to ask Mr. Sandison to desist from wasting the police's time. Mr. Sandison explained that he had called the police at eight o'clock and the crowd had been there until close to 9:30. It wasn't his fault that the police hadn't arrived on time to prevent his loss of trade and so many people getting hurt. The policeman rejoined that he was not at the beck and call of the white man. Those days were over and he worked on a first come first serve basis. White or black, Mr. Sandison reminded him, he had failed in his duty to keep the peace and protect the people.

Chapter 21

Mrs. Dembar had gone to New York to shop for Judy's wedding. Except for the food, she was buying everything there, even the champagne. Mr. Dembar and Judy had to fend for themselves in the food preparation while she was gone. For the first two mornings, Mr. Dembar made breakfast for himself and Judy. For lunch and supper, they ordered take-away. On the third morning, Mr. Dembar revolted. Why should a rich man like himself be doing menial tasks because his wife refused to have helpers? It was ridiculous. What was the use of money, if not to buy one's comforts? This was the last morning that he was going to cook his own breakfast.

Not forgetting his English traditions, he fried himself bacon, sausages and egg. He boiled an egg for Judy and warmed some beans for her also. Before he took his seat at the table, he took a tray with cornflakes and milk, orange juice, the egg and beans up to Judy's room. Then he sat down to eat, forgetting that he had not toasted his bread or put on the kettle. Ah, he thought, I will just eat what I have here then drink some orange juice. I'm not getting up from this table. This is my wife's fault.

He didn't get up right away. His thoughts went to Judy. It was honourable of that young man to marry her at this juncture in his life. Many would not have done it. He hoped and believed that Judy would have a son. He hoped his wife would change her mind and buy the stuff for the nursery on this trip. She had said that they could wait. But he would have preferred them now, so that he could go into the nursery and look at them and pretend that his grandson was already there. Ah, he thought again, I'm going nutty over a baby. Know what? My wife is right this time. We'll all wait for my grandson to arrive in style.

He got up from the table when the clock chimed nine o'clock. After clearing the table and drinking the orange juice, he took the comfortable one seater sofa next to the drawing room phone. Then he searched for the employment agency and called the number. He asked for a cook to work from 8:00 am to 4:00 pm and a housekeeper to work from 9:00 am to 5:00 pm, if possible, beginning from the next day. He listened to their terms and conditions, agreed to sign all documents to be sent to him and then hang up.

Anna, the cook, arrived promptly at 8:00 am the next day. Mr. Dembar showed her the kitchen and told her it was her job to keep it clean. More-so, breakfast was served between 8:00 am and 8:30 am, lunch between noon and one o'clock and when she left at 4:00

pm, she should leave supper on the table. Also, she should find out what each person desired for each meal. In addition, the cake and bread bins must never lack and the refrigerator must have an ample supply of fried fish, roast beef and baked chicken.

When Jem, the housekeeper arrived at 8:55 am, he gave her a tour of the house and told her that it was her job to keep it clean as well as do the laundry and ironing. Mr. Dembar determined that Alma and Jem were staying, no matter what his wife said. After all, it would give her more time for him and the baby. He was sure that things would work better this way.

***

Ruth looked at her mother, refusing to believe what she had just heard, although she knew that her mother was telling the truth. "Mom, today is Monday. If those people had not caused this disturbance, you had no intention of telling me anything."

"You can say that," answered Mrs. Sandison defiantly.

"Why?" asked Ruth trying to contain her anger.

"Because you do not listen to reason where that boy is concerned. You want me to sit by and watch him wreck your life?" asked Mrs. Sandison.

"You can go to jail for this," Ruth reminded her.

"If I succeed in breaking you up, it will be worth it."

Now Ruth let loose.

"Mom!" she screamed. "You yourself told me that I am just eighteen and have nothing to worry about, and before you let time take care of things, you nearly killed Jamie!"

"Sweetheart, if I did not have regard for some of your feelings, I would have bashed in his face as well," said Mrs. Sandison, rising as if to indicate that enough was said. Ruth rose too.

"You don't like Jamie because he is a Christian," wailed Ruth, now sobbing. Now it was her mother's turn to be angry.

"Save your tears, Ruth. I have no sympathy for them right now. I have nothing against Christians. I just don't like hypocrites, and the whole McKenzie clan and their congregation fit that label. I am just trying to remove the scales from my daughter's eyes."

"Yeah." Sobbed Ruth. "But you behavior is not only potentially damaging to my self-concept, but is highly likely to intimidate any would-be suitors, and where would that leave me? You don't care about me at all, mom. This is a personal vendetta against a Christian. I hate you, mom. I really do!" And with that, still sobbing Ruth went into her bedroom and closed the door behind her. Mrs. Sandison left Ruth to herself, knowing that after the initial shock, she would see sense.

Ruth stripped and sat in the dry bath tub, crying her heart out. "Oh Jamie, Jamie I'm so sorry. I'm sure you didn't meant to get that girl pregnant. Oh Jamie, oh Jamie." Jamie had been keeping his distance but had respected her enough to call and tell her that Sheridan as pregnant. Now, he would never talk to her again. Even if she tried to visit, Mrs. McKenzie would never allow her to see him. What had her mother done? She didn't want it to happen this way. Ruth cried until she had developed a headache, forgetting that she had not eaten breakfast. Finally she turned on the taps for a warm bath, followed by a long, long sleep.

***

When Sheridan returned later on Saturday, she found Jamie's door unlocked and went in, assuming that he had not gone far, she performed her self-appointed chores. She even decided to surprise him and cooked him a fish tea, her own brand consisting of boiled redfish with ochro and cabbage and green pepper. She left it in the pot so that he could re-heat it. Then she sat down to watch TV and await his return. It was already eight o'clock. She thought that he was probably at one of the neighbours, because he had left the TV going, and there was still a half filled bottle of malt near to his newspapers. It would be inept of her to go knocking on doors, so she would just wait. But at 11:45, overcome with tiredness, she stretched out on the sofa and promptly fell asleep, with the TV still going.

When Sheridan awoke, it was morning and a check revealed that Jamie had not come home. Now she was worried. Something was wrong. For the second time, she was forced to call at his parents' home to enquire of his welfare. Mr. McKenzie answered. After ascertaining who she was, he told her that Jamie was in hospital. Sheridan thanked him and hung up. Hospital again, she thought. She had not asked what the matter was since his father had not volunteered the information. She decided to go home and freshen up before visiting Jamie and also to eat the fish tea instead of leaving it to spoil.

When Sheridan knocked on the door of the private male surgery, Mrs. McKenzie opened the door. She looked Sheridan up and down.

"Are you the slut who deliberately got pregnant to trap my son?" asked Mrs. McKenzie. Sheridan flushed red with guilt. How does she know? Wondered Sheridan. Aloud, she made no reply.

"Guilty conscience, eh?" Mrs. McKenzie continued. "Look how much trouble your selfishness has caused my son, you bitch!"

"Mother," called Jamie in a barely audible protest from his bed.

"It's alright, son. I'm here to protect you from scavengers," she said, closing the door in Sheridan's face.

Sheridan stood rooted to the spot, awash with guilt, shame, anger and rebellion. She also felt slapped and wished that she could return the insult. Who did that woman think she was? Did she think that her son was an angel?" Wasn't it him who had tried to mess up her life, use her like a spare tyre and stopped for that good-looking bitch from Lowmans Hill? Why didn't he stick to his woman? She had every right to trap him, concluded Sheridan. She would get even with that woman.......calling her names.....

"You have to knock if you wish to go in. His mother is there with him." It was a nurse addressing Sheridan having seen her standing at the door looking lost. The nurse smiled.

"Oh, hmm…ah… I was just leaving," stammered Sheridan so lost in thought that she did not realize that she had attracted attention. She thanked the nurse and left.

Sheridan was just about to cross the road from the hospital when she remembered that she had locked Jamie's apartment and brought the keys for him. She therefore returned to the hospital and asked the nurse to give the keys to Jamie. As she turned to leave again, she knew that she would find some way to make Mrs. McKenzie pay for the way she insulted her.

***

Jamie's manager decided to fire him because he was being regarded as a liability to the business. This was the second time in two months that they would have to award him sick leave with pay for getting himself

216

embroiled with physical confrontations. Perhaps outside of the business premises he had poor inter-personal skills and therefore was not a good representative of their values. He received the letter the same day that he was released from the hospital. He had spent four days in hospital and was sent home to heal and recuperate. He was with his parents.

They were all appalled at the judgment of the letter. Jamie felt betrayed and now his physical pains seemed even more severe. He couldn't believe that he was being punished when, in both cases, he was at the receiving end of the stick. Where was justice? Was his manager playing judge, jury and executioner? It wasn't fair, he thought. It just wasn't fair. Now Jamie blamed Ruth for all of his misfortunes. Now he was out of a job. It was all her fault. It she had agreed to have sex with him, and then he would not have had to seek it elsewhere. Then Tony would not have had to bash in his face and her mother would not have had to break his ribs, hearing that Sheridan was pregnant. Ruth was bad luck, Jamie concluded.

But his mother offered him a solution in one respect.

"You can move back home until you find a job dear."

She was very disappointed when he replied, "I pay rent by the quarter, in advance. If by the end of September, I'm still out of work, I'll think about it. But thanks for the offer, mother."

***

Mrs. Dembar's two new employees, Anna and Jem, fitted the stereotype of black women - full lips, fleshy nose and big bums. Anna was fair with reasonably long hair. Jem was very dark with bold, almond shaped eyes. Both were in their early twenties. Anna was reserved and business-like. Jem was out-going and attention-seeking.

On the first day of work, Jem changed into a respectable house dress before beginning her tasks. Having learned that mistress of the house was overseas, she changed into very short hot pants and midriff top on the second day. Mr. Dembar was propped up in bed, around ten o'clock, reading the weekend paper that had just been delivered when Jem knocked on the door and asked him if she could clean his room now. Mr. Dembar told her that he did not feel like getting out of bed to accommodate her at the moment. But she insisted that she would just tidy up and clean the bathroom and change the sheets later, so she let herself in.

Her tidying up was very noisy and distracting, and each time he was distracted and cast his eye to see what had caused the noise, their eyes met. Was this woman trying to attract his attention? He went back to his paper. There was another noise. This time, he looked directly at her with a 'What do you want, woman?' unspoken question. She smiled. He just held her eyes.

"When is your wife coming back?" she asked.

"She left last Saturday for two weeks."

"Well, if there is anything I can do for you until she gets back, please let me know," she said holding his gaze. Then she moved her eyes to his groin and let it linger there, then back to his eyes, and finally she scratched between her thighs gently.

Mr. Dembar was a sophisticated man but not a stupid one. His wife doled out sex as if it was a rare delicacy, always complaining of tiredness. But he had never sought to complement her lack in any way. The business, combined with running a large plantation, kept him busy. With the coming of his grandson, he had decided to take things easy and appointed his nephew as manager. Now here was this woman handing him sex on a plate, he had never had sex with a black woman before. But there is always a first.

"What about now?" he asked casually.

"Fine with me," Jem replied, smiling.

"Meet me in the guest room then," replied Mr. Dembar, laying aside his paper. He rolled off the large bed and left the room. About five minutes later, Jem did the same thing.

Mr. Dember was standing in front of the full-length mirror. His partly bald head glistened and his thin serious business-like mouth was very serious. He did not like his big nose, but thank God, it was straight. He turned his sharp grey eyes on Jem as soon as she came through the door and asked:

219

"Are you clean?"

"What you mean by that?" asked Jem, clearly offended.

"Do you have STD's?"

"What's that?"

Mr. Dembar was now annoyed.

"Sexually transmitted diseases, you know, sickness that you can acquire by having unprotected sex with a carrier of these diseases."

"Nah, nah," she said, shaking her head vigorously.

"I clean, you can smell me if you want," And with that she pulled off her pants and knickers with one sweep, threw herself on the bed and spread herself wide; she used both of her hands to part the lips of her vulva, revealing a clean looking red passage. Mr. Dembar's eyes widened, his jaw dropped and his penis shot outright with desire.

"God!" he whispered.

Keeping these eyes firmly on the red passage, he hastily peeled off his drawers, and scrambled into the bed, hovering over her. Instead of smelling as she had invited him to do, he entered her, hard.

"Oh," he whispered. "Oh."

It was as if he was experiencing sex for the first time, and he just rested in her, not moving, savouring the moment. Her vagina therefore began to convulse spasmodically, resulting in more 'oh's' from Mr. Dembar. Then he withdrew somewhat and began to thrust into her, one, two three and whoosh, he ejaculated. There was a long 'oh' from him and he dropped into her for a moment.

Then he got up and went into the bathroom, telling her to hold on. He cleaned his penis and brought a wad of toilet tissue for her to clean herself. Then he took it from her and flushed it. His testicles filled up to bursting every three days or so, and usually he would masturbate in the toilet and empty them. He smiled as he flushed the toilet. How much more gratifying to empty them into a woman than a toilet? He thought to himself.

At forty-five, with little exercise, that two minutes' sex had tired him. But he wanted more. He lay next to Jem.

"You come on top now," he invited, lying on his back. She obeyed and positioned herself into a stoop over him. Then she went down onto his upright penis until all of it was into her. It was only five inches erect and medium stoutness, so it was no problem to her. Gripping it with her vaginal muscles tight, she went up and down, on him resting her palms on his chest. Then she changed her actions, now swinging her hips from side to side. Soon, she began to cackle like a yard fowl and then exploded with her climax. She had suspended all motions as she had her orgasm, her face contorted as she successfully suppressed her scream.

During orgasm, her vagina convulsed rapidly and Mr. Dembar could feel his penis awash with liquid. Then she began again, this time, turning her body around in a circle on him without the penis slipping out.

After three turns, Mr. Dembar stopped her. That action was painful. Could she do something else? So she lifted her lower body as if she was withdrawing, but when she got to the tip of the penis, she stopped and caused her vagina to convulse around the tip of it, as if the vagina was kissing it. Then she went back down on him, wiggled, and up back, slowly to the tip again, repeating the kissing actions. After several motions of this act, she invited him to sit up and they hugged each other with the penis fully into her. Here, she did some gentle wiggling and then he, feeling intense pleasure let out a long sigh of 'oh's', while she laughed. Then they finally came together, waited a while and then fell away from each other. She went to the bathroom. Mr. Dembar went to sleep.

Chapter 22

It was about 7:30 on a Saturday evening. Chloe and Dinah, decked out like twins with close fitting blue jeans, blue and white oversized striped shirts and two inch black thimble heels with a bow, were waiting at the bus stop in their village on their way to rendezvous with Alma on a night out. They had left their children with Chloe's mother, who had to be paid $20, from each of the young women, in advance. Chloe's hair was parted into two from to back and plaited into two cascados, sometimes called corn rows. Dinah's hair was too short for this hairstyle, so was parted into several sections from the base all around to the centre of her head. Each section was plaited into a cascado, the ends of which were held together with a black pompom. They wore no jewelry and carried no purse, putting their money and penknives into their pockets. Soon, a minibus bearing the name 'ANGEL' and pumping deafening dub music came hurtling along. They pushed out their hands and it stopped. They jumped in and were off, happy as larks.

After ten minutes, they arrived in Kingstown and alighted at the shell gas station at Paul's lot and walked the rest of the way to Alma's home at Level Gardens.

The streets were busy as was customary for Saturday evening. Kentucky Fried chicken was full as usual and the Rastafarian shops along the way to Alma's were not doing too badly either. The night was clear and the sky was ablaze with stars.

"What a beautiful night," whispered Dinah.

"Sure is," replied Chloe.

The yard lights were on and Alma's car was facing out. She must be ready, they thought. They let themselves in and heard men's voices coming from the restaurant area and suspected that one of the men of the house was having a meeting of friends. They slipped by unnoticed and went up of Alma's bedroom and knocked.

"Chloe and Dinah," said Dinah

"I'll be there in a minute," returned Alma. The girls went back down and out and waited on the porch. They took in the familiar well-cut lawn and hibiscus hedge and the chatter of the few passers-by as they waited. They did not wait long as Alma was down in five minutes, resplendent in ruby earrings and bracelet, a plain three-inch, a plain three-inch thimble heel and red, and a black, sleeveless, squared-necked, close-fitting plain velvet dress, reaching about two inches above her knees. Her hair was pulled back into one mass and held together with a black ruby encrusted comb.

"Wow!" said both girls simultaneously.

"You make us look like if we are going to now the lawn," commented Dinah admiringly.

"Oh no," demurred Alma graciously. "We all look fine, come, let's go."

"No way," said Dinah stubbornly. "Lend us some jewelry first."

"What do you wish to have?" asked Alma pleasantly amused.

"Let's see what you have," ventured Chloe and they turned re-entered the house and went back to Alma's room.

The room was affluent and fragranced with Jasmine. Everything was of gold and white except for the carpet which was all white. There were gold handles on wardrobes and drawers. Gold frills on curtains and pillowslips and spreads. Even the sofa had a golden border. "Come," said Alma guiding them to her dressing table with its several jewelry boxes.

She opened all of the boxes and the girls gasped, and then said again, "Wow!"

"Come, come," said Alma. "We don't have all night. Take your pick." Chloe chose a star sapphire pair of earrings with a matching bracelet and Dinah chose a flower with a central pearl pair of earrings and two plain golden bracelets, both of which she wore on one hand. Their appearance now enhanced, they all took a last look in the mirror and left.

"It's ten past eight," said Alma. "We're late."

"Do you know of any show that starts on time in St. Vincent?" asked Dinah. "I can bet they're not starting until 8:30. Don't worry." Dinah was right. In spite of the traffic, they arrived at the Peace Memorial Hall at 8:23. The hall was almost full and they had to ask for a kind exchange of seats so that they could all sit together. Alma was getting a lot of attention from jealous women and admiring men. She was more beautiful because she did not appear to know that she was outstandingly lovely and it enhanced her appeal. At 8:30, the master of ceremonies apologized for the late start of the variety show and asked that everyone stand for the national anthem.

The first item on the program was a short skit. It was titled, 'HOPE'. Concisely, a man had a common law partner who was not keen on faithfulness but yet blamed him for all of the problems in the home. There was constant bickering and fighting, the man often getting the shorter end of the stick. Sarcastically, it was she who decided that she had, had enough. And the house being hers, she took all of his belongings and threw them out of the window and they landed into the main village road. With threatening machete, she demanded that he leave right away. He was not willing to wager with his life, neither was he willing to go to jail for this woman. He knew that he could beat her but he did not like to pit his strength with a woman. More-so, it was her house. So, backing away from her and keeping his eye on the machete he picked up his shoes from the porch and left.

He sat outside the house by the road on a retaining wall feeling despondent and angry, wondering where he could find lodging before night. He didn't want to crawl back to his mother. He would have to go to one of those expensive hotels, but he was not going to bend down and pick up those clothes. As he was pondering, along came a woman.

"Are these clothes yours?" she asked compassionately. He nodded affirmatively.

"You got throw out?" Again in the same tone of voice he answered. He looked back at the house without answering.

"Don't worry, sweetheart." She came forward and caressed his head kindly. "My house has plenty of room for you."

And with that she went about collecting all of his belongings and stacking them into three heaps. Using his shirts as carriers, she tied the stuff into three bundles. She gave him the largest one, she put one on her head, stuck the other under one arm through his arm, saying: let's go, love."

Without looking back and with relief on his face, they left and the curtain closed. The audience cheered and clapped. A man jumped to his feet and said, "That's right sister. Woman gone, woman still dey. No horrors, fellars!" The skit was followed by a few calypsos and ballads and a dance troupe. It was now time for the comedy slot, the most anticipated item in variety shows. People just love a laugh.

Devious Joker was the first on and the audience welcomed him with applause, their eager faces waiting to burst into laughter. But they were greatly disappointed and their faces fell as they sand back into their seats. There was nothing devious about Joker's jokes. He had chosen some old, stake jokes about a dumb guy called Dum-dum that most Vincentians had heard told over and over again.

He began with, "there was this stupid guy called Dum-dum. He saw a mango on a tree. He climbed the mango tree and felt the mango. He climbed back down and pelted the mango with stones to dislodge it from the tree." Of course, nobody laughed.

But he went on. "This other time, Dum-dum was sitting on a wall in his village when a drinks truck, laden down with crates of beverages, pulled up alongside him and stopped. The driver and his assistant came out and spoke to Dum-dum. They asked him to watch the truck for them while they went to fetch a snack and a drink at the nearby shop, Dum-dum agreed. Word soon got around that an unattended drinks truck, fully loaded, was parked by the village wall. People came from everywhere and helped themselves to as many crates as they could carry and the truck was soon empty. Eventually, the driver and his assistant emerged from the shop and were horrified to see their truck standing empty. Dazed, they found their way to Dum-dum who was still sitting on the wall, the truck. "Sir we asked you to watch the truck for us. Why didn't you call us when the drinks were being stolen?" asked the driver in a hurt, stunned voice.

"You asked me to watch the truck, not the drinks," replied Dum-dum.

Still no one laughed. Where did this man come from, with his Standard English and old jokes, England? Do people tell jokes in Standard English? Why is he still on stage? Everyone wondered. He was just about to start his fourth joke about Dum-dum again, when the MC decided to rescue the show before people began to leave. He hustled on and grabbed the microphone with one hand and patted the joker with the other saying, "Thank you, thank you, thank you.

The joker seemed glad to be rescued and slunk away having evoked not even a smile. Turning to the audience with an apologetic grin, the MC asked them to welcome the other comedian, 'COMEDY KING'. But having been let down by the previous act, the audience kept their hands in their laps. But as Comedy King came towards the centre of the stage and stood beneath the full glare of the lights, the audience began to snigger and giggle. He stood watching them and still they sniggered even more. He walked to the left of the stage, rolling his shoulders and jostling his hips as if one leg was severely shorter than the other; now there was controlled laughter. Now he walked to the right of the stage and then back to the centre, as it were, waiting for the laughter to stop. It continued and then he smiled. Upon this, uncontrolled shrieks of laughter erupted, with persons stomping their feet and holding their tummies. Comedy King was an ugly man. He looked as if he was created by someone who had won the competition for creating the ugliest and most comical man in the world. His looks would evoke laugher even at a funeral parlour. His forehead was pointed but the back of his head was broad and bulging. The bulges at the side of his head were clean-shaven seemingly by accident than by design and his hair was grubby and held in hundreds of little balls of hair. His ears were elf like and his eyes small and deep-set but sharp. He had no nose bridge and his nostrils were so fleshy and large that they made the tip or middle part of the nose seem diminutive. His mouth couldn't close because the upper row of teeth hung over his lower lip and seemed as if someone had pulled his plate both outward and upward, forcing his upper lip back. When he smiled, the upper lip touched his nose.

If people tried to stop laughing and looked away from him, as soon as they looked back, they would start laughing again. More-so, every antic, genuine or otherwise, brought more laughter. For he was tiring of this laughter, willing to begin his stint, but every time he put up his hand and said, "OK, OK," they laughed more.

If he sucked his teeth, and shrugged, that brought even more laugher because he was even more comical when he sucked his teeth. Finally in exasperation he sucked his teeth and walk off. He had exhausted people from laughing without giving one joke. He was so rightly called Comedy King.

Once again the MC hurried on, himself full of rains, and asked the audience to take fifteen minutes' intermission. The audience filed out, still laughing and talking about Comedy King. Dinah and Chloe were describing him to Alma as if she had not seen him herself and they began to laugh some more.

"Oh, I'm so glad that I came. Laughter does relieve stress. I feel so happy," confessed Alma.

What are you so stressed about? asked Dinah, stilling her laugh.

"Oh, mainly my friends," Alma answered. "How I wish they were here."

"You asked them, didn't you? I'm sorry that you are sorry but I'm glad because if they had come, I would have missed this." And Chloe began to laugh again and in spite of Alma's regret, she and Dinah joined in.

Chapter 23

Ruth dried her tears and finished her bath. Then she stepped out and pulled a towel from the rack and wrapped it around her. She faced the full-length mirror but didn't really see herself; instead she saw her dreams slipping away from her. Or was it her plans not taking shape? In her mind's eye she could see Judy beautifully dressed in white lace with a trail of bridesmaid and flower girls and all of the other trimmings. When was she going to get married? Where had she gone wrong? And now her own mother was dishing dirt on her last hope. There was no way that Jamie would come back to her now, not after what her mother had done.

Suddenly her stomach reminded her that she had not had breakfast. She looked at the time. Wow, after ten! She returned to the bathroom and dropped the towel into the laundry basket. Then came back to her dressing table and pulled out a top drawer and took out a pair of knickers and slipped them on. She closed that and pulled a lower one and took out a simple house dress, sleeveless with buttons down the front. Then she pushed her feet into her house slippers, closing the drawer simultaneously. Then she was out through the door and down to the kitchen.

"Martha, Martha," she called. "Did you save any breakfast for me? I'm starving."

"Yes, missy. I put it all in the food warmer. Shall I get it for you?"

"Yes, please, and thanks, Martha."

"You are welcome, Miss Ruth." Martha placed a bowl of oats in front of Ruth and then returned with a plate containing fried plantains, a bun, scrambled eggs and bacon and an orange. Then Martha asked Ruth what she would like to drink. Ruth wanted hot chocolate with added milk. In a jiffy, it was served.

"Thanks again, Martha. You're an angel," complimented Ruth. Martha beamed.

"It was my pleasure, missy."

After breakfast, Ruth lay on the sofa, but there was that clock again. That was the last time that Jamie had visited her. She wanted no reminders and changed position. She was now facing the opposite wall and looking at a painting showing mountains in the background and a road that was lost between the hills, on which walked a man and his dog. The man had a bunch of green bananas on his head and machete in his hand. He looked like a farmer. A simple man, thought Ruth. She believed that she was a simple woman too. All that she really wanted was to get married but her plans had gone awry.

Perhaps she should listen to her mother. Why was an eighteen-year-old worrying about marriage? Was she subconsciously competing with her sisters? They had both married under the age of twenty-one. Was she competing with them? Oh, no, she thought. Perhaps she should have had sex with Jamie. They would have been together now. No, no, no she thought again. Others had done it and the men had still left them for new flesh. No way, marriage first, sex after.

Then she thought of her mother. I think that I have been too hard on mom, she thought. She was just doing what mothers do best, looking out for their children, although in mom's case ,a little over-zealously. She would have to apologize to her mother. Sally, when last did she speak to her? Tony called last night but she and her parents were having a little family time and she had asked him to call another time. Alma, Judy. Ruth sighed. Right now she just wanted to be by herself. But she didn't feel like staying home all day. Perhaps she should go shopping. But she had never shopped alone before. It was always her and the girls, and before that her sisters and mom. There was always a first. She would walk the town and window shop. She didn't really need anything. She always kept her bank cards in her wallet, though. She got up. She would go into town, alone.

So she got up. On her way to her room, she poked her head through the dining room door and called Martha.

"Martha, I'm going into town, but I would really like some boilin when I return. Could you keep some warm for me, please?

"Sure, missy. What exactly do you want in it?

"Well, for fish, I prefer some cavali today. And for vegetables I would like green bananas, eddoes and cabbage. That's all."

"It will be ready, missy."

"Thanks, Martha."

Ruth proceeded up the stairs to her room. She was a little depressed and did not feel like dressing up. So after moisturizing her body and using deodorant, she put on a pair of stone-wash jeans and a green and white striped shirt. Then she brushed back her hair and held it together with a diamond clasp. Last of all she chose a white thimble heel pair of shoes and a silver tip and white purse with diamond. She wore no jewelry and make-up, but as usual, she didn't need it in order to look stunning.

Before she left, she passed by her mother and apologized. Her mom was very understanding and forgiving. She waved her dad who asked if she had enough money and she assured him that she had. She decided to wait outside her gate for a minibus.

A 150 metres walk would take her to the highway where the buses ran frequently but after the disturbance that morning, she preferred to keep a low profile. In fact, the street was still littered with debris from the protest. After ten minutes though, a minibus bearing the name

JOURNEY, came along. She pushed out her hand. It stopped and she hopped in. There were a number of admiring glances, but she paid no attention.

As the minibus approached the hospital, Ruth's heart couldn't allow her to go past. She asked the conductor to stop around the corner. She paid her fare and climbed out hesitantly as if wanting to change her mind. But she persisted. She waited for the traffic to clear and then crossed the road and winded her way to the hospital gate. She passed through the gate wondering which ward he would be in. It should be surgical, she reasoned, and turned right to steps that would take her to see Jamie.

She mounted the last flight of stairs and read the sign, male surgical. Her heart and legs became heavy and she could not find the strength to go on. That woman would be there, she mused. His mother would be there. She hates me. She wouldn't allow me to see Jamie. No, she wasn't going to take any insults or blame from Mrs. McKenzie. She turned and ran down the steps and out of the hospital compound as if someone was chasing her. Ruth stopped running when she was safely outside the gate and looking back, breathed a sigh of relief. She crossed the road and stood outside daddy's shop to collect her composure. It was very hot.

Having stopped off at the hospital, Ruth would now have to walk the whole length of the town, since she intended to reach Sharmin's boutique which was at the south end of Kingstown. She now regretted her action.

She should have known better. Anyhow, she had come into town to walk, so she would. She passed Victoria Park and Bentick Square and turned up Tyrell Street.

There was nothing worth seeing around here. Then she crossed over to Grenville Street. Here was something to admire, and she always did: St. George's Cathedral with its Greek and Roman architecture of arch windows and decorated columns and stained windows. Opposite it was the Methodist Chapel but that was plain and uninteresting. She was tempted to cross over to the side of the street with the Methodist Chapel because there was more cover from the sun from the many buildings which extended over the sidewalks with arches.

But she resisted the temptation because there were more opportunities for window shopping on the side that she was walking. She passed the Shell gas station hastily and crossed the road into Paul's lot. She stood in front of Grand Bazaar's show windows. There were a number of souvenirs. She was not interested and walked on. None of the remaining stores along Grenville Street tempted her beyond their show windows.

She was now in the centre of Kingstown. There was the court house on the left with its stone walls and cream brick decorated windows. The war memorial was in the middle and on the right, the dilapidated vegetable market. She decided to walk through the market, not that she needed anything, she just delighted in the sights and smells of the market. One could smell ripe bananas at a distance. Yellow plums and java plums were in season. The blacker the java plums, the sweeter and juicer they were. There were white plumroses as well as red ones. There were marmie apples and tamarind and all sizes, shapes and types of mangoes, but Ruth loved Julie mangoes the best. The ladies with tubs of lettuce kept sprinkling them with water to keep them fresh. And the tomato hucksters were shouting, "Tomatoes, only one dollar," over and over again. The price of tomatoes had dropped from $4.00 because there was glut on the market. Some vendors were shelling green pigeon peas so that they could sell them at a higher price.

She left the market using the pedestrian crossing over to Bata Shoe store. She didn't bother to examine the show window. Bata always had attractive shoes. She walked around the store admiring everything. Then she settled for a pink thimble heel with a multicoloured gold metal appliqué on the front, as well as a three coloured thimble heel; yellow, green and black. she had not meant to buy anything, but she loved nice shoes.

The heat was now getting to Ruth and she was a little tired. She therefore abandoned her original plan to walk the whole town and decided to make one more stop at the wedding shop. So she went up Middle Street and into Cobblestone Inn ground floor. There were a mannequins in bridal gowns and bridesmaids gowns. Ruth was sure that one of those bridal mannequins looked just like Judy. She turned away from the gown with a heavy heart and went to the showcases of rings and wedding bands.

Now Ruth was excited. She adored handsome rings, ooh, she thought, they were all wonderful. But there is a beauty in simplicity that doesn't escape the eye and she saw it. An engagement ring with the top in the shape of two isosceles triangles touching each other at the apex of the unequal angles, and a diamond at the point where they converged; simple and gorgeous. Ooh, breathed Ruth. I'm going to buy that and wear it on my right hand since I can't engage myself. I'm not leaving you for anyone, sweetheart. She called the attendant. It cost $895.00. She paid for it and put it on right away on the third finger of her right hand. Satisfied, she decided to call it a day. All that was left to do was to pass through the market and this time, buy herself some yellow and java plums, then go home to eat her boilin.

Chapter 24

"You know Donald, my dad was saying how he wished that more young men your age were as responsible as you," commented Judy thoughtfully. Donald reached over and pecked her cheek. They had done some resistance exercise on the sand and had then gone swimming up and down along the beach, instead of out to sea because Judy was afraid of deep water. She was adhering to one of her mother's sayings: 'Sea water doesn't have any backdoor.' They were now relaxing on a towel, enjoying the fair weather and gentle breeze and admiring the clouds, satisfied in each other's company. It was late mid-morning on Sunday.

"What have I done to deserve that compliment?" asked Donald.

"For not deserting me when I got pregnant, as many others do."

"Desert you!" exclaimed Donald. He rolled over on his tummy so that he could look her in the face. "Men run when they are not in love with the woman and the thought of a child makes them feel trapped, so they put wheels on their heels. But I love you. I fell in love with you the first time that I saw you, remember?"

"How would I know the first time that you saw me, Donald?" laughed Judy, pinching his ear lovingly.

"You can't have missed that moment", insisted Donald, pretending shock.

"It was after the 1979 Independence celebrations. Your group had gone to our house with Sally. Then I came with one of my friends. When I pushed the door, you were sitting facing the door so I looked straight into your amber eyes. I felt like someone had thumped me in my chest and this strange feeling rolled down my chest, tummy, groin, knees and right down to my toes. I was literally weak at the knees. I just stood there, transfixed. You kept looking cheekily back at me with the expression: 'what are you looking at me for?' You were eating popcorn. I was fourteen, you were twelve and seemingly not yet into boys. I wasn't really into girls as yet, just enjoyed teasing them. But that day I grew up. I fell in love. Then Alma asked Sally if I was her brother. Sally looked around and saw me and said yes. Then Alma said that I seemed very interested in you and you all began to giggle. I blushed and my friend and I went to my room. I have never stopped loving you."

He drew her close and began to kiss her hungrily. He was getting hot and hard between the legs and said, "Let's go into the water." They went waist deep into the sea. He advised Judy to hold him about his shoulders and wrap her legs around his hips. He maneuvered his bathing trunks and her bikini until part of his penis was into her vagina, but it kept slipping out. So he instructed her to change position and stand with her back to him. He held her around her waist and told her to lean forward. Again, he got a little penetration, but the wave motion kept unbalancing them and made intercourse impossible.

"Let's get our towel and go to the end of the beach," said Donald in frustration.

"No, honey, let's go home. I have a queen-sized bed remembered?"

"Yeah, let's go," conceded Donald.

They hurried out of the water and picked up the towel. They then headed for the car which was about eighty metres from the beach. As they neared it, Donald unzipped a pocket on his bathing trunks and took out the keys. But when he approached the driver's side of the car, he realized that he would not need the keys. Someone had broken into the car and had left the door open, with its window smashed.

Donald stood there dumbstruck. "Are you alright?" asked Judy. Donald still couldn't answer and Judy flew to his side thinking that he was being taken ill. Then her eyes fell on the vandalized car and she drew back as if struck. "Oh!" was all that she could say as she stood in amazement. Then Donald's face flushed with anger.

"You know what? The person who did this knew that this car was ours. He must have done this when we were swimming or else we would have heard this smash." He checked inside the car. Its radio was gone and all his cassettes and his wallet which were all in the glove compartment. His NIS card was in his wallet, as well as money.

"What are we going to do?" asked Judy sympathetically.

"Take out the mat. Get the hand brush from the boot and sweep all the splinters and broken glass onto the mat. Put the mat and its load into the boot until we meet a garbage dump. I'll drive you home. Then I'll drive this car to a garage and leave it there. I'll buy a new car tomorrow. This car is tarnished."

"You can take my car, dear. We don't need two cars between us now."

"Oh yes we do! A car is a convenience, not a luxury. I work, you have places to go. We need two cars. And besides, the car belongs to Sally and me."

"But you can still take mine and I'll ask dad to buy me another," persisted Judy.

"You'll do no such thing, honey. Except if you allow me to take your car and buy you a sports model instead. That Mercedes is too big for you."

"OK then. I suppose that can work," Judy conceded half-heartedly.

***

Mr. Sandison pulled up outside the McKenzies' home. It was a beautiful house: white with brick red roof and trimmings, a high roof and sash windows. He opened the gate, admiring the well-kept lawn, walked up the short drive and knocked on the door. Mrs. McKenzie opened the door and scowled.

"This is not a good time to visit, Mr. Sandison." She said and was about to close the door in his face.

"Let him in, Ethel!" said Pastor McKenzie firmly. Mrs. McKenzie moved aside grudgingly, giving Mr. Sandison glances of death. Mr. Sandison ignored her glances, stepped in and the door closed behind him.

"Thank you for letting me in, Pastor and Mrs. McKenzie; and good afternoon to you."

"Please, sit down Mr. Sandison," invited Pastor McKenzie.

"Thank you," he replied, taking the sofa closet to the door.

But Mrs. McKenzie was still standing, scowling and swinging her hands indicating that she hoped his visit wouldn't be long. He wasn't welcome.

But her husband would have none of it. "Ethel!" he said, casting his eye from her to a seat. She sat on the edge of the chair. Then Pastor McKenzie turned to Mr. Sandison.

"So, sir, to what do I owe honour of this visit?"

Mr. Sandison cleared his throat.

"First of all," he replied, "how is Jamie?"

"In pain and out of a job, thanks to your wife," returned Mrs. McKenzie before her husband could even open his mouth.

Pastor McKenzie ignored her and said, "Jamie is recuperating very well, thank you. In pain, as you may expect though. Due to this incident, his manager has fired him. He claims that these things that Jamie gets himself into are costing the company. This is even more difficult for Jamie to handle than the pain. You understand."

"Sure, sure," replied Mr. Sandison. "I am very sorry to hear that, and on behalf of my family I express our deepest regret and apology."

"On behalf of my family, and for the sake of peace, I accept," responded Pastor McKenzie. But Mr. Sandison wasn't finished. "In addition, I would be grateful if we could settle out of court. I had intended to offer ten thousand dollars; I would increase it to twenty, since the young man is out of a job. He can start a small business of his own with twenty thousand dollars," he finished hopefully.

Once again, Mrs. McKenzie, bursting with rage and contempt, interjected. "No thanks. this is a case we can't lose and when it is over, we'll sue your pants off you and the snob out of your wife."

"Ethel!" almost shouted Pastor McKenzie, rising to his feet in outrage. "Are you trying to undermine my authority? You'll be quite or leave!"

In response, Mrs. McKenzie sat fully back into her chair, indicating that she wasn't going anywhere but at least she would keep her mouth shut; not before throwing hateful menacing looks Mr. Sandison's way. Pastor McKenzie took is seat again.

"I'm sorry about that, Mr. Sandison. Yes, er… your proposal is worthy of consideration, but it is for Jamie to decide. Would you like to speak to him yourself?"

Mr. Sandison shook his head slowly.

"No," he replied. "In the circumstances, he would find my presence revolting and that could cloud his judgment. If I am not asking too much, I would be grateful if you could convey my apologies to him and also table my proposal for deliberation. Then he can let you know is decision and I'd be grateful if you'd let me know. If you would allow, I would prefer not to burden you any longer. But thank you for your kind indulgence." He rose. So did Pastor McKenzie.

"Thank you for coming, Mr. Sandison. I would convey your compliments to my son and I'll be in touch. God speed."

They shook hands and Mr. Sandison took his leave without approaching Mrs. McKenzie who had her arms firmly folded across her breasts. Mrs. Sandison had not informed her husband before she had committed her heinous act, so neither did he forewarn her of his visit to the McKenzies. When or if the Pastor called then he would let her know.

***

As Sally sat in the pew that Sunday morning, her attention was elsewhere. Her mother had already spoken to her Aunt Enid in England, she was all packed and tomorrow she would book her flight. Perhaps she shouldn't rush away like this. Perhaps she should wait until her tummy started showing. She smiled. What a ridiculous thought. Wait until her tummy showed indeed! So that all the tongues that were not already wagging, could start? No, her mother was right. She'd go; out of sight, out of mind. She would miss church thought. She looked around. Here were most of the elite of this little society; little indeed. That was the problem, too small. Everybody knew everybody and their affairs too. She should go and never come back.

Tony called soon after she got home and asked if she would like to go to the cinema later. She didn't, but apologized for her mother's behavior on Saturday and told him of her imminent departure. He responded that it was the best option in the circumstances and that she should keep in touch and be sure to send him her telephone number. She could have given it to him right then, but he seemed relieved to be rid of her so she did not force the issue. Donald poked his head around her door and asked if she would like to go to the beach with him and Judy before she left for England, but she reminded him that two are company and that three is none.

Then Sally felt guilty. How thoughtful of Donald to want to show her a good time before she left for London. She had forgotten all about his wedding so caught up in herself. And the wedding was only two weeks away on the fifteenth of August. Surely she could wait that long

247

for her brother and avoid them having to explain to all and sundry why his sister wasn't there. She hurried into the kitchen where her mother was cooking.

"Mom!" she called excitedly. Her mother turned quickly and expectantly.

"We have forgotten Donald's wedding!" finished Sally.

"I haven't," said her mother, arms akimbo. "I've already ordered his cake, paid for the venue, organized the drinks and personnel for the bar. Mrs. Dembar is taking care of the food. What have I forgotten?"

"Don't you think people would be asking you guys all sorts of questions as to why his sister was absent? Especially since it's only two weeks away?"

"That's true, sweetheart. But with Donald's welfare is under control, I was only thinking of you. Now, as you foresee, I am not looking forward to telling everyone why you are not there. I'll call Enid to expect you after the wedding, OK?"

"Yeah, Mom." They hugged and Sally went back to her room.

***

Arlene opened her bamboo gate and let herself in. She closed the gate then turned and admired her empire, as she always did on returning home, even if she had only gone to the shop. Her heart swelled with pride. It was a dirt yard but it was always well swept because Arlene swept it several times a day, even if the wind blew two leaves into her yard. Her rose shrub with a circular seat right around it was the envy of the village. Arlene's house did not have a porch, but that circular seat meant that, apart from midday when the sun was directly overhead, she could always find a shady spot to sit and knit. At the opposite end of the yard was a vegetable stand on which she grew lettuce, tomato, sweet pepper, and chive. On the ground adjacent to the stand were two small patches bearing cabbage and carrot. Behind the stand were half a dozen pigeon pea trees, not yet in bloom. Conveniently outside the kitchen door at the corner of the house, were a hot pepper plant and two pots, one bearing thyme and the other peppermint.

Satisfied, Arlene climbed the three steps and turned the key in the door of her house. She went in, dropping the keys into the drawer of a small desk. She took off her shoes, then sat at the desk and took up the phone. She conveyed to a few notable members of the church what sister McKenzie had told her and hung up. Then she sank into an armchair to think.

She needed to find a husband. Even Esther who didn't know how to care for a husband had one. Anyway, she scolded herself, she must be doing something right because Dan, though mauger, always had a smile. Esther didn't work, but she came from good family, had a fair complexion and was pretty. That was why an educated man like Dan married her. Good lucks were really handy.

Arlene knew that she wasn't ugly. There just were not enough men in the church, especially ordinary men who wouldn't mind her not having academic qualifications. She had been waiting on the Lord to send her a husband, but faith and works go together, so it was time that she did something to find a husband before time passed her by. But what could she do? She couldn't date a man who was not a Christian, and most of the available men were not Christians.

Then it was if a voice spoke to her and said, "Why don't you tell God all of these things? He is wonderful in counsel and excellent in guidance." So she got up right away and went into her bedroom and fell onto her knees and poured out her soul to the Lord with tears streaming down her face. When she was finished, she got some tissue and cleaned her face and blew her nose. Then she heard that voice again.

"Do like Abraham's servant and ask for a sign." So she went back to her desk and got her Bible. She turned to the chapter of Genesis where Eleazar went to Mesopotamia to seek a wife for Isaac. When he had gotten to the well where the community drew water, the servant asked God for a sign. "Let it be that damsel to whom I shall say, give me some water, and she shall say drink and I will draw for your camels also, let that be the one that you have chosen for my master's son." Before he had done speaking, there was Rebecca, who did exactly as Eleazar had asked.

Arlene closed the Bible, she was excited. What sign could she ask for? She thought and thought. Then she had it. "Let it be that the one whom I shall invite to church and he agrees to go with me, let that be the one that you have chosen for me." So she knelt again at her bedside and asked God for that sign. Then she got up from her knees, but she was not happy. Perhaps she had asked for a highly improbable sign. The men in her village didn't go to church. After work, they sat in the rum shop and drank and played domino and cards until midnight. She doubted if they had suitable clothes for church. Perhaps she should ask for an easier sign. Then she chided herself, isn't God the God of the impossible? And if the sign comes to pass, then I will know that it is God's hand.

Now she felt better, hopeful and even happy. So she went off to the kitchen to bake her weekend bread singing, "Tell it to Jesus, tell it to Jesus, he is a friend that's well known. You have no other such a friend or brother, tell it to Jesus alone."

Still singing, she secured a large tumbler of warm water and set aside. Then she sifted almost two kilograms of flour into a large bowl and made a valley in the middle of it with her hand. Into the valley she cut 125 grams of shortening and fifty grams of margarine. Then she added half a cup of brown sugar and few teaspoon of salt. She reached for the yeast but there were just a few grains in the tin. How could she have forgotten? She stopped singing. What a bother. Now she would have to go out again. She got the money and her shoes and hurried to the shop, not bothering to lock the door since she wouldn't be long.

She went to the grocery section of the rum shop and called for a small tin of yeast. Jomo, who was in the rum shop but close to the grocery said, "Arlene, you going to bake bread? I would like to have a woman like you to take care of me."

The other men laughed. One of them said, "Yes, Jomo. We know that you like homemade bread." They all laughed again, but Jomo ignored them. Arlene just smiled. But Jomo wasn't finished.

"Arlene, ain't it time you get married and get a man to keep you company?"

"Same thing I'm saying too, but Christian men are hard to find," replied Arlene with a laugh, remembering what she was indeed just praying about.

"But I can become a Christian, I'm thirty-five. Time for me to settle down with a good woman like you, and study God."

Now the whole shop was silent and listening. No more laughing. Jomo seemed serious. Were they witnessing a proposal? Arlene too was aware of the change of temperature in the shop. Her heart quickened as she remembered her prayer and sigh. Could it happen to quickly? Should she try the sigh? Jomo was ordinary, just like her. He was managing, just like her. She looked at Jomo. Both of his lips were heavy and putting. His eyes were almond shaped and pulled back like a

Chinese's, but for a black man, his nose was too small. If one concentrated on his nose and mouth, he failed. She looked into his eyes and smiled.

"Are you serious?" she asked.

He kissed his hands and swore, "So help me God." There were sniggers. Arlene hesitated and said a silent prayer.

"Then would you come to church with me tomorrow?" There, she had done it.

"Sure," said Jomo. "I still have me suit that I wore to Andy's wedding."

Arlene was in a daze but she managed to say, "well, get ready for half past nine tomorrow."

"Where should I meet you?" be asked.

"Just knock on my door. I'll be ready." And she took up the yeast and her change and left, still in a daze.

Chapter 25

Ruth was glad to get home. She could hardly wait to strip off her sweaty clothes. She stopped in front of the shop door and waved to her parents then proceeded to the kitchen. She asked Martha to wash the plums and put them in a bowl. Then she hurried to her room. She dropped the two bags of shoes in front of the wardrobe, kicked off her shoe and headed for the bathroom. She stripped off her clothes and dropped them into the laundry basket. Then into the shower she stepped.

Although the day was hot, the water was still very cool. Ruth relished it. It was so exhilarating after that heat that she just showered herself for a good while before using any gel on her body. After twenty-five minutes, she stepped out of the shower and toweled herself. She saw the reflection of the ring on her finger and for the first time since arriving home, she paid it full attention.

She shouldn't be wearing this ring on her right hand; it should have been on her left. She shouldn't have bought it herself, Jamie should have. Why think about it? He had not even suggested getting engaged to her. Why did she end up with someone like Jamie? Why didn't she find someone like Donald, just twenty and getting married even though it was not his plans just yet? That was an honourable young man.

Jamie was twenty-one, called himself a Christian, wanted to have sex outside of marriage: clearly a non-Christian practice, and chided her for refusing to go along with him. Now he had gotten that young woman pregnant, and it didn't sound as if he planned to marry her. Well, at least, she was glad that he had no such plans or else all hope for her would have been gone. Oh, she thought, it's so hard to give up Jamie. He's so tall and handsome. He commands attention.

There were not many tall good-looking white, young men around. She might have to go to England to find one if she lost him. She could never settle for someone less than Jamie now. But the thought of starting all over again was daunting. It would spoil her plans. She had been prepared to wait at least two years, but with Judy soon to be married, two years was too long. She still couldn't believe that Judy was getting married before her. Then she felt hunger pangs. She dropped the towel into the baskets, hurriedly slipped on a pair of knickers and a house dress, pushed her feet into a pair of slippers and was out of the door.

Ruth forgot her troubles a while as she savoured her boilin. It was one of her favourite dishes. Plus, she still had her bowl of plums to relax with later. She smiled. She loved simple things. Perhaps she was a simple woman at heart and that was why she was so hung up on marriage rather than her career. She put down the spoon and looked at the ring again. Perhaps she should not have bought it. Suppose she gave herself bad luck?

That thought bothered her and immediately she lost her appetite. There wasn't much left in the dish, anyway. She got up, taking the bowl of plums with her. She had meant to stretch out on the sofa in the drawing room, but she went to her room instead. Suppose she had given herself bad luck by buying herself an engagement ring? Suppose she never got married?

It was a sobering thought and it filled her with fear. She knew a lot of beautiful women who never married, so she couldn't rest on her looks. She also knew a lot of women who were of barely average looks who were married. Things were certainly not going well for her, at least, not according to her plans. For the umpteenth time she asked herself, suppose I never get married? No, she thought. I will get married. You know what, for safety's sake I'll marry Tony. Better to marry a black man than never marry at all.

Ruth knew she was only eighteen and had all the time in the world to get married. But Judy was eighteen too, and would be married in a few weeks. Ruth was not prepared to wait for years. After all, she was the one who was always thinking and talking marriage. Life was not fair. Why was Judy getting married before her? She would start being nice to Tony and if asked again, she would say yes.

The phone rang. It was the Ministry of Education. She was to come for an interview and bring her GCE results, the next day at 9:30. It was while she was on her way to the interview that she saw Jamie in his father's car and so realized that he had been discharged from the hospital. She had told her parents and Mr. Sandison had secretly decided to pay them a visit the following day.

The interview had gone well and she had been appointed a probationary assistant teacher. She was happy. At least, that had been in her plan. Now she had to get married for the plan to come to fruition. She would get married; she would do whatever she had to do. After all, one couldn't always wait for things to happen. One had to sometimes make things happen.

***

Jamie did not wish to hear anything about the Sandisons and wanted nothing from them, but out of respect for his father, he listened. Then Mr. McKenzie left his son to his own deliberations. Jamie was enraged. Imagine those contemptible people trying to buy him off. They would all meet in court, that's for sure. He wouldn't touch their money, not even with a pole. Then he reconsidered. If he sued them, it would still be their money but at least, he comforted himself that would be the right way to obtain it. Not as a pay off as if he was hiding something.

Then he tried to be objective. Suppose her defense argued that he had provoked the attack by his behavior towards Ruth? Suppose they used his low standard of Christianity to question his integrity and make him look like a villain and Mrs. Sandison as the aggrieved victim, pushed as it were by him? And there was Sheridan's pregnancy. He could see the weekend papers, 'SON OF PASTOR KICKED SENSELESS BY AGGRIEVED MOTHER.' He shuddered. How would his father feel? He would take that money. This case was no done deal in his favour. He had no intention of facing those nasty defense lawyers in court.

***

Three days later, Mr. McKenzie called Mr. Sandison and conveyed his son's decision to him. Mr. Sandison was grateful and promised to be in touch. When they were in bed that night, Mr. Sandison told his wife what he had done. She wasn't pleased but her husband wasn't asking for her opinion. He was simply informing her. It was now his wife's job to inform Ruth.

***

Mr. Dembar and Jem had sex around the same time the next day, Saturday. As soon as he penetrated her, she began to spin her hips very fast almost throwing Mr. Dembar off.

258

"Hold it," cautioned Mr. Dembar. "This fast is not sexy, I find it scary. Slow down."

She slowed down and it was heavenly. He liked that swirling movement of her hips. It meant that he had very little work to do, but to keep his balance. He also liked when she contracted her muscles and pumped up and down his penis as if her vagina was massaging his penis. Where did this woman learn all these vaginal tricks? He would pay any money for sex like this, but here he was getting it free. No, he would have to pay this woman a bonus on her wages. She deserved it. They came almost together and he rolled off her. After cleaning up, he did not go to sleep but discussed with her how they would work their intrigue around his wife who was due back in a week's time.

They agreed to have sex every day for the following week. Sunday was her day off. He would miss her. When his wife returned they would not have sex if she was at home. But as soon as she went out, the sign for Jem to go into the guest room would be the sound of his wife's car rolling off. Then Mr. Dembar would meet her there shortly after.

"I didn't offer to help out for free, you know. I noticed that you talk strategy, but no money," said Jem pointedly. Mr. Dembar was a little taken aback by her forthrightness but managed to compose himself.

"That is understandable," replied Mr. Dembar. "How much do I owe you?" he asked.

"Well, I never have money on weekends, and there is always a lot to do and places to go. So I'd like one hundred dollars every weekend," she finished.

"That is reasonable," said Mr. Dembar. "Beginning today, each weekend I'll put that amount of money for you under this end of this mattress and you will collect it at your convenience."

Pleased, Jem took her leave and proceeded with her chores, hustling to finish by the half day. Funny, thought Mr. Dembar. When I was inside her, I thought I would pay any amount of money for that kind of sex, and a few minutes later, she dropped it like that. But I'll pay. Her sex is captivation. Then he went down to the kitchen and told Alma that from now on, he would have ochroes and eddoes boiled up with fish as his mid-morning snack and that he would now like to have linseed drink every afternoon. Linseed and ochro are extremely slimy and eddo, mildly so. Because of its property, some Vincentian men believed that these foods would enhance their sperm producing capacity.

***

The wedding was a high profile splash affair. The 'who is who' of the Vincentian elite were there. Sally was chief bridesmaid. Ruth and Alma were among the six bridesmaids. Donald's best friend Markie was best man. Judith Duncan sang 'Together forever' and the SVG Cadet Force's band played the wedding march. Judy's headpiece was held together by a diamond studded tiara and her train as well as the close fitting bodice of her gowns was bedecked with hundreds of pearls. The sleeves were puffed at the upper arm and then close fitting down to the elbow. The skirt was gathered at the waist and was very full.

It was all lace and satin and very conservative because the bodice was stopped with a pearl studded turtleneck, so none of Judy's skin was seen except her face and hands. She carried a large bouquet of white roses with two red ones in the middle. Donald, who was wearing a tuxedo, also had a red rose on his lapel.

Mr. and Mrs. Dembar were the happiest people at the wedding. The Clarkes were reluctantly so. At the receptions, the guest were very happy, the food was served buffet style and there was more food and drinks than there were guests to eat and drink. But with foresight, Mrs. Dembar had ordered hundreds of takeaway containers, and the guest were encouraged to take home what they could not eat in order to avoid spoilage, which they were most obligated to do. So everything went well and that same night Mr. and Mrs. Dembar flew to Miami to meet their ship for a Caribbean cruise.

Chapter 26

Seven months later in March 1986, travelling bags and suitcases were being checked and double check to ensure that every necessity for both mother and baby was packed. It was nearing the end of March when Judy and Sheridan, along with Sally in England, plus many other women, were expecting babies. March is always a busy time for the maternity ward in St. Vincent coming nine months after carnival when most people let their hair and many other things down.

Jamie was happy. No not at the imminent birth of his child. He had started his own business, a taxi service and his taxi was the only one that offered twenty-four hours service. Pregnant women and their partners depended heavily on McKenzie's Taxis. He had started with four cars and had now progressed to six. His mother worked with him during the day at the taxi stand in Kingstown as receptionist/ cashier. After eight o'clock, she took the calls from home. This left Jamie free at nights.

***

Mrs. Clarke had flown to London to be with her daughter at the delivery. On the 22nd March, Sally delivered as healthy seven pounds baby boy at St. Charles Hospital. Mrs. Clarke's heart sank. The baby had his father's nose and lips. She had hoped that he would have more of their features. Anyway, he had Sally's forehead and eyebrows. But he had something all his own: honey coloured eyes. There was no one on either side of the family with those eyes. He almost looked white and had no hair.

Tony did indeed keep in touch with Sally, so when Mrs. Clarke got back to her sister's house, she called him to tell him the news and that both baby and Sally would be discharged the next day. Tony thanked Mrs. Clarke and called his parents. They were thrilled. Then Mrs. Clarke called her husband.

"Now Betsy, you bring my grandson home. Don't leave him up there."

"Are you crazy?" asked his wife. "You can't make that decision without Sally."

"Of course I can. I've already promised Sally that I would take care of him. Remember that day when you were saying that you didn't want it in your house. You bring him home, woman. Hear me?"

"When Sally comes home tomorrow, you talk to her. I'm not even going to tell her what you've just said."

"Fine," conceded Mr. Clarke. "I'll talk to Sally."

But Sally's aunt had asked Sally to allow her to babysit the child. She had never married and did not have any children. It would be her pleasure to have a little one running about their house. She would just have to cut back on some charities. She had stopped working since she was forty-five, having delegated someone to manage her business to give her more time for fun and leisure. But now, at fifty, a child would be great. Sally had agreed.

Mr. Clarke was not pleased. He had hoped to have his grandson to spoil more than he had time to spoil Donald. Why couldn't Enid foster or adopt a child? Mr. Clarke would shelve the matter until the child was weaned. That would give Enid enough time to decide her way forward without his grandson. Enid agreed.

But Sally couldn't understand her father. It seemed that he had forgotten that she was off to university in October. Did he expect her to send her son to St. Vincent, to be away from his mother at so young an age? Or did her father expect her to postpone university now that she was a mother? Sally wasn't yearning for St. Vincent. In fact, she wasn't sure that she would ever go back. How could she? Ruth was engaged to the man she loved, her son's father.

Sally did not understand Ruth's game. Ruth didn't hate black people, she just didn't believe in interracial marriage. Yet here she was, engaged to a black man. Each time Tony called, Sally would end the conversation by telling him that she loved him. But his response was always 'OK love, keep in touch.' It was she, Sally, who had fallen in love with Tony from the first time that she laid eyes on him. And he knew it too. But he had chosen the woman who was giving them hell.

On the other hand, perhaps it was better to send the child to St. Vincent and get on with her life. He looked so much like his father and she would be constantly reminded of Tony. But did she really want to forget about Tony? No, she loved him. Ruth was a bitch, a real bitch. Instead of redoubling her efforts to take her man from Sheridan, she found it easier to take Tony; who knows, to hurt me, thought Sally bitterly. They were friends. But she sure wasn't making any effort not to hurt her. What a dilemma. Fate was so cruel.

Mrs. Clarke stayed three weeks with her daughter and it made Sally feel a bit like home. Mrs. Clarke didn't do much shopping for there was really no need, just bought a few solid shoes for her husband and Donald and a foot sauna for Judy. She took lots of pictures of the baby, whom they had decided to name Noel Caleb, every day. She went to the opera and theatre with her sister and visited a few galleries. Finally, she visited her mother's grave and laid some flowers. Sally was sad to see her go but kept a brave face.

***

While Mrs. Clarke was enjoying almost exclusive right to her daughter's son, Mr. Clarke had to share the birth of his son's son with the other half of the family. Donald witnessed the birth while the rest of the family waited in the waiting room. But Mr. Dembar couldn't sit still. He was now more concerned for his daughter than for the baby. He kept pacing up and down, hands in pocket.

"I hope she is alright."

"Please sit, John. You are making me nervous," complained is wife.

"Don't worry," put in Mr. Clarke. "She is in good hands."

After saying, "I hope she is alright," more times than anyone could count, Mr. Dembar's anxiety was finally alleviated when a midwife came out and said that Judy had delivered a healthy baby boy. Now Mr. Dembar changed his tone.

"I Knew it was a boy. I knew it, I knew it!" Any way they had to wait until after the cleaning to see both Judy and the child. There was no anxiety in this wait.

Donald and Judy had not changed their accommodation. This was Judy's idea and Donald had gone along with it. They would continue to visit each other whenever they felt like it and sleep at whichever home suited the occasion. Judy wasn't ready to feel like a married woman. She still wanted to feel eighteen years old. After all, she had gotten married to please her mother, encouraged by Donald, so he could not argue with the arrangements now. But he would have preferred otherwise. A married man still living home didn't sound right to him. The only comfort was that he was not doing it because of economic constraints.

***

With Sally in England, Judy married and Ruth teaching, Alma had to learn to walk lonely paths and occupy her time wisely. So she decided to start a hospital ministry, Monday through Thursday. During visiting hours 11 am to 12 noon, she visited the pediatric ward and read fairy tales for the children or told them the Bible stories. During afternoon visiting hours 3 pm to 5 pm, she roamed all of the adult wards, looking for those who had no visitors. She offered to run errands for them, such as buying little things at the shop opposite the hospital or she would read similarly from the Bible, a book of short stories or the newspaper.

She also decided to teach herself to sew and so bought several instructional texts on sewing. Soon, she was making herself simple tops, skirts and home dresses. She and her younger sister were now spending more time together, going shopping and to the beach and places, sometimes accompanied by Dinah and Chloe.

Chapter 27

Ruth was on the school's Easter vacation and was really enjoying the challenge of teaching. She had been given a mixed class of twenty-two seven year olds. She had discovered that their reading was extremely weak. She immediately launched a crash course in remedial reading, introducing the children to phonetics. She explained the importance of the vowels and taught them the long and short sound of each of them. Then she showed them how to put sounds together in that order would give the word 'at'. If they put certain letter sounds in front of 'at', they could make other words such as bat, cat, mat and so on. Then she introduced consonant blends such as SH, PH and BL, and digraphs such as ie, ea, and oe.

To motivate them to read, she bought each of them a book of poetry, and encouraged them to join the library. Each Friday afternoon, any child who recited from memory one of the poems from the book that she had bought them, would receive a small gift. Children love gifts and each Friday afternoon, she was privileged to hand out twenty-two gifts. Now children were attacking new words with fearlessness and Ruth was very proud of hers and the children's success.

But she was not in St. Vincent. She had used her vacation to travel to London to meet her sisters: Megan and Dawne, who were going to help her to shop for her wedding. She was going to be a June bride.

***

It was after five in the morning when Sheridan felt her first pang of pain. She woke her mother and they got ready to go to the hospital on foot since they lived near to the hospital. Her mother stayed there till 7 am, and then left promising to return in the evening, by which time she should have delivered.

"First babies always take long," her mother reminded her. "And don't tire yourself by crying and writhing," she warned. "Save your strength to push."

She patted Sheridan's head and was leaving when Sheridan reminded her to call Jamie and tell him around ten o'clock. Sheridan's mother, Amy, entrepreneur a small shop in her front yard where she sold a number of little things, that households usually ran out of, such as salt and sugar, matches, detergent, tinned beef and sardines. She made enough to pay her bills and maintain her home. She was hoping that Sheridan would have a son because her son had died at the age of five, run over by a minibus.

***

When Amy called Jamie, he told her to call back after the baby was born. He was busy and couldn't go to the hospital just to hang around. Jamie had stopped Sheridan from visiting his home since he did not wish her to encounter any of the number of ladies who now frequented his apartment. They might think that because of Sheridan's pregnancy, she had a monopoly on him.

With Jamie's height and good looks, he was on the list of most eligible bachelors around town. But since he had become an entrepreneur, sitting behind the wheels of a Hyundai, his status had trebled. Women were literally throwing themselves at him. His taxi service was right in the centre of town, adjacent to the vegetable market. When he was not on call, he would either be standing around the petite office or sitting in the car; either way he was visible to all.

Sometimes women would call and insist that they wanted to be driven by him. In a number of cases, they were prepared to wait if he was out. Then they would direct him to some long distant, made up destination to get more time to try to entice him or set up a date. If the woman met his approval, he would play along. Otherwise, he would claim that he was already committed.

Jamie loved his new life and Ruth was now a distant thought. Not that he was no longer interested in her but he just felt that Ruth needed time to grow up and become more aware of the real world.

He told his mother that Sheridan was at the hospital's maternity ward. Mrs. McKenzie hoped that it would be a girl since she did not have a daughter. She promised to accompany Jamie to the hospital after work. Just as Jamie and his mom were about to lock up for the night, Amy called to say that Sheridan had delivered a healthy baby girl. Mrs. McKenzie was delighted and wanted to go right away to see her granddaughter.

When they arrived at the hospital at 8:15 pm, the nurse had to seek Sheridan's permission to let them in so late, especially since she had had a late delivery and was very tired. The nurse told Sheridan that a Jamie McKenzie and his mother wished to know if they could visit her.

"Jamie can, but not his mother," said Sheridan vengefully, recalling how Mrs. McKenzie had insulted her when she had attempted to visit Jamie that last time. The nurse delivered the message just as she got it. Mrs. McKenzie's hand flew to her face as if she had been slapped.

"Oh!" she said stepping backwards. She caught herself. "Oh, OK, that's ….. that's alright." And she turned to leave feeling humiliated.

"I'm leaving, too, nurse," said Jamie. "But thanks for your time." And with his arm about his mother's shoulder, they left.

Sheridan was too tired to care. It was her mother who had paid for the private room for her. Why should the McKenzie's have their way after the way they had treated her, both mother and son? Exhausted, she fell asleep.

***

The next day Amy came to take her daughter home. She had hoped for a grandson, but God knew best. With a blonde mother and father, the child was also blonde with blue eyes and very pretty. Sheridan was grateful for her mother's help. What would she have done without her mother? Her manager had given her only six weeks' maternity leave and her mother encouraged her to resign and stay with the child for a year. She would maintain them until Sheridan found a job after the year's leave. Sheridan couldn't appreciate her mother more.

Amy was not rich, but she had saved well. She had never married. After her fiancé jilted her for her best friend, she had left England in shame, vowing not to marry or trust men again. She had done well enough in St. Vincent, working at several jobs until she had bought her own house and started her small shop.

Now she was wondering if her daughter was also unlucky with men. Or was it because she and her daughter had average looks? It couldn't be that. We are just unlucky, she thought again. Anyway, her granddaughter was pretty, even perhaps beautiful.

Having the child had changed Sheridan's perspective. With her mother to support her, and her child to give meaning to her life, she was no longer going to force herself on Jamie or any man, for that matter. She and her mother and her bay who she ad now decided to name Rose-Ann Amy, were going to do and enjoy, a lot of things together.

***

Mr. Dembar was just about to penetrate Jem, her legs spread wide, when she said, "I'm pregnant." His penis went limp, his face drained of colour and he fell over as if in shock. She waited a while for him to say something but after no response, she said:

"Come on, you must have notice something."

Seething with rage, he said, "I notice that your cat was getting fatter, but I thought that you were just putting on weight. How can a big woman with two children make a third mistake? Haven't you learned how to protect yourself by now?"

She sat up, enraged by his attempt to belittle her. "I am on the pill, mister! I am on the pill. Why didn't you protect your fucking self if you didn't want to breed a black woman? You fire me and see if I don't sue you for rape," she finished replacing her clothes hurriedly. "And no more sex for you, yo bald head cunt." And she was out of the room before the stunned Mr. Dembar could compose himself.

He didn't make attempt to put on his clothes. He just lay there. It was his wife's fault. If she hadn't starved him for sex, he could have willingly turned down this woman's offer. Now what was he going to do? He had indeed wished for a son, but not like this. And perhaps God might punish him and give him another daughter. He sucked his teeth and got up and began to put on his clothes. He just would not tell his wife anything. He would work something out with Jem. That was that.

Mrs. Dembar had not put up much resistance when she returned to meet two helpers in her home. God know she could do with some help. Why had she been so stubborn? Now with her daughter's wedding and child on the way, she'd let her husband have his way. He was right this time.

Anna and Jem got along well with Mrs. Dembar because they did things the way she wanted and so there was hardly any conflict. Mrs. Dembar even told Jem that she would miss her when she went on maternity leave. She gave Jem some money when she was leaving at the end of March for maternity leave. She promised to hold the job for Jem although she was quite busy with her grandson who was now only four days old.

On the 20th April, the Dembar received a call from the hospital. The message said that one Jem Molac wished the Dembars to know that she had delivered a baby boy and would be leaving hospital the next day. Mrs. Dembar reasoned that it would be easier for them to visit Jem in the hospital instead of going all the way to Prospect, so they decided to pay her a visit during afternoon visiting hours.

Mrs. Dembar reminded her husband to take a gift for the baby. When they arrived, Jem was feeding him. Mrs. Dembar was surprised to find the baby so white from a mother so dark. So she commented, "Jem, your baby has a white father, I see." Jem smiled and looked at the baby. Then she withdrew the breast to give the baby a breather and he opened his eyes.

"Ooh, what beautiful grey eyes!" complimented Mrs. Dembar. Jem Smiled again.

"That straight nose, those serious eyes, business-like lips; he looks like someone I know," said Mrs. Dembar smiling. She turned to her husband, "John…"

She was about to ask him if the baby did not remind him of someone in their sphere of acquaintances, but she stopped short. She looked back at the child again. Now back at her husband. Now at Jem who was looking at the wall.

"Jem, your baby's father is not only white; he is here in the room, isn't he?"

"Yes," replied Jem, still looking at the wall and Mr. Dembar shifting his weight from leg to leg.

"So all the time that I befriended you and treated you better than most, you were playing me for a fool?"

Now Jem looked at Mrs. Dembar.

"Mrs. Dembar, what you don't know don't hurt you. So I thought it best to keep it a secret. I didn't expect the child to come so white, seeing that I am black. And I really didn't expect him to take off his father's face. So I called you because it can't be a secret when the child looks so much like his father. I'm really sorry, Mrs. Dembar.

"I am sorry to Jem. You can't imagine how much." And she turned and left the room, widening her eyes to prevent tears from falling. So a black woman had given her husband the son that he wanted.

Mr. Dembar hastily gave Jem the letter containing the gift, and without a word, followed his wife. He caught up with her and tired to put his arm about her shoulders, but she shook him off like a snake and he did not persist. She got to the public telephone in the corridor; she stopped and called for a taxi.

"You are not going home in a taxi, Judith. You are going home with me," stormed her husband.

"Try and make me if you want to make a scene."

Mr. Dembar did not wish to make a scene and walked to where his car was parked and drove home without his wife, angry with everyone but himself. If he had known that the child resembled him so closely, he would not have gone to the hospital and would have done everything in his power to keep his wife from seeing the child. Jem was wrong and foolish to do what she had done.

Mrs. Dembar got home fifteen minutes after her husband and went straight to the nursery and informed Judy that she had some issues to deal with and wouldn't

276

be able to help with li'l Alan for the rest of the day. Then she proceeded to the bedroom that she shared with her husband, gathered a few essentials, and took them to a spare bedroom, locking the door behind her.

After putting the things away, she threw herself on the bed, but found that her feet felt funny, only to discover that she had not taken her shoe off. She kicked them to the floor and relaxed visibly. Then the tears flowed. She did not have a sob. The tears just flowed with the thoughts. Her self-esteem was severely damaged. She had not given her husband a son, but he had helped himself to a helper, right under her nose. It was a real secret, because even now looking back; she could not detect any treacherous conspiracy. What a wicked betrayal.

Mrs. Dembar was certain that Jem had something up her sleeve. If she wanted to maintain the secret, she could have. It was not imperative for Mrs. Dembar to see the child. What did Jem want?

One of the first concessions that Jem wanted was for her son to carry his father's surname. Now that he was obviously his father's child, surely they could not object to his name? So she had called them to subtly verify her claim. So when she was leaving in the morning and the staff nurse asked, name of father, she could boldly say, John Dembar. What's his occupation? Plantation owner. And her son would be proudly Johnny Jemaut Dembar.

Although Jem had stopped offering sex to Mr. Dembar, he had continued to give her the money so that she could eat well for the child's welfare. Now he would have to treble that amount. But money was not the problem for Mr. Dembar right now. His wife and their relationship were. She had just passed by the lounge, her expression as hard as a mask, pretending that she had not seen him or blatantly ignoring him.

He knew her well enough to give her some space until she was ready to talk.

Chapter 28

Being on TV, young, good-looking, Tony was not only among the most sought after bachelors in SVG, but among the happiest. On Christmas Eve night at a dinner, Ruth had agreed to marry him. He had gotten out of his seat, pulled back her seat and lifted her up in his arms. He had whirled around the tables with her until he found himself on the dance floor still cradling her. He began to waltz, although no music was playing, planting kisses all over her face intermittently.

Needless to say, he was the centre of stunned attention. Everyone knew him, the presenter at GrenTV. Was he extremely happy, or was he going bonkers? As he finally put Ruth down and they walked back to their table, hand in hand, nervous and suspicious glances followed them and stayed with them for the rest of the evening.

Fortunately or unfortunately, the act was caught on camera by the production team that had been hired to video tape the evening's proceedings. It made the front page of the first issue of all the papers after Christmas. When Jamie saw it, he just laughed, dismissing it as a publicity stunt by Ruth to obtain his attention, stir his jealous and probably force his hand in marriage. That lap dog of hers would do anything to get her attention. They don't expect me to fall for this, do they? thought Jamie. He was not won over by the fact that Tony had stated in the interview that he was overjoyed because Ruth had agreed to marry him.

From that night Ruth and Tony became regulars, especially since Tony had bought himself a car, a white Rover. Ruth had never invited him back to her bedroom. They occupied Jamie's former place on the sofa, facing the clock, which now no longer bothered Ruth. She was not in love with Tony the way she was with Jamie. He did not stimulate her desires and set her heart racing the way Jamie did but his coming pleased and excited her in a comforting way that Jamie did not. She had peace and assurance with Tony and she knew that she could live with that and honestly say, until death do us part.

***

Mrs. Sandison sent out the wedding invitations just before school went on Easter vacation. Mrs. Clarke was still in England, so when Mr. Clarke received it, he read it and put it in a drawer in the pharmacy and promptly forget about it. The whole family was invited but he was not interested and therefore told no one, not his wife, not Sally.

It was when Alma asked Sally if she was planning to come home for Ruth's wedding that Sally found out about it. She astounded and in shocked disbelief. But she called her parents for verification. Mrs. Clarke knew nothing but asked her husband if he did. Mr. Clarke confirmed that the family was invited. Sally confided in her mother that she had distantly hoped that she would get Tony in the end but now all hope was gone. It was not going to be easy for her. She was glad that Aunt Enid was such a great help.

Her mother told her not to bottle up her feeling and stress herself out. Cry if she like it for it was an effective way of flushing out pain. When the tears dried, she would feel refreshed and could look to the future with hope. She was now nineteen. Her whole life was still in front of her and there was someone out there for her. It was not the end of the world.

Sally thanked her mother and hung up. Then she went to her aunt and explained her situation, trying not to cry. Her aunt assured her that baby Noel would be cared for, so she could go and have a long cry. Sally did just that. She cried until she fell asleep again. When she had the strength, she cried. She did not leave her bed to eat or to shower for three days and her aunt threatened to call her parents so she got up and ate some fish and chips and took a quick shower. Then she went back to bed. Poor baby, thought her aunt.

***

Jem was happy. She had landed a big catch. She had a child for a rich man. She was now a baby mama. What better job could there be for a woman of her status? Being paid by a rich man to maintain and look after his child, her own child. Mr Dembar was now giving her $300 per week. That is what she used to work for, for a whole month. She knew that Mrs. Dembar would not now want her back, but she had no intention of working for anyone now. She was moving up in the world. As soon as she had saved enough money, she was going to stop her mother from doing road jobs and open a grocery shop in their front yard and let her mother manage it.

For herself, she could now learn sewing, and floral decoration and icing of cakes and those things. She could even go evening classes and study for some subjects. Who knows, the sky was the limit. She was going tell Mr. Dembar that her mother's house was now not convenient for her son, because it had only two bedrooms and Johnny needed his own room. Of course he should realize that I want him to buy a house for John sooner than later. Her mother was only forty-four. If Jem and her children moved out, somebody might be likely to propose. Marriages worked better when both parties were looking for old age security and companionship, their wandering days now over.

It was almost a week before Mrs. Dembar spoke to her husband. She had to admit to herself that she had unwittingly pushed him into the young woman's arms, but that did not stop her from feeling inadequate and a little jealous of Jem. She was really overjoyed at the birth of his son. So one night, she had gone back to their shared bed and lain next to him and asked him how he felt about the birth of his son.

He put his arm about her and reminded her that he was never dissatisfied with the one child that she had given him. All that he had wanted was a grandson, and Judy had given it to him. Johnny was a bonus that he had accepted.

"You know that I love you, Judith. Perhaps that's why you took me for granted to some extent and did not pay enough attention to some of my needs. But nothing or no one can undermine our relationship or my love for you. I have never loved anyone else, and I never will."

He went on to explain that during those years that her willingness for sex had diminished, it had never crossed his mind to look for sex elsewhere. It was Jem who had handed him sex on a plate, and he had not refused. Then she had turned around and asked for money. He believed now that he was set up. He thought that she was a gold digger and if his wife didn't mind, he would seek full custody when the child was weaned. In the meantime, when the baby was three months, he would ask her to send him for weekends so that he could begin to become acquainted with them.

Mrs. Dembar didn't think that he should go to court for custody. Gold diggers could be bribed. Mrs. Dembar's plan was to tell Jem that if she handed over the child when he was weaned, then Mr. Dembar would buy a house for the child and Jem could live in it until the child was grown and had need for it.

In the meantime, she could rent out the downstairs to enhance her earnings. Warn her that if she does not agree, then you will stop supporting the child and if she dares to carry you to the court, you will truthfully tell the court that you used to pay for sex and therefore it was up to her to protect herself from pregnancy.

Mr. Dembar agreed that his wife's idea was brilliant but told her that they should now stop talking about Jem. They began to kiss and caress, fondle and pet and before long, they were transported back to their early years of marriage and were making love with the passion of two twenty-plus-year-olds. Mrs. Dembar did not have Jem's antics but this was the woman he loved. At least she was not hastening him and making feel as if he was a bother. Her attitude had changed and he was overjoyed. He had almost forgotten what a great vagina she had in those years of scarcity when he had to hurriedly make a few quick thrusts and then roll off. Perhaps, who knows, Jem's intervention was a blessing in disguise.

***

When Ruth joined the staff of the Lowmans Leeward Anglican School in September 1985, she brought the number of white member of staff to four, and she was the youngest. There was one Indian and all of the others were black, including the head-teacher. The school was one-story as most primary schools were then, and consisted of open classrooms. In fact, there were only three walled partitions, one at the north end, enclosing a very small utility room, used mainly for storage. Another was in the middle of the school separating the infants from the juniors and seniors and the third at the south end, enclosing the head-teacher's office. But they were so cramped for space that the head-teacher kindly shared her space with the common entrance class. Thus everyone in each section could see each other.

Things went well at first. Everyone got along with each other. But then a problem developed. Mr. Barker, the only white male on staff, attached himself to Ruth as a self-appointed guardian, as if she needed one. If Ruth was speaking to a female member of staff or an all female group or even a mixed group, it was alright. But if it was a male or all male group, Mr. Barker would join them in a flash, even if he had to interrupt his lesion to do so. This act or behavior on his part was not missed by the staff and gradually the male members began to give Ruth distance in order to avoid a clash with the obnoxious Mr. Barker.

He tried to force his attention upon Ruth but she told him that she was at a crossroad in her love life at that time, and needed to sort things out before deciding which road to follow. When he discovered that one of those roads could lead to a black man, he scorned her choice, flabbergasted as to why a beautiful young woman like herself would waste any form of energy on a black man when there were willing and eligible bachelors like him around.

Ruth smiled at his consternation and simple solution, selfish as it was. Ruth knew that she would rather have a black man any day, especially a handsome one like Tony, than a short, ugly, stocky, overbearing white man like Mr. Barker. She had never told him that she was desperate, so she did not know where he got the notion, but she preferred to smile than to hurt his feelings.

Thus it was, during the Christmas vacation when the male members of staff saw Ruth in the arms of a black man on front pages of all the papers, they could hardly wait for school to re-open to gloat. And gloat they did, throwing Mr. Barker knowing loaded glances. He must have seen the papers too because he was now giving Ruth the cold shoulder and the male staff happily resumed their camaraderie with Ruth.

**

Ruth had visited London before, but she still wanted to pack as many sights as possible into her two weeks as well as go for a ride on the Thames. But first she had to visit all the of wedding shops in town and visit and revisit them until she could make up her mind. So her sisters took her to all the wedding shops on Oxford,

Regent and Bond Street. She finally settled on a mid calf length dress in Debenhams. It was mainly lace with a large V-shaped insert of chiffon at her upper chest, bordered with diamond-studded appliqués. There was also a chiffon turtleneck collar embroidered with diamonds. The rest of the close fitting bodice and full gathered skirt was liberally dotted with pearls. The lace sleeves reached her elbows and down the back of the dress was closed with tens of pearl buttons. She also chose lace shoes and a lace hat with simple ribbon and one rose. Everything was white. She and Tony had agreed that he would buy the rings. Megan advised her to buy a pair of gloves, but she wasn't interested.

Her sisters did not like her contemporary choice. They preferred the traditional gown, with headpiece and veil and train and the lot. Ruth confessed that she had always dreamed of the traditional way, but since Judy had married before her, she wanted to look different. Dawne begged to disagree, telling her, her reasoning was infantile and irrational. Most people, especially the young, chose the traditional, her sisters pointed out. More-so, Ruth's choice suited someone who was marrying for the second time. Why didn't she take the stuff back and go for the whole traditional works? But Ruth stuck to her guns. She would keep what she had bought. The bridesmaids and ushers were having their clothes tailor made in SVG but she had to buy the girls' shoes since it was difficult to find that colour of pink shoes back home. Megan was going to be chief bridesmaid but she had time to shop and certainly didn't want any help from Ruth, being not satisfied with her choice for the bride.

With her shopping done, Ruth was eager to get home so that she could spend a few days with Tony before school reopened and so her sisters accompany her to Heathrow and saw her off, promising to see her soon.

Tony was glad to have her back and went to the airport to await her arrival at 11:00 am the Friday before school was due to reopen after Easter. When she came through customs, they hugged and kissed briefly, leaving their rejoicing for private to avoid making the papers again.

Chapter 29

Ruth was getting married on the 28th June. On the 12^{th,} a call came to McKenzie's taxi service. The Manager of Floral Designs would like to be picked up in front of the Anglican Church and taken to Prospect. She would like the driver to be Jamie.

Jamie obliged her and soon they were on their way. Unsolicited, she began telling Jamie that she had secured the contract to decorate both church and reception venue for Tony and Ruth's wedding.

"Ruth Sandison?" asked Jamie, taking his eye off the road. It couldn't be.

"Keep your eyes on the road," warned Mrs. Jones. She was a young divorcee and had a thing for Jamie. "Yes, Ruth Sandison. Do you know her?" she asked, watching Jamie closely.

"She's from my village," confided Jamie, trying to sound casual. "I've always admired her but she would have none of it."

"Really, she refused you and is marrying a black man, albeit a very good-looking one?" replied Mrs. Jones incredulously.

"It's really her parents' influence. You see, my parents are Christians and the Sandison don't like Christians."

"Oh," replied Mrs. Jones, relieved. "But you don't follow your parents' way, do you?" she persisted.

Jamie winced a little. Then he shrugged his shoulders. "I try my best, but I have a weakness for good-looking women," throwing her a sideways glance. She giggled and asked him about his plans for later. He told her that he was already engaged. Ruth was actually getting married. The last time he had spoken to her was to tell her that Sheridan was pregnant, almost a year ago.

Tony had women crawling all over him, young women as well as middle-aged and even a handful of older ones. Who did Ruth think she was? He couldn't believe that she was really leaving him. He had decided to give her distance so that she could come to her senses, not to leave him; and for a black man at that. What was wrong with that girl? She had not visited or even called when her mother had broken his ribs and so he had decided to punish her even more. He had ignored her. But he certainly did not expect her to leave him. He pressed the accelerator. As soon as he dropped off this pest, Mrs. Jones, he was going to call Ruth.

Jamie dropped off Mrs. Jones, collected his payment and sped off. He took only twenty minutes to get back into town and hurriedly parked at his business premises. He told his mother that he wouldn't be available for about twenty minutes and headed for the

Cable and Wireless private telephone booth. He called Ruth's number but it just rang and rang. Impatiently, he called the house number and Martha answered. He asked for Ruth.

"Oh, Miss Ruth is at work, sir," replied Martha. He did not know that Ruth was working.

"Where is that, may I ask?" he asked.

"Who is this?" responded Martha in surprise. 'What friend could this be? Miss Ruth's been working since September, thought Martha.

"I'll tell you if you promise not to tell Ruth's parents," answered Jamie.

"OK," conceded Martha with curiosity.

"This is Jamie, Ruth and I have not spoken for some time," he confessed. "Now, where is she working?" Martha hesitated.

"Please, Martha," begged Jamie. Martha liked the way he said her name, stretching the 'r' and the last 'a'. She smiled. What harm could be done?

"She's at the school up the road."

Jamie thanked her with lots of love and she blushed. Old bother, thought Jamie as he hung up and took up the directory to find the school's number. He found it and dialed. When the head-teacher identified herself, he asked if he could speak to Miss Ruth Sandison as a matter of urgency. He was asked to hold.

In about two minutes Ruth answered, "Hello?" When Jamie identified himself Ruth was angry.

"You are not allowed to call teachers during instruction time unless for an emergency," she hissed in a low voice.

"*This is an emergency*," Jamie responded emphatically. "Is it true that you are marrying Tony?" he asked, almost angrily.

"Why do you want to know? The last time you called me was to tell me that Sheridan was pregnant. Why have you suddenly remembered me?"

"Ruth you haven't answered me," responded Jamie trying to be patient. Ruth hung up the phone and thanked the head-teacher for calling her.

Jamie felt slapped. He couldn't believe that Ruth had hung up on him. He replaced the receiver and sat there boiling with rage. He was as angry as a bullfrog. He was sure that if someone even touched him he would explode. He was sure that he couldn't work for the rest of the day. He just couldn't pretend to be pleasant. He didn't want to go home and sulk because he might smash everything in his anger. He needed tempering. He would go to see his child. She was nearly two months and he had not seen her as yet. It was Sheridan's fault. Anyway, she shouldn't have insulted his mother.

He walked blindly back to his taxi stand and told his mother that he had something to attend to and would not be available for the rest of the day. Then he got into his car and pulled away, tyres screeching. Jamie had never visited Sheridan's place but he knew the direction; a shop in the front yard, a yellow cottage with a blue porch – first street below the hospital. He would find it.

Just as he suspected, the premises were not hard to find, but a place to park was. He had to drive around the block twice before he found a cosy spot on the reclaimed bay front. So he had to walk back about a block and half but he did not mind. As he turned in at the gateway, he was certain that the lady behind the counter in the shop was Sheridan's mother although they had never met in person. She and her daughter resembled each other.

"Good afternoon, Sir. Jamie?" she asked.

"Yes, that's me," he replied with a wry smile.

"After all of this time, I wasn't expecting you. What brings you?" asked Amy cynically.

Jamie winced.

"I'm sorry," he apologized. "But may I visit with the baby please?" begged Jamie, looking straight at Amy who looked straight back at him. She put her hands on her hips.

"For my part," she said coolly, "no. But for the baby's sake, I suppose you may." Then she looked past him as if he wasn't there.

"Thank you," said Jamie as he turned on his heels, knowing that he was dismissed without blessing.

He walked the few paces from the ship to the house, then into the porch and knocked on the door. Momentarily, Sheridan opened the door and couldn't hide her surprise. She just stood there as if she had seen a ghost. So Jamie helped her.

"May I come in?" he asked, smiling in spite of himself.

"Oh, sure, sure," said Sheridan drawing herself up and stepping out of his way. He came in and she closed the door. She looked at him.

"May I see the baby, please? He asked. Sheridan was offended. He had no manners. He had not even asked how she was doing, even for protocol.

"Does my mother know that you are here? She asked coldly. He looked at her. Why this coldness? He asked himself. Anyway, he had to admit that he had sidelined her after he opened his business. Sidelined? No, dropped her like something hot. Why expect open arms from her and her mother? They were right to treat him this way.

"Yes, I have her permission," answered Jamie hesitantly, wanting to add, 'but not her blessings'. Sheridan pointed out the way to the nursery and took her seat again on the sofa. She was revising high school biology, planning as it were, to apply for a teaching position at the end of her maternity leave.

The nursery was airy and pleasant, with white frilly curtains with cherubs and soft classical music coming from a stereo set in one corner. But the room was definitely crowded, filled with stuff that the baby was not yet ready for, such as a walker, stroller, playpen and toys. But they made Jamie feel guilty because he had not contributed to the purchase of any of these things. He stood over the crib and looked down at the sleeping child. She was blonde and beautiful. He was sure that she looked just like him and wondered if her eyes were blue too, but did not intend to ask Sheridan. He would come back again, hoping to meet her awake. He put his index finger between her tiny fingers and smiled. Why hadn't he come before? He longed to hold her, but instead just looked and looked.

Finally, he withdrew his finger and pulled out his wallet. He took out ten twenty dollar notes and put them at the baby's feet. Ten twenties, the last time that he gave that amount of money to anyone was to that call girl who went home with him from the bar. No, he must give his daughter more. He pulled out five more and added them to the pile. Then he bent over and kissed the baby's cheek and left, feeling like a new man.

When he re-entered the drawing room, Sheridan continued with her reading. He stopped in front of the door and said, "I'm sorry that I have not come before. I'll come again when she is awake." Sheridan ignored him. He continued. "What's her name?"

"Rose-Ann Amy," replied Sheridan without looking up. But he still continued.

"I didn't like the way that you treated my mother," he said remonstratingly. Sheridan looked up. Calmly, she said to him:

"It was the same way that she treated me. Remember, in the hospital?"

"But that is my mother!" he retorted. Sheridan saw red.

"And I, who am I, nobody, nothing, shit? I'm sorry, what's good for the goose is good for the gander. I take shit from nobody," slapping the book in her lap. Defenseless, Jamie turned, opened the door and left.

Jamie passed by the shop and bade Amy goodbye, but she merely nodded her acknowledgement as she minded her customers. Hands deep in his pockets, he trudged back to his car. Perhaps he shouldn't have come. But he was glad that he had. He was a dad. How he wished the child was Ruth's; oh, Ruth. He quickened his steps. He must get to her before school dismissed.

But as his car came into view, he groaned. The car that had been parked a reasonable distance from his car was gone, and its place taken by a big truck that left no space for Jamie to maneuver his car out. Instead of crossing the road to his car, he decided to visit all the shops opposite the parked vehicles to ascertain whether the driver of the truck or that of the car behind his car, was around. The search was futile and frustrated, Jamie crossed the street to his car, determined to get out even if it took a miracle.

He was passing the truck, when from the corner of his eyes, he saw most likely the driver of the truck stretched out on the front seat with his back to the door; a box of Kentucky Fried Chicken in his lap, a litre of Pepsi in his hand, eating. Jamie was initially surprised and showed it, but then he couldn't help laughing. The driver continued to eat, giving Jamie a look that asked, are you nuts? Soon Jamie contained himself, but still chuckling, explained to the driver that he had been scanning the shops, looking for him to ask him kindly to move forward a little so that he could come out, and here he was having lunch in a most relaxed and unconventional way. The whole episode was humorous, Jamie told him, as if to justify why he had laughed.

The driver decided to humour Jamie, so he swung his legs around to his foot pedals, screwed his Pepsi shut and then drove forward a little then promptly went back to his lunch. Jamie laughed again and raised his fist in appreciation to him and thankfully went to his car. Checking that his way was clear, he pulled out and away up Queen Street and then onto the Leeward Highway. He was going to wait for Ruth right at the school gate. They had to talk.

Jamie could now see that he had been arrogant or even over confident, or perhaps, he had taken her for granted. How long had he not spoken to her in his efforts to break her? Anyway, old fire sticks are easy to rekindle. He and Ruth had a special love for each other that no one could take away. She would listen to him.

Although Carnival was in the air again, Jamie had not gone to any shows, not wanting to embarrass his father but more-so, concentrating on taking people to those shows thus enhancing the bank balance of his business account.

As Jamie drove along, his eyes were on the road, but his mind was on Ruth. He looked at his watch then stepped on the gas. It was 2:35. Some schools dismissed at 2:45. He wanted to be there before the bell went. She had hung up on him, but face to face, surely she would talk to him.

But he had not spoken to her for almost a year. Among other things, he was punishing her for what her mother had done to him. More-so, she had not visited him during the illness inflicted by her mother. He had not felt obligated to talk to her in a hurry. But he had not expected her to run off and get married to a man who also had put him in the hospital. Where was her loyalty? How much did she love him? Perhaps he should just forget about her. No way, she was his. He had thought that she understood that.

With relief, he turned off the highway and down the school's road. He parked where everyone who was leaving the school could not miss him. Then he got out of the car and stood, leaning on it. He looked fondly at the school. It was his alma mater. There was a huge flamboyant tree with its bright orange blossoms. It was a pleasant setting and it evoked many memorable days there. The ringing of the school bell dissipated his reminiscing and he looked eagerly at all the doors, not knowing which one Ruth would come through.

He heard the singing of the evening song, then the familiar prayer and then dismissal. He was getting excited. She would soon be out. But it was children who

298

came pouring out, followed by a few teachers. He was a little disappointed. It was the infant section that had been dismissed. So she was either in the junior or senior school. How long did he have to wait? He shifted his position and now rested an elbow on the top of the car for support, keeping his eyes firmly on the school doors.

The extra ten minutes seemed like eternity to Jamie and he kept shifting his weight from leg to leg, and sometimes changing position. But finally the school bell rang again and his heartbeat quickened. He was getting nervous and was surprised at his behavior. It was only Ruth. Why was he behaving like this? She had pulled the rug from under him and he had not even known it. Now he felt like a fish out of water. He wouldn't like all those other women to see him now, the most eligible man around town indeed.

Now the older children were leaving. Soon the teachers followed. There was Ruth. He was sure that he was blushing and was glad that she was too far way to see it. He collected himself. Ruth had seen him to, and had paused momentarily but kept walking, looking straight at him. It was difficult to look anywhere else since he was directly in front of everyone who was coming that way. She hadn't seen him for a long time and was shocked to find that he still made her weak with longing. But she would not forget that he had abandoned her. She would not forget.

So she kept right on walking and passed as if he wasn't there.

"Ruth," he called. She kept walking.

"Ruth," he said again, running after her. She kept on walking. Then he caught up with her and held her hand.

"Please, Ruth. Talk to me."

"Let go of my hand, Jamie. Do you want to go back to the hospital?" hissed Ruth, trying not to make a scene; which was inevitable since this tall handsome man had already attracted the attention of the senior girls and his car was being inspected by the senior boys. They were precocious enough to realize that this handsome man was interested in their beautiful teacher and she was giving him the chill. They watched, fascinated.

Jamie let go of her hand in a jiffy and instead, fell into step with her.

"Please, Ruth…" he began again, but Ruth stopped him short.

"Cut it out, Jamie. After a year, it's kind of arrogant to think that you can just walk back into my open arms, isn't it? Well, my arms are already full. Please leave me alone. I don't want mom or Tony to lose their cool. I don't want to see you or talk to you. I don't want you to walk next to me either. Goodbye."

Jamie knew that he was dismissed and for the second time during the day, he felt defenseless. So he just stood there, hands in pockets looking at her elegantly clad figure walking away and turning the corner to her home. The children were looking at him with knowing smirks and grins and, embarrassed, he turned and walked back up the road to his car.

What a difference a day made. He felt as if the world was on his shoulders and boulders were tied to his legs, for it took a ton of effort for him to put one foot in front of the other. But finally he got to and into his car. He slumped down into the driver's seat but his elbows felt so weak that he just rested his arms in his lap and sat there. Most of the children and teachers were now gone so he did not feel pressured to move on, but right then, he just didn't care about public opinion.

Chapter 30

Megan and Dawne had come home for Ruth's wedding and had brought a friend with them. So for the next two weeks, Ruth and Tony were more than busy. Although the major preparations for the wedding were contracted, there were still little things to do like choosing the baskets for the flower girls and furniture for their new apartment. Thankfully, Tony had the two weeks off plus two extra weeks for the honeymoon. During the day he and Ruth took Megan and Dawne's friends hiking, ferrying, boat riding, yachting and shopping and at nights they patronized the Carnival shows.

***

Jamie did not sleep well that night. He kept dozing on and off. Each time he took a little snooze, he dreamed about Ruth. Finally he woke suddenly, all hot and sweaty with his boxers full of sperm. In his dream he was making love to Ruth and it was heavenly. Why did he awake, why such a dream? It was just 5:30 in the morning. As soon as it was nine o'clock, he was going to the registry to see if there was any announcement of

Ruth's marriage there. He still couldn't believe that Ruth was getting married. Ruth was his, always would be. She couldn't leave him.

At eight o'clock, Jamie called his mother and told her that he had things to do and might not be in that day. At ten to nine, he parked his car in the yard of the court house and waited until the registry opened before leaving the car. He wasn't the first one to enter the registry, though. There were quite a few persons who were before him. But as soon as he stepped through the door, he felt a stab in his heart; Ruth Haden Sandison and Anthony Samuel Blake, teacher and TV presenter. Jamie turned away and went back outside, standing in the gallery, hands into pockets, looking stunned as if the truth had finally been absorbed.

He just stood there starting, seeing nothing. All of a sudden, his promiscuous lifestyle didn't seem so glamorous anymore. It had, when he had believed Ruth was his. But now, no one mattered but Ruth. He would get married if that was what she wanted. He would go back into the registry, take out a marriage licence and call Ruth later and propose to her. He went back into the registry and joined the queue.

It was the longest and most miserable day of his life. Time simply stood still. But finally, it was 3:30 and he dialed Ruth's number. In response, he heard, "The number you've called is no longer available." Jamie replaced the handset slowly. He couldn't call her, couldn't visit her, he couldn't wait for her after school;

what was he to do? He would write to her care of her school. He had never written a love letter before, but there was always a first. Sometimes on the sofa during those Sunday night visits, they used to write each other short love lines rather in play, but now this was serious. He decided to write to her right away.

But there was no paper. He therefore grabbed his car keys and ran out to his car to try to reach the stationery shop before it closed at 4:00 pm. Once again, he parked at the court house and walked the rest of the way to Reliance Variety shop. He was in time and bought a writing tablet and a pack of envelopes. He had a lot of pens at home. With his precious package, he hurried back to his car and home.

***

After eight days, Sally pulled herself out of bed. She needed to be a better mother and needed to get on with her life. She should do something instead of feeling sorry for herself. But what could she do? She couldn't force Tony to love her. But yes, that was what she would do. Write to him and let him know how much she loved him. After all, she was the one who had loved him from the first time that she had set her eyes on him. Ruth had had nothing but contempt for him. How was he sure that Ruth wouldn't leave him for a white man? Wasn't it better for him to be with someone whose love was sure, like hers?

Sally had written and posted the letter in May, but now, two weeks away from the wedding; she had had no reply. Not even a call. Now she felt snubbed and did not feel like going home for the wedding. But she knew that she couldn't stay away. She had to look Tony in his eyes. She would let her eyes love him if he wouldn't listen to her words. And so she went shopping for a wedding outfit and then began to pack.

Sally and Ruth had not spoken to each other since that verbal confrontation in Judy's car. How could they? It was as if Ruth had gone out of her way to prove a point to Sally. Why, Sally wondered, didn't Ruth make a bigger effort to secure Jamie instead of falling helplessly into Tony's arms? Or couldn't she just find another man? Didn't everyone rave about her beauty? How could she succumb to Tony as if she was desperate and couldn't find anyone else? Surely, she must indeed want to hurt me, concluded Sally.

Alright, so Ruth has won, continued Sally in her thought, I wonder how she feels. She can't call and tell me that she doesn't wish it was Jamie, laughed Sally in her thoughts. Anyway, when Ruth drops him, I'll be here for him. He's the father of my child, and more-so I love him, Sally finished as she zipped close her suitcase.

***

When Jamie got home, he went straight to his small dining table and sat down. He then took out the writing tablet and opened it at the first page. How did he start? What should he say? He twiddled with the pen, beginning to feel nervous. Suppose he failed? This was no exam he reminded himself. And this was not really a love letter either. That thought made him feel a little better. Of course it was not a love letter. He was just going to put on paper what he couldn't, or more, what he wasn't allowed to tell her by other means. Thus he began:

My dearest darling Ruth,

I am sorry that I have to resort to this method to reach you, but I am desperate. I am desperately sorry, confoundedly sorry, that I played with your feeling so foolishly; and you had every right to move on.

But my darling, on bended knees, I humbly ask you to forgive me and give me another chance. I made a grave mistake. I took your love for granted and thought that you would always be there no matter what I did. I was wrong. Please, take me back.

I have loved you all of my life although my actions showed otherwise. Yes, I was arrogant. I got carried away by the attention of so many women. But none of them mean anything to me now. Nothing is anything without you, Ruth I am literally sick, just wanting you and the thought of losing you is driving me mad.

Please, Ruth, please give me another chance. You do not have to change your plans, just change your man. Let me be your man, your husband. Please, Ruth, will you marry me? Please find enclosed a copy of the marriage licence that I have procured for both of us, same date as your wedding. You see, my dear, just change the man and let all of the other plans stand. I will refund Tony any contributions that he has already made. But even he should not mind giving way. You are mine, my darling. We belong together.

Please Ruth, think about my proposal carefully. I am now ready for marriage. I am ready to spend the rest of my life with you. Please, do not say no. Please do not turn me away. I love you.

Forever yours
Jamie.

Jamie read the letter again and again. It sounded alright to him, but he was still a little worried wondering if he had omitted any essential points. Finally he put it, along with a copy of the marriage licence, into the envelope and sealed it. Then he addressed it to Ruth care of the school. He had always given her stuff face to face, so he did not know her mailing address.

Now he was restless. He would have to wait until the next day, Saturday, to post it, which meant that she would not receive it until about Wednesday. If he sent it by courier, there was no guarantee that Ruth would be the person at the door to sign for it. For he would be utterly humiliated if her parents or even Martha were to find out he was forced to write to Ruth. It was a safer route to her school, but longer. He groaned. If only he could call. Did she change her number to avoid him? Of course, wasn't it yesterday that he had called her number and it had rung? He had better try again. Perhaps, he had made a mistake.

How could she acquire a new number so quickly? So he got up and went over to his sofa and took up the handset. This time he made sure that he dialed correctly. He listened. "The number you've called is no longer available." So he had not made a mistake. He felt sick. He stretched out on the sofa. He would just have to wait. How cruel time could be sometimes, always crawled when you wished for it to sprint.

***

The Sandisons and the Blakes were getting together for the first time, and they preferred and informal but impartial setting. So Alma suggested to Ruth that their kitchen/ restaurant would be the ideal place, and everyone agreed. It was to be the last Saturday before the wedding. They would do the cooking so that they could get to know each other better while they worked. But they decided to provide simple dishes in order to ensure that they wouldn't spend the whole evening in the kitchen while the others socialized. The menu was to be the local favourite of rice and green pigeon peas with stewed beef, cooked and fresh vegetables, and some baked chicken with homemade bread for takeaways. The Sangues had provided cake, ice cream, and fruit salad on the house.

The evening came and went well. While the women cooked, the men played dominoes and talked about everything except the wedding and the young women played scrabble and snakes and ladders and eavesdropped on the men's conversation.

Since Ruth and Tony did not have an engagement party, they decided against having separate hen and stag parties. Instead, they would stage a big moonlight beach party for all of their friends on the Wednesday before their wedding. There was going to be a lot of mutton, goat and fish prepared in a variety of ways and drinks galore. They also contracted two steel band to play for the party.

Tony felt blessed. He was marrying the woman of his dreams, who only a few months before had made him feel that it could only happen in his dreams. Sometimes he had to pinch himself to believe that it was really happening.

He regretted what had happened with Sally, although he was glad to have a son who resembled him. But he could have preferred that son to be with his wife. Sally had written him a letter that had made him feel a little guilty because he couldn't return her love. He had hoped that he had made it plain right from the start that he was in love with Ruth. So he did not take kindly to Sally now hinting to him that Ruth was using him and that she was the one who really loved him. Tony didn't care whether Ruth loved him or not. As long as she was content to spend the rest of her life with him, he had enough love for both of them. He was happy knowing that he would be having a woman like Ruth to come home to.

He had not bothered to respond to Sally's letter. What could he tell her? 'You asked for it.' Or, 'forget about me, I can take care of myself.' 'You should find yourself a man.' No, she was a nice girl and he had enjoyed her sex, so he couldn't hurt her feelings. He had thrown the letter in the waste. But still he wondered if she was coming for the wedding. He would really like to see his son.

***

It was just after the morning break when the head-teacher brought a letter to Ruth. She was a little surprised and showed it. The head-teacher smiled.

"A secret admirer does not know your mailing address," she suggested to Ruth by way of explanation.

Ruth returned the smile and thanked her. But her smile was quickly wiped away when she recognized the unmistakable handwriting of Jamie. Sitting at her desk to avoid attention, she put her hands under the table and tore the letter to bits angrily. This is harassment, she fumed to herself. I told him to leave me alone. I changed my number and now this. I don't want to get Tony or Mom involved in this, so the next time that he bothers

310

me, I'll report it to the police and ask them to warm him. She put the shredded letter into her bag to be disposed of when she got home. She wondered if she should call him and warn him herself but decided against it. Jamie had put her on a shelf, made her feel useless because she wouldn't have sex with him. She would not forget that either. He had hurt her more than he ever could imagine.

Now as far as she was concerned, it seemed better to have someone who loved you than someone who you loved. Those who loved you appreciate that love and didn't seek to exploit it and take you for granted. If Jamie hadn't been aware of her how much she loved him, would he have treated her the way he did? No way. But he thought that he had her all sewn up and that gave him the prerogative to do anything, thinking that she would either wait on him or bend to his wishes. Yes, she did love him, but not more than she loved herself. He probably did not think that she had any self-respect. He was wrong.

Jamie did not work all week. He had neither the desire nor the will to do anything but sleep and drink his malts. At half past two on that Wednesday afternoon, he could no longer resist the temptation to call Ruth's school and ask to speak to the head-teacher. He identified himself as a secret admirer of Ruth Sandison, and ask if the head-teacher had seen a letter addressed to Ruth come to the school recently. The head-teacher smiled. It was just as she thought.

"I delivered it to her myself this morning," she replied, glad to help this poor soul out. Jamie thanked her profusely and hung up, relieved. Now, he had to wait for Ruth's response. What would she say?

Chapter 31

Ruth awoke startled. What was that? Had someone woken her? Had the phone rang? She listened, but nothing. Then she remembered, today was Saturday 28th June, 1986. She was getting married today. It was eight o'clock. She wasn't due in church till two o'clock. Had her subconscious woken her? Anyway, it was better to be fresh and early instead of hot and in a hurry.

Ruth smiled, evaporating the sleepiness. Her plans had now fitted like a glove. She was already teaching. She was getting married today. She would have children. Then she would get a degree and move up to secondary teaching. She rolled from side to side on the queen sized bed. Wow! She didn't have to get out of bed if she didn't want to, either. Everything was being taken care of.

But she would miss her room. She looked around it lovingly as if trying to personify it. She listened, there were birds. She would miss them too. And that view of Mount St. Andrew from the front porch. And Martha's cooking. Oh, perhaps she should have followed her parents' advice and lived at home. Sure there was room for everyone. But she wanted to feel like she was married and that involved moving out of your parents' home.

Anyway, what was she grieving about? Their apartment in Villa had a glorious view of the sea and of Young Island. She would still be teaching at the same school with its wonderful surrounding and Mount St. Andrew viewed from the yard. Plus, she would be eating lunch at her parents', thus Martha's food. She really was having the best of both worlds. Today was to think about today.

She was dressing at home. She had asked the florist to deliver her bouquet by 12:30. Her father was taking her and her mother to the church. Two minibuses were taking her wedding party: cushion and flower girls, bridesmaids and ushers. They were to be there for 1:30. She touched her hair. It had been done the day before. All that she had to do was to flip out the curlers and brush the curls. She rolled off her bed and went into the spare room next to her and peeped into the wardrobe. Yes, everything was where she had left it. She was just making sure. She didn't regret not buying a traditional gown.

"Aren't you tired of looking at your outfit?" asked Megan groggily. Ruth was startled a little.

"I thought you were still sleeping, Meg," laughed Ruth.

"I am," answered Megan. Ruth laughed again.

"So you are talking in our sleep then?" she asked. This time Megan ignored her and turned on her side with her back to Ruth.

"Now, don't be rude," said Ruth. "It was you who started this." Then she checked her shoes and stockings and left.

After the wedding, she was off on her honeymoon, to Australia and New Zealand. She smiled remembering the fight that she and her mother had had when she announced her choice of countries.

"You're not serious," her mother had responded.

"Why not?" Ruth had asked, surprised.

"St. Vincent is too far away from those countries for you to go for a honeymoon."

"Mom, we aren't walking or even going by ship. We are jetting, for God's sake."

"Watch your language, Ruth," reproved Mrs. Sandison.

"Sorry, mom. But I can't see the fuss. That's my choice and Tony agreed."

"Well, Tony should have disagreed with you. It's eight hours and forty-five minutes from SVG to England where you have to change planes. Then it's twenty-six hours to Australia. By the time you get there, you'll be so jet-lagged and tired that there'll be little time or energy left for honeymooning. Why don't you stay within the Caribbean basin like most people? Go to Florida, or Cayman Islands or even Curacao. Somewhere near, not to the other end of the world."

Ruth became angry. "Do I have to do what you think is best, or what everyone else is doing? Can't I be different for once?"

"Look, sweetheart, I am only doing what mothers do best. Make suggestions, give advice and speak wisdom. You want to leave the Caribbean? Then go to the Mediterranean to Malta, Cyprus or even the south of France. But Australia and New Zealand means that you'll be spending more time in the air than in your husband's arms."

"Thanks for the advice, Mom. But I'm not changing my plans."

"You do know that it's winter in July in the southern hemisphere?"

"I did geography, mom!" snapped Ruth annoyed to breaking point. "I wouldn't go there in summer anyway; it's hotter than in the Caribbean. You do know that?" finished Ruth sarcastically. Now her mother was annoyed.

"I did geography too, Ruth. And I don't understand why you are trying so hard to be different. Sameness has its place, you know. We belong to the same human race. We have the same colour blood in our veins, and we have the same mortality. It's only our colour and beliefs that are so different. Who are you competing with? You did the same thing when you were choosing your outfit, now this. Be careful, sweetheart, be careful. Do what is best for you. What you enjoy as long as it is within the ambits of the law and a good conscience. But I rest my case. Enjoy Australia and New Zealand."

Ruth had apologized for snapping at her mother and they had made up.

***

Tony's father was driving him and his best man to church. His younger brother was taking over the apartment, so he had left everything intact as a gift for his brother. His brother was his best man.

***

The evening the Sandisons and Blakes were having their get together, Alma had decided to make herself scarce. She was just leaving the house when the Blakes had come in. Kenaz had seen and fallen in love with her immediately. On inquiry, Ruth had told him that Alma was not yet interested in dating. He was sure that he could convince her to change her mind, since like Jacob in the Bible, he was already sure that he was prepared to wait seven years for her if he had to. She was so beautiful, he was blown away. He himself was not as gorgeous as his brother but bore a resemblance and was quite handsome.

That very night he had asked his brother for the apartment. Now all that was left to do was for him to ask the Ministry of Education for a transfer. He was teaching for a while before going off to university in order to ease his parents' financial obligations towards him while studying.

**

St. George's Cathedral has a long walkway from the sidewalk to the main road up to the main entrance. Ruth had therefore commissioned four video crews, two outside the church and two inside. She did not want anyone to be missed. The church was spectacularly decorated, every column and every pew with ferns, buttercups and yellow roses.

The wedding party arrived on time but waited outside for Ruth. All the girls were in yellow nylon dresses reaching mid-calf as Ruth specified, with lace sleeves to elbows and V-shaped lace inserts at the chest bordered with a lace edge. There was a lace edge at the hems also, and the dresses were all gathered at the waist with a stain bow at the back. They all had a yellow rose with a baby satin bow in their hair. The bridesmaids had a white long stemmed rose in their hands. The flower girls had baskets of flowers. The two cushion girls had two heart-shaped cushions in their hands. All had white shoes and white lace stockings for the younger girls and white fishnet stockings for the older girls. The ushers were in black suits, white shirts and black bow ties.

Tony arrived about five minutes after the wedding party. He was dressed like the ushers, but with a yellow rose at his breast. He was accompanied by his best man, who was dressed in dark grey but had the same style as the ushers. Tony took his place at the altar and waited. Then, as if by a signal, the guests began to stream in. There were three hundred invited guests. But usually weddings cater for a least fifty extras that include persons who come with friends and relatives.

Exactly at 1:55, the bridal party arrived and so the wedding party took their rehearsed position in front of Ruth and her father, who was escorting her to the altar. Alma, who was chief bridesmaid, came last and Kenaz was waiting to escort her. She was styled like the bridesmaids but in blue and carrying a yellow rose. Kenaz was absolutely delighted with this task of escorting Alma. She had agreed to date him but with a hands-off policy until she had returned from university.

All of the guests turned towards the entrance to witness Ruth and her party walk down the aisle accompanied by the wedding march played by the cadets' band. Ruth was radiantly beautiful, wearing very light make-up and her curls bouncing and glowing below her hat. Her sisters had eventually persuaded her to wear gloves because it was a gloved hand that was clutching her bouquet of yellow roses and another gloved hand lined in her father's arm. As the wedding party took their places, her father guided her to Tony's side, then Alma and Kenaz took their positions.

At this juncture, Mrs. Sandison decided that it was time to take her place in the church. As soon as she stepped in the minister asked:

"Who givest this woman to be married?"

"I do," replied Mr. Sandison.

The Minister then asked the guest to stand to sing the hymn, 'O Perfect Love' no. 1 on the hymn sheet. Mrs. Sandison was proceeding down the aisle to take her place in the front pew next to her husband, when from the corner of her eyes, she was sure that she had seen someone who was certainly not welcome at her daughter's wedding. She stopped to make sure and turned to face the person. Sure enough, it was Ethel McKenzie and her son Jamie, and Ethel had a baby girl on her shoulder. Mrs. Sandison glared at them, her eyes blazing, but keeping her mouth shut.

True, she had invited Mr. and Mrs. McKenzie, but it was just to taunt them. She hadn't expected them to be so dumb as to turn up and with Jamie. But of course, nosy Ethel would come. And since her husband, who had some sense, probably refused to drive her, she had brought that abominable son of hers. She glared at them, they stared at her. Now Mrs. Sandison was attracting attention. So with one last withering warning glance, she went on her way, far from pleased.

The song finished and the Minister asked the guest to sit. Then he proceeded to say a few words about how marriages are made in heaven and such like that. Now they were to stand again to sing hymn no.2, 'Love

Divine'. Mrs. Sandison stood but she wasn't singing. That child on Ethel's breast is Jamie's, she thought. They are the ones who are now taunting me. She was tempted to go and throw them out of the church, but decided against it. The song finished.

"Please remain standing," said the Minister. Then he continued:

"Dearly beloved, we are gathered here in the sight of God and these witnesses to join together in holy matrimony this man and this woman. If anyone knows of any cause or impediment why these two should not be joined together, let him speak now or forever hold his peace."

The Minister looked all around the pews and after ascertaining that there was no one who seemed likely to stop the proceedings, turned again to his script and was about to open his mouth when Jamie jumped up and said:

"Stop, there is a cause! This woman is mine. I love her and that man brainwashed her and stole her from me," and he began to walk towards the altar.

Everyone, including Ruth and Tony turned to look at him. Then Ruth and Tony looked at each other reassuringly and then turned back to the altar. Mrs. Sandison had already assayed to leave her seat to take charge of the situation, but her husband held her hand and looked her straight in the eye. She stepped back.

"Young lady," asked the Minister, "should we proceed?"

"Yes, please," answered Ruth.

"Well then, young man," said the Minister, to Jamie, "Please sit down. I mean, retake you place or leave the church."

Jamie did no such thing. Instead he ran forward and fell on his knees in front of Ruth. At this gesture, his mother ran forward and began to shout.

"Don't grovel, Jamie! There are a lot of women out her for you, let her marry her black man!"

Before Mr. Sandison could stop her, he himself being shocked by the turn of events, Mrs. Sandison was in front of Mrs. McKenzie and had slapped her hard on both cheeks. Then she grabbed her hair and pulled her towards the church door and chucked her out.

"Come back in here, and I'll kill you. I would have done it now had it not been for that child in your arms." Then she turned and calmly walked back to her place as if she had just gone to get a breath of fresh air.

Jamie had not vacated his position to help his mother. He was humbly waiting on Ruth because she was looking at her mother in horror, as was everyone else. To say that the guests were shocked was an understatement, especially when Mrs. Sandison returned as if she had done nothing wrong. The Minister was in consternation. Ruth was visibly shaken. Tony was in disbelief and Jamie was desperate.

Thus Jamie grabbed Ruth by one leg with both hands and wailed.

"Please, Ruth. I'm sorry for the way I treated you. I was wrong. Please, please, forgive me. I love you, Ruth. I am ready to get married, right now. I have a marriage licence right here. Please marry me. Ruth, we belong together," he finished sobbing like a five-year-old who couldn't find his mommy.

The guests were now transfixed, wondering if they were watching one of those crazy movies. Ruth's heart softened and she looked up at the Minister.

"Well?" asked the Minister, not knowing what else to say.

Tony just stood there, hardly breathing. Jamie was still holding on to Ruth, still sobbing. Ruth looked around at her parents but could read nothing from them.

"I don't know," she said.

Everyone gasped. Tony felt like wetting his pants. She didn't know, she didn't know! This was not good enough for him. This meant that she wasn't sure if she wanted him. He was utterly humiliated. He turned, and as fate would have it, looked straight into the eyes of Sally. Now he felt shame, look at those eyes, full of love.

As if drawn by a string he took slow, stumbling steps to Sally, not taking eyes off her. All eyes were on him. He fell at her feet, putting both of his arms around her waist and began to cry, then to sob. Between sobs, he told her that he was sorry and asked her to marry him. Sally said yes, then she too, began to cry and everyone was dabbing at their eyes.

Then Kenaz came to his brother and advised him to go outside and Mrs. Blake followed and drove them back to Tony's old apartment, now Kenaz's.

Once again, the Minister asked, "Well?" Ruth looked down at Jamie. She really did prefer to marry him. She still loved him. But he had made her so angry. He did seem sorry. Perhaps, they could work things out. She looked up at the Minister.

"Yes, I'll marry him." The guests clapped.

"You may now be seated," the Minister said to the guest.

To Jamie, he asked, "Young man, do you have a marriage licence?"

Jamie stood up and handed him the document. Then he took out his handkerchief and dried his eyes and wiped his face. Then he blew his nose.

"Ahh," murmured the guest, sympathetically. Then he took Tony's place and Mrs. Sandison shot up as a bullet and said:

"Wait!" and she sped out of the church. She went all the way to the main road where the cars were parked. There was Mrs. McKenzie, standing near her son's car. Mrs. Sandison hurried to her.

"Mrs. McKenzie, I am sorry for the way that I treated you. If you can forgive me, please come back to the church. Your son is getting married."

Mrs. McKenzie gave Mrs. Sandison looks that could kill and said nothing, but she went back to the church, again, the guest clapped.

"Shall I proceed?" asked the Minister in a voice which suggested that things had been taken out of his hands.

"Yes," answered Mrs. Sandison.

Without further ado, the Minister proceeded to the exchange vows. There were no rings so he invited them into the office to sign the register and certificates. During this period, Yolande Haynes sang, 'I'll still be Loving you'. On returning to the altar the Minister asked them to kneel and he prayed a blessing on them. As they stood, he said:

"I now pronounce you husband and wife. You may kiss the bride." Which Jamie relieved, did.

Everyone breathed a sigh of relief. What tension, what drama, what a wedding! Ruth cast her eyes around the church, then at her parents. She smiled. In her mind, she said:

'I'm married, at last!'

Tony kept the new apartment because it was he who had procured it and more-so, he and Sally were getting married at the end of July.

Ruth and Jamie had to wait until Monday to get new airline tickets. But because Jamie had been so depressed for the past two weeks, he couldn't savour a long flight to the southern hemisphere so they settled for Curacao. They also decided to buy a house but would leave it until after the honeymoon. They therefore spend the weekend at the same hotel where the reception was held.

Jamie refunded Tony and the McKenzies refunded the Blakes. Mr. McKenzie regretted not going to the wedding, but admitted that it was his son's fault.

Sally did not go to the reception because she was comforting Tony but she did call Ruth the next day and asked that they let bygones be bygones so they could all be friends again.

The Sandisons and the McKenzies decided that they would have to get along with each other for the sake of their children and grandchildren. So they planned to have a get together when Ruth and Jamie bought a house.

Ruth and Jamie bought rings on the Monday and carried them to the Minister to be blessed. Tony returned his rings and bought new ones for himself and Sally.

The End